Ocean Boulevard

a novel by

John Robert Schmierer

Ocean Boulevard is a work of fiction. Names, places, characters, and incidents either are products of the author's imagination or are used fictitiously. Any resemblance to actual events or persons, living or dead, is entirely coincidental.

Copyright 2010, 2013 by John Robert Schmierer

ISBN 978-0-9888981-0-3

Ocean Boulevard

PROLOGUE

NO ONE dies in Corona del Mar. Once you look past the small businesses crowding Pacific Coast Highway and experience the old part of town, it's not hard to imagine. The narrow, tree-shaded blocks sandwiched between the highway and the sea consist of well-tended homes, remodeled cottages, and overdone mansions that ooze enough wealth and privilege to form a barrier against the world. Not a mean street in sight. If death happens to call, it shows up behind closed doors, an unwelcome guest with at least the good manners to arrive quietly and collect its toll without causing much of a stir.

Maybe that's why it took so long for the morning joggers to notice the corpse.

The usual crew was out running that day, scattered along lonely sidewalks skirting the edge of a seaside bluff. The predawn glow lit the way, while out in the mist an unlikely shadow developed definition on the beach below. Nobody stopped for a better look until the sun came up.

A paramedic team responded within minutes of the phone calls. Newport Beach Police Officers and a medical examiner from the Orange County Coroner's Office set up shop after the body was pronounced dead. Streams of neon tape shouted out the location of a possible crime scene at the top of the bluff and cordoned off a block-long section of the street overlooking the beach. The growl and stench of diesel engines filled the air as a forensics walk-in van lumbered up among the emergency vehicles standing by at the curb and prodded them for a place to pull over.

Residents peered out of windows, stood in open doorways, or came out to their front yards. A few were already dressed, but the majority had on nightclothes under clutched robes. They gathered onto the street and milled about like passengers on the deck of a lost ship, asking questions to any of the uniformed personnel willing to engage in conversation.

News spread fast. The town buzzed with word-of-mouth accounts of one of its own being zipped into a body bag and hauled away. The following days passed without an official explanation, a lack of response that only created more anxiety for the locals wary of outsiders passing through their breached enclave.

When the news media lost interest, life began the slow process of returning to normal. A superficial calm eased the surface tension, then sank deeper as time wore on without further incident. Weeks turned into months. Underlying worries stopped festering and healed over. Everyone finally relaxed, mistaking the remission for a cure.

ONE

WES MARSHALL looked across the empty cockpit and thought of the old man. He thought of the long hours they had spent on his boat, a forty-four foot sloop Marshall bought last year and where he now stood alone at the helm. He was more than familiar with the rigging, well schooled in its design and purpose and able to carry out the required tasks to sail the boat by himself. But this was his first time solo, and he was nervous.

Lingering traces of the old man's presence seemed to stir behind the breeze. If Marshall listened hard enough, he could almost hear the old man's commanding shout, its edge rasped with age but still sharp enough to cut through the wind and rise above the usual shipboard clamor of singing winches and stressed rigging and snapping sailcloth fluttering out of trim. The trick was to keep him quiet, and over time Marshall had figured it out—as long as the sails were trimmed and he held his course, the old man would say nothing. Their last time together had been filled with silence all the way back to the harbor, neither one of them breaking the spell while they made fast the mooring lines and completed their docking procedures. They had walked away from the boat and were halfway down the wharf when the old man, staring straight ahead, finally spoke.

"Maybe we'll make a sailor out of you after all."

It was the closest thing to a complement the old man was capable off expressing, and Marshall smiled as he relived the moment. It helped him ignore the percussive clap of large waves hitting granite boulders off in the distance.

When the channel came into view he watched bursts of spray from the breaking waves rain over the tops of the jetties protecting the harbor entrance. Second thoughts about going out alone began to gnaw on his confidence the moment the first serious gust grabbed hold of the headsail. The boat pitched and rolled toward the open water, running with the tide, everything happening too soon and moving too fast. The mainsail wasn't up yet and Marshall spat out a curse aimed at his own negligence. The sail should have been reefed and set in preparation for the conditions outside the harbor. Now he was out of time, with little room to maneuver and bearing down closer to the piled boulders that made up the southern jetty.

He hove to and began hoisting the mainsail with the full force of the wind upon him. It whistled through the shrouds and tore at the unfurling canvas while the deflated headsail flapped like a wet rag against the mast. Loose sheets whipped about and threatened to tangle with the rigging. Shifting wind and uncooperative sails kept him too busy to notice the drift until he saw the windward jetty coming up fast on the port side. He gave the halyard winch a final yank just as a strong gust swirled in from somewhere off the stern. The sail caught air and sent the boom swinging free against the slack mainsheet in a wide, powerful arc before it slammed to a dead stop at the end of the line. No time to savor his relief that the canvas and rigging remained intact—the wind breathed life into the boat and she lurched forward with a burst of acceleration he would have thought impossible. He was able to steer away from the jetty, but any hope of reducing sail was already gone. All he could do was hang on and fight his rising panic.

Turning back wasn't an option while still inside the harbor entrance. The swell direction and northwest wind wanted to force him into the jetty but his only course was to continue alongside its flanks for the last thousand yards to the open water. If he were to expose his broadside to the swells and lose forward momentum he'd be swept into the rocks as he came about. He was making headway, but not gaining much actual distance. Whenever he angled too far away from the jetty the air would begin to spill out of the sails as they turned into the wind.

It took a conscious effort to draw a long, deep breath and let it fill his lungs. He looked up at the ragged sails and maybe the added oxygen to his system helped clear his thoughts.

Just trim the sails and the boat will sail herself.

How many times had the old man drummed that into his head? Marshall relaxed his two-fisted grip on the wheel and then removed one hand altogether and used it to secure the starboard jib sheet. *No shit. Trim the goddamned sails.*

But how? His initial reaction bogged down as the tried to think it through. Thinking only made it worse. He froze. *What do I do?*

Whatever it takes.

The words rang in his mind, as if the old man were standing over his shoulder, shouting into his ear. It gave Marshall the assurance to push aside the fear long enough to let his training take over. He sheeted in the sails, getting as close to the wind as he could while still allowing the boat to plane, then played the mainsheet to keep her as upright as possible. He eased the bow toward the swells and tried not to focus on the alarming shudder sent down the length of the hull when it plowed through the steeper faces.

It didn't take him long to recognize that all was as it should be. The boat was in her element, performing as designed. He began to work with the conditions rather than fight them. Once clear of the harbor jetties his proficiency improved with every tack. He worked his way up the coast and didn't turn away from the wind until he had long passed Huntington Beach and could see the backside of the Palos Verdes Peninsula.

His new course allowed him to ride the swells, a welcome relief from taking them head on. The pitching and rolling settled into a relaxed rocking motion as the boat gathered her downwind pace. He coaxed her along instinctively, helped her find her stride and let out as much sail as he dared, unaware of the speed he had picked up until he saw how quickly the features along the shoreline came into view and moved across his field of vision.

When the harbor jetties reappeared, a sense of well-being warmed his insides, sudden and unexpected, like you get with that first glance of recognition when you happen upon an old friend. He stared out at Saddleback Mountain, a prominent landmark standing watch twenty miles inland. Although high enough to jut above the inversion layer on smoggy days, the twin peaks were now dwarfed by the taller San Gabriel and San Bernardino Mountains looming another fifty miles out, dusted with snow and etched razor sharp against clear blue skies. For a few moments he lost track of time and what he was doing, caught up in the view. It took a while longer for him to get it, that he was actually feeling good for the first time since Kathleen had died.

* * *

The wind was still a factor inside the harbor, but the calmer water allowed Marshall to take his time lowering the sails. He drifted by a new house under construction along the waterfront and watched the framers pound nails and walk the roof trusses. The hammer strikes beat out a familiar cadence, accompanied by occasional shouts of mostly young guys stripped to the waist wearing cut-off jeans, toolbelts, and steel-toed boots. Electric saws whined in the background and Marshall could smell sawdust amidst the fragrance of raw lumber. There were no hardhats in sight—obviously a non-union crew, and Marshall smiled appreciably.

He sometimes wondered if he would have made it without Kathleen, or if he would have remained a lunchbox carpenter working for wages the rest of his life. He thought of himself climbing a ladder—and pushing fifty—as he watched the framers. He wished them well, and sent Kathleen a silent thank you.

She had always been the strong one, even in high school, when her father got his promotion with 3M and moved the family to Minnesota. They stayed in touch as best they could, and he flew back to marry her the month they graduated. He wasn't interested in college and she stood by him and supported his dreams. After the baby was born, they used their savings and all they could borrow to invest in an empty lot in Newport Beach. The house Marshall built turned a profit. He used it to buy more lots in Big Canyon, continued to reinvest the proceeds back into his expanding business, and set up Marshall Development in 1985.

Years passed and the business continued to grow. Marshall got out in the field less and less, until his days of pounding nails and walking trusses were gone forever. But as he watched the framers on the shoreline, he held on to those old memories, then let them slip away as he drifted around a bend and lost sight of the house.

He continued through the harbor with the sails down and the diesel running. He was getting pretty good at arriving under sail but wasn't up for it today. Gliding in close enough to dock without motor control or an extra hand to lend help was a tricky maneuver.

He was appraising the boat traffic near his slip when he noticed a sport fisher had run into the wharf and was in the process of sinking. He couldn't imagine how a boat that size could get up enough speed in the close confines of the harbor to run aground. He came up closer, the scene unfolding before him, when he finally recognized the remnants of his own slip reduced to splinters beneath the foundering hull. He was about to heave to when a familiar shout rose over the noise of his diesel. He cut the engine and looked back over the stern at Walter Jenkins, the old man, hailing him from a Zodiac.

Barely within earshot, the old man yelled, "You sure picked one hell of a day to go out."

He maneuvered in close enough for Marshall to catch a line, who then hauled in the slack and brought the inflatable boat up to the starboard gunwale. The old man clambered aboard with an agility that defied his years. He picked up the conversation from where he'd left off.

"I guess it's fortunate you lacked the good sense to check the weather and postpone your maiden voyage." He looked over at the wreckage strewn across the wharf. "There's no way your pretty little boat would have stood up against *that*. You should have heard the noise the collision made."

Marshall finished tying off the Zodiac as he spoke. "What the hell happened?"

"Don't know yet. I still have to sort it out. For now, you'll have to use one of my offshore moorings. There's nothing else available. I might be able to scrounge up a skiff you can use to ferry yourself back and forth, but it'll only hold a couple of people. If you're going to need something bigger, give me a heads up and I'll see what I can do."

Walter pointed the way to a mooring buoy about one hundred yards offshore. Marshall was lucky. He knew only too well the difficulty in obtaining mooring space in Newport Harbor, choked beyond capacity with more than 9,000 boats competing for space. Most of the waterways were narrow, especially where they wound around the seven residential islands scattered throughout the bay. All the boats, the restricted space, and the strictly enforced five mile per hour speed limit on powerboats had Marshall wondering once again how the sport fisher was able to inflict so much damage.

He turned to Walter. "Just how long are the repairs going to take?"

"Who knows? Could be a week, could be a month. You know how things work around here. I'll know more when I get a better look at the damage and find out who owns that sport fisher. Whoever he is, I hope he has his insurance paid up."

After securing Marshall's boat the two of them jumped into the Zodiac. Walter started the outboard motor and dropped Marshall at the Dry Dock, a local watering hole a few doors north of the damaged slip. Marshall walked up a gangplank bridging the wharf to the unheralded rear entrance to the bar. He pushed inside, observing the usual assortment of deckhands, fishermen, and local boat owners scattered about. He knew a few of their names but limited the greeting rituals to a nod of recognition or a "How-are-you-doing?" Behind an ancient mahogany bar stood another shopworn fixture, the bartender and resident sage, Dick Larkspur.

"How's it goin' Wes? I take it you missed all the excitement around here. Too bad about your slip."

"Do you feel bad enough to buy me a drink?"

Dick gave him a sidelong stare, squinting from the smoke rising from the perpetual cigarette dangling out of the corner of his mouth—California antismoking laws be damned. He said, "I don't know . . . ol' Wally's kinda cranky today."

When he served up a light-beer, Marshall winked conspiratorially. "I won't tell if you won't."

They bantered a few minutes until Dick moved down the bar to attend to a new customer. Marshall turned on his barstool toward the back windows facing the bay. The view trying to shine in through the weathered panes did little to brighten the interior. A narrow, elbow-high counter with accompanying foot rail ran parallel to the bar and a dozen dining tables took up the floor space beyond. No potted plants or artwork. What passed for decoration amounted to a limp fishing net strung against one of the walls and a couple of crossed harpoons nailed onto another.

A meager scattering of faded black-and-white framed photos attempted to fill the some of the remaining voids.

He returned his idle gaze to the bar and wondered how many years of accumulated dust and infrequent cleaning it had taken to tarnish the large gilded mirror mounted behind the cluttered countertops and shelves. A permanent haze clouded the surface of the glass and conspired with the fine cracks that must have webbed its silver backing to render an aged, gray patina upon all it reflected.

The rest of the afternoon slipped by. Marshall nursed a few more beers, kept a running conversation going with Dick between interruptions from the bar patrons, and eventually moved to a quiet corner of the dinning area for something to eat. As he finished his meal, Walter joined him at the window-side table, muttering obscenities into his beard.

"What's the matter," Marshall asked, "still upset about that boat parked in my slip?"

"I wish it *was* your slip", Walter said.

"I'll be glad to stop paying rent on the damn thing if you'd like to hand it over."

Walter wasn't smiling, but Marshall knew better than to take his hard stare personally.

"I just got through talking to that deputy sheriff with the harbor patrol," Walter continued, still simmering. "You might know the lad, Larry Walker? Anyway, he tried to run down the registration on the sport fisher and came up blank. There's no paperwork on board and he says the numbers on the bow are useless. What's left of them look freshly stenciled. Probably bogus numbers, just to look good."

"Anything on the stern, a name or something?"

"Nothing."

"What about the skipper? He should be able to come up with some answers."

"That's the best part. Whoever ran the boat over my wharf managed to disappear in the confusion." Walter looked down at his gnarled fists resting on the table. "This whole thing is starting to royally piss me off."

Marshall bought him a drink and changed the subject. They talked about sailing, and the old man's attitude mellowed. His scowl lost some of its vinegar, directed at Marshall now with a hint of respect, an unspoken nod to a protégé who had just earned his membership in a select fraternity.

When their conversation had run its course, they finished their drinks in a shared silence while the sun descended behind a forest of masts and rigging visible through the windows along the back wall. Marshall shoved off, saying goodbye to Walter, then waved to Dick on his way out the front door.

The euphoria he'd felt out on the water seemed a distant memory as he climbed into his Suburban and headed for home.

TWO

SHADES OF faded rose petals lingered over the horizon as Marshall pulled up to his house on Shorecliff Road. His daughter's car was parked in the driveway. Marshall drove by the brick gateposts guarding the entrance and managed his way past the vehicle and into the garage. He entered the house through a back door, walked through the utility room, kitchen, and large family room before finding Jennifer leaning against a railing on one of the outdoor decks overlooking the ocean.

He stood still for a moment behind the sliding glass door, watching her standing out there on the deck, looking so much like her mother. It was disconcerting sometimes. The blond hair, faded freckles, and wide-set green eyes were obviously handed down from mother to daughter. But it was the way Jennifer moved and her subtle, unconscious mannerisms that truly made her a younger version of Kathleen. Marshall was glad he'd seen Jennifer's car in the driveway; it provided advance warning that she was at the house. Although he enjoyed meeting her every week or so for lunch, he didn't like that sudden implosion in the pit of his stomach when he ran into her unexpectedly.

He slid open the door, substituted a greeting with, "Working late?"

"Uh-huh." Jennifer pushed away from the railing, slowly, as though reluctant to turn away from the water. "Debra wants me to go over your master bedroom tonight. You know how she gets. She doesn't like the color we painted the walls. I'm going up to mix some new batches. I'll brush out some samples for her to look at later. While I'm at it, I'll go ahead and paint my old room. It needs a fresh coat."

"Didn't we hire painters for that?"

"Yeah, but I want to do it. I want to stay connected."

Marshall tried to smile but his heart wasn't in it, as much as he appreciated what Jennifer was trying to say. Before the break in the conversation grew noticeable he asked, "Where *is* Debra, anyway? I noticed her car's not here."

"She called me from her parents house. Thought it would be a good time for me to take care of this." Jennifer took a close look at him. "Are you okay? You don't look so hot."

"I've had a few beers, but I'm all right."

Marshall turned away from the doorway and headed for his favorite chair in the family room. He wished it *was* the beers, or the onset of fatigue after a long day. But a familiar, dark funk was bearing down on him. Jennifer followed him inside and sat on the closest end of the sofa. He tried to sound upbeat as he told her about his sailing experience from earlier that day.

". . . and I'll admit, I was probably in a little over my head, but if I was going out, it had to be *today*. I'd been planning it since I'd bought the boat. I barely slept last night, and when the wind came up I almost backed out. I'm glad I didn't. Something happened out there, toward the end, when I was heading back to the harbor. It was like I could feel your mother's presence, watching over me . . ."

Jennifer was shaking her head. "Why do you do it, Dad? Wasn't losing Mom bad enough? Now you're out there risking your life on that damn boat."

Marshall came up to the edge of his seat, leaning toward her. "I know I've been a little obsessive about the sailing lately, but I'm okay. I'm not playing out some kind of death wish. It's just the opposite. It's about concentrating on the here and now, living life. Besides, the weather's usually pretty calm around here, there's really nothing to worry about."

Jennifer wiped her tears. "Who are you kidding? I know what day this is."

She reached over and grabbed his hand and squeezed hard. Marshall squeezed back, feeling the energy of their souls pass between them. She let go of his hand, came up and hugged him around the neck. He closed his eyes and felt the two of them connect for one of those rare, unsustainable moments he wished could last longer, sharing thoughts that were already gone before they could be formed into words.

Marshall opened his eyes, looking over her shoulder. "I still can't believe she's really gone."

"I'm not over it, either." Jennifer backed away and returned to her seat. "I'll go for days, sometimes weeks, feeling all right. Then out of the blue something happens that reminds me of Mom . . . and that I'll never see her again."

"People don't die jogging in Corona del Mar," Marshall said, unable to stay seated. "Not like that. Not without having a heart attack or something."

He paced aimlessly, staring through the darkening windows bordering the room, reliving once again the worst day of is life: the phone call, recognizing Kathleen's broken body lying in the sand when he arrived at the scene. It was an image always close by, ready for instant recall.

"And how can people forget? It hasn't been *that* long ago. Every day they jog along the same sidewalk and lie out on the beach where she fell, oblivious to it all. And no one's done a goddamned thing about it."

"What could they do?" Jennifer said. "It was early. The sun wasn't even up yet. Nobody saw her fall—"

"She didn't just *fall*," Marshall interrupted. "She didn't trip or keel over or have some kind of epileptic fit. She was in perfect health. No matter how it happened, she couldn't have just rolled off the sidewalk and over the cliff on her own. There are too many low shrubs growing alongside to allow that to happen."

"Don't do this to yourself," Jennifer said. "The police were very thorough. They went over and over the area, searching for clues, talking to residents . . ." She paused, bringing up a hand to cover her brow, as if she'd momentarily lost her balance, then took it away and let out a deep breath.

They looked at each other in unspoken agreement to talk about something else. It wouldn't be about Debra. Jennifer had already mentioned her when he first walked in, and Marshall didn't expect to hear her name spoken again.

He tried not to think of what Jennifer must think of him, remarried so soon after her mother had died—and to a woman his daughter's age. After he figured it out, when he understood what had possessed him to go through with it, he'd find a way to explain it to Jennifer. In the meantime, the less conversation about Debra, the better. The tension between the two women was palpable. They had once been friends, right up to the moment Jennifer had introduced her to Marshall.

Jennifer looked at him knowingly, as if reading his mind. She stood up and motioned for him to follow her, saying she needed his opinion on the color she had in mind for her old room. Although she no longer lived there, he was glad she wanted to preserve her place in the house.

Maybe after they talked more about the painting and the latest plans for the remodel, they could get back to what was important. He regretted his outburst. And as he calmed down, he wanted so much to recapture that fleeting moment of peace he'd found on his boat. He wanted to share it with Jennifer, let her know that everything was going to be all right. If only he could find the words . . .

The phone interrupted his thoughts on his way up the stairs. He turned back to answer it. Jennifer was already opening paint cans when he returned from the call to tell her he had to leave.

* * *

Marshall should have been feeling satisfied. He lay quiet on damp sheets. A soft breeze from the forced-air ducts cooled his chest. He had just made love to a beautiful woman who made sure he got everything a man could ask for. He'd reached his climax just in time. Another few seconds and he would've pushed her away, like a plate containing the last morsel of a delicious meal that was too much to finish.

Yet at the same time it wasn't enough. Why was it, when they made love, that their passion sometimes felt like a fragile veneer in danger of wearing through to an empty void? Whenever it happened, all he could do was go through the motions and try to hide his disappointment.

He used to think it was him, some kind of guilt trip, but now he wasn't so sure. He looked over at Debra lying next to him on her left side, her back facing him. He tried not to think about it, that déjà vu sort of feeling that he hadn't been able to shake since the day he'd met her. It was the first thing that had attracted him to her, and even now, as they lay there, it served as a conduit that linked the two of them together.

Debra finally stirred. She rolled toward him and stretched her arms over her head and arched her back in such a feline gesture that he could almost hear her purr. Her black hair spilled across the pillow and covered her shoulders like wisps of smoke, allowing glimpses of skin to peek out with a warm luminescence. It seemed to radiate from some secret source, dimming the thoughts that were troubling him.

They almost disappeared when she smiled the words, "Have I told you how much I love you today?"

Marshall gathered her in his arms and pulled her on top of him. He felt big, hard, and young, detached from the cold grip of mortality that sometimes chilled his spine. Maybe that's all there was to it. Middle-aged craziness looking for a place to hide inside that warm luminescence.

* * *

Sleep wasn't part of the deal. Debra made it clear with a playful wink as she dialed room service.

"How hungry are you?" she said, placing her hand over the phone's mouthpiece. "Should we get a bottle of wine?"

"Sure, something white and dry."

Debra completed the order and hung up the phone. She snuggled up to Marshall, using his chest as a pillow while he kept her close with an arm around her shoulder. He dozed off until the food arrived.

Over the second glass of wine, Debra asked, "Well, aren't you going to ask me why we're here?"

Leaning against the headboard, Marshall said, "There's a lot of work going on at the house. They're upstairs making a mess of things and you're not in the mood to deal with it."

"You're pretty close. I hope you're not mad at me."

"Are you kidding? I think we should do this more often, maybe get a suite next time."

"You are mad at me, aren't you? I'm sorry I didn't think you'd—"

Marshall didn't allow her to say another word, smothering her mouth with a long, passionate kiss. He came up for air and said, "I'm not mad. You should know when I'm kidding by now."

"Then you don't mind? Everything's all right?"

"Sure. I understand how you feel, having to live in the house I shared with someone else for so many years. I should be the one who's worried—that you're mad at me for insisting we stay there. When the work on the remodel is finished and we've had time to get used to it, and if you're not happy, we'll move."

"That's not going to happen. I know how much your home means to you. I'll never ask you to leave. It would ruin everything. Before long you'd hate me for it. Besides, I like the house. I'm also glad Jennifer's taking control of some of the decoration and comes around to keep things on track."

Marshall was back against the headboard. Debra snuggled in tighter and lowered her voice. "I have to tell you, though, I am uncomfortable with the work going on upstairs, especially with your old master bedroom. I like the bedroom we use now and would rather not get too involved with the room you shared with Kathleen. I just want to keep a low profile for a few days, until the work there is finished. I'll be fine after that."

"How many nights have you reserved here?"

"Don't be silly." Debra leaned across for the wine bottle standing on the nightstand and poured the remainder into their glasses. "This is a one-night party. I was on my way home from my parents house, that's all. I haven't made further plans."

She settled back on her side of the bed, taking her wine glass with her. After a slow sip, she said, "Tomorrow, why don't we spend the night on your boat?"

Marshall was surprised by the request. She'd never shown the slightest interest in his boat.

"Well," he said, "the boat's not exactly at her slip."

Debra cocked her head, a slight frown wrinkling her brow.

"There was an accident at the wharf," Marshall continued. "I'll have to keep her moored offshore for a while."

"Is your boat okay?"

"The boat's fine. I'd been out sailing when the accident occurred. Wally lent me a skiff for the time being. He keeps it tied up next to the Owens cabin cruiser down from his office."

"That's not so bad," Debra said. "In fact, I think it could be romantic, out on the water. Let's meet there tomorrow night."

"Why not drive out from the house, together?"

"A sly grin crept up on Debra's face. "Oh, I forgot to tell you. You're going to be busy tomorrow. I'll just meet you afterwards."

* * *

The time spent battling rush-hour traffic the next morning annoyed Marshall almost as much as his golf date with Debra's father. Marshall had been at a loss for words when she informed him of his obligation. According to Debra, her father had been asking about him, telling her how much he wanted to get together for a round of golf.

Marshall didn't appreciate Debra accepting the invitation on his behalf, but it was obviously important to her. Maybe she was trying to patch things up with her old man. Now Marshall had to fight the traffic back to Corona del Mar for his clubs and a change of clothes, then grind it out for the return trip to LA.

He arrived at the guardhouse blocking the Wilshire entrance to the club with no time to spare. He left his clubs at the bag drop, parked his car, and was directed to the men's locker room and assigned a locker. Too bad about the golf shoes, the ones with the metal spikes. He'd picked up the old pair by mistake in his hurry to get back on the freeway.

He put on the shoes and attempted to tread lightly, but the clatter of steel against concrete announced his arrival outside the pro shop. A suited, gray-haired gentleman appeared from out of the landscape and politely informed him that soft spikes were the rule and that he should return to the men's locker room, where an equally courteous attendant changed them for him. Marshall stepped up to the first tee twenty minutes late, greeted by a cordially perturbed Paul Cappannelli, Debra's father.

Marshall professed his apologies and was introduced to the remaining two members of the foursome: a couple of big, rough-looking men who had done their best to blend in with the genteel surroundings by sporting salon haircuts and wearing expensive golf outfits. They answered to Luke and James. As for last names or what they did for a living, they didn't offer and Marshall didn't ask. Talking was kept to a minimum as each of them, in turn, teed up a ball and knocked it down the fairway.

As they played on, Marshall began to appreciate the golf course. It was challenging, as expected, but what impressed him most was the timeless quality of the surroundings. The location was as urban as it gets, between Westwood and Beverly Hills, yet the ambiance was pure country. The loamy scent of the woods framing the rolling fairways mingled with stronger fragrances of budding eucalyptus acorns and citrus blossoms, bringing back fond memories of growing up in Orange County before the asphalt and smog took over. While walking along the third fairway he enjoyed secluded vistas that hadn't changed in seventy years, save for the height of the trees. They were now tall and dense, effective barriers from the steel, concrete, and glass that had long ago sprouted up along the Wilshire Corridor.

After nine holes the foursome made a quick stop at a covered food stand next to the tenth tee. They sat around an outdoor table wolfing down hotdogs and guzzling beer. Cappannelli and his buddies conversed among themselves.

When they walked off the eighteenth green, Marshall expected Cappannelli to offer him a drink, maybe open up a little. By now, he was more annoyed than ever about Cappannelli's invitation.

All the man said was, "Nice seeing you Wes. We'll have to do it again sometime." Not even a handshake. Cappannelli checked his watch and turned for the clubhouse, not waiting for a reply.

Marshall saw to his clubs, retrieved his shoes from the locker room, and headed for the parking lot.

"What an asshole," he said, throwing his clubs into the back of his suburban, taking a cursory glance around to see if anyone nearby had heard him, not really caring if they had. He marched around to the driver's door and tried not to think about the traffic backing up on the 405.

* * *

Marshall pulled into his usual parking space near his slip. The two-hour drive from LA had given him plenty of time to wonder what the hell was going on. What was up with Debra's old man? Of course he wasn't that old, not much older than Marshall, which was troubling enough. And then there were the two guys

Cappannelli had with him. They were about as subtle as a couple of streetwalkers receiving communion at The Good Shepard.

Marshall couldn't figure it. He had no idea why it was so important to play golf with Cappannelli, when all the man had done was treat him with open hostility. Marshall was going to have a long talk with Debra about it, just a soon as she showed up.

He was about to call her on his cell phone when Jennifer's gray BMW pulled up next to the passenger side of his Suburban.

Now what?

Marshall was half-way around the hood as Debra stepped out of the BMW.

"Hi. I had to borrow Jennifer's car."

Marshall stood there, speechless.

"The Mercedes conked out on me and I had to leave it at the dealership. I was running late and didn't want to wait around for a loaner."

Marshall kept staring at her. "What did you do to your hair?"

"Oh, do you like it?" Debra tossed her head to flick back a few strands of blond hair away from her eyes. "I thought it was time for a change."

She regarded him with a smile Marshall didn't recognize, then came up and pressed her body against his and kissed him on the mouth, hard and long.

Marshall didn't know how to respond. He had to look at her again, and he pried himself loose and stepped back, not taking his eyes off her. This wasn't déjà vu. Never had been. Debra met his stare, her smile reduced to a disturbing grin, and for all the world she looked just like Jennifer.

He couldn't believe it. He'd seen the two women together countless times, never noticing anything like this, at least not consciously. Until now, Debra had always seemed so much darker, her eyes and skin shaded with obvious Mediterranean tones, her features more pronounced. Yet here she stood, a mirror image of his own daughter. His own flesh and blood.

Debra was still within arm's reach. She narrowed the gap and whispered, "Where's the boat?" She stayed close and encouraged Marshall to lead the way.

They walked to the docks, arm in arm, Marshall not really sure who was leading whom. He helped Debra into the skiff, fumbled around with the outboard motor, and piloted them across the water to his boat. While he was tying off the skiff, Debra grabbed the keys to unlock the companionway. Marshall followed her down the stairs a couple of minutes later. As he came off the last step, a powerful blow against the base of his skull sent him crashing onto the deck of the main cabin.

THREE

THE SMELL came first. It seeped into his consciousness and brought him around in slow, fretful stages He was in bed. His clothes were off, the sheets sticking to his body. He stared into the darkness after a few alarmed blinks assured him that his eyes had really opened. A sharp pain shot through his skull when he raised his head. He lay back, afraid to move until the throbbing aftershocks subsided.

But the pounding intensified, punctuated by loud thumps that somehow shook the bed. It couldn't be coming from his head. It was more like the sound of intruders clambering aboard his boat. Shouts and muffled replies echoed in the near distance, drifting closer. The voices had been there all along.

One of them called out his name.

"Wes Marshall . . . are you aboard? Is *anyone* aboard?"

The door to his cabin burst open. Flashlight beams swept across the berth and zeroed in on him. A swarm of dark, rough shadows pulled him off the bed, slammed him face down onto the deck, and handcuffed his wrists behind him. A large foot across his neck held him in check, his right ear scraping against the hardwood when he turned his head for a look. One of his assailants broke away and ran back through the galley and up the companionway, then came the ragged hack of a man throwing up over the gunwale. No one else made a sound.

A light flicked on. Out of the corner of his eye, Marshall had a floor-to-ceiling view of two uniformed men surveying the cabin.

The one with the large feet stood over him, keeping the pressure on his neck.

Returning footfalls shuffled down the companionway steps and stopped in the main saloon, out of sight. The two men inside finished their visual sweep and looked across at each other.

Without a word, the smaller man's eyes said, Hold it in. If you lose it, so will I.

Marshall strained against the foot on his neck, trying to shout. It came out as a hoarse whisper.

"I can't breathe."

"You piece of shit."

The big man's foot pressed harder. His partner spoke up.

"Frank, take it easy, the guy's turning blue. This is Newport PD's problem. Let's call it in."

"Yeah . . . let's call it in." The big man pulled back his foot. He reached down and grabbed Marshall's upper arm and almost yanked it out of the shoulder socket as he dragged him across the deck and shoved him into a sitting position against the bulkhead. "Stay there and don't move, or you'll wish it was your ass on the bed."

Marshall groaned, still hurting, then craned his sore neck to look around the man and up at the bed. The man stepped aside, and for a brief moment of disbelief, the world stood still.

Marshall squeezed his eyes shut, waiting for the moment to pass. He waited for his friends to jump out from behind their hiding places and for Debra to spring to life, all of them laughing and clapping him on the back, as if he had been nothing more than the victim of a sick joke.

He opened his eyes. Debra didn't move, sprawled across the stained sheets, her limbs frozen in an unnatural pose. The blond hair startled him, like before, until the memory of the events leading up to his blackout came rushing back. Now her skin was far too pale, almost translucent. Blood had sprayed across the teak walls, soaked the sheets, and collected in random pools on the deck.

He looked down at the swaths of congealed blood on his body. The smell hit him again, stronger and more visceral now that he knew what it was. He swallowed hard against the acrid taste of bile rising in his throat.

His two captors stood over the bed.

"I know it's academic," the big man said, "but we have to make sure."

He reached out and felt for a pulse at the carotid artery. The head was poised at a pivotal angle, waiting for a slight nudge to help gravity move it. Marshall sat transfixed as it made a slow, half turn toward him. The blood-caked blond hair spilled away from the face.

It wasn't Debra.

Marshall lurched onto his knees and stared straight into his daughter's green eyes, searching for a glimmer of light beneath their fixed glaze. The contents of his stomach spewed across the deck before he had time to brace himself. He tried to breathe, but nothing happened. It was as if an unseen hand had grabbed him by the throat and cut off his air supply. The cabin walls closed in on him, the varnished teak losing its color, turning gray before his eyes. When he looked up at the men staring at him, they seemed to posses the same deathly pallor as the body on the bed.

Marshall caught sight of the blood again. Jennifer's blood. He turned away and looked out the door and up at the companionway. The unseen grip on his throat finally lost its purchase and he managed a few deep breaths. Crouched on his haunches, he stole a furtive glance back at the men on the other side of the bed.

The look on their faces, framed by all the blood and the unrelenting sight of his daughter's body before them, finally struck home. They knew he did it. No need for questions. Marshall wanted to talk to them, but he couldn't find the words.

How do you explain the unexplainable? Couldn't they see he was more shocked and sickened than they were? That there was no way he was capable of doing this? Were they blind?

This can't be real. I know I'm not crazy yet Jennifer's lying there and these guys are ready to crucify me and I can't even catch my breath long enough to spit out a word . . .

He was hyperventilating. First he couldn't breathe, now he couldn't stop gasping. And between each quick breath his fear grew stronger, acquiring a life of its own and about to overwhelm him. Marshall really did want to say something, but the uncontrolled scream rising out of his chest ended any hope of a sensible resolution. He bolted through the doorway, panicked, trying to run away from the fear more than anything else, speeding past the third man seated on the bench behind the galley table and climbing up the companionway steps as his scream finally gave out. The lifeline fencing in the cockpit was his last obstacle. He focused on the water beyond, his only salvation, the only way to wash off his daughter's blood. Feeling it on his body, knowing how it made him look, the thought of them dragging him into custody branded with this red badge of a monster—it was more than he could bear. If he could just keep going, make it to the water . . .

The big man caught him halfway across the lifeline. He spun Marshall around and slammed a fist into his stomach.

"I thought I told you to stay put."

He must have worried about Marshall retching again, allowing him lean across the lifeline to aim over the water. The rest of the crew came up from behind and gathered within earshot.

"We can't take him ashore like this." It was the smaller man's voice. "He needs some clothes. If we can't find anything handy, I'll grab a blanket out of the fireboat."

Marshall didn't acknowledge them. The spasms wracking his stomach subsided, but he couldn't stop shivering in the cooler air outside the cabin. With his hands manacled behind his back, he had no way to warm himself. He stared down at the water while the big man, the one they called Frank, answered his partner.

"You're right. Newport PD should be standing by on land any minute. We'll cover him up before we make the transfer. Leave the crime scene alone and take a look in the other cabins. Try not to disturb anything. I'll let dispatch know what's up."

Marshall scanned the perimeter of his boat. The fireboat the smaller man had mentioned was secured alongside. A vacated one-man patrol boat bobbed next to it. They belonged to the harbor patrol, which meant the uniformed men who had come aboard were Orange County Sheriff's Deputies.

He backed away from the lifeline and collapsed onto the nearest bench in the cockpit. Two deputies went below, while the third kept watch. Marshall looked over at his keeper. The deputy's body language discouraged any thought of talking.

A few minutes later the cavalry arrived. Marshall faced the west shore of the harbor and had an unobstructed view of the police vehicles threading through a parking lot off Pacific Coast Highway. The sirens were off, but the light bars mounted on the units were all fully lit. Bright patterns of red and blue and yellow hues flashed against the buildings next to the parking lot and danced across the water.

The deputy had his back to the action. When he turned his head, Marshall rolled under the lifeline and slid off the side of the boat. He sank into the black water, chased by shouts that quickly faded in the distance. The sputter of a powerful inboard engine coughed to life overhead.

He let out all the air in his lungs to insure his continued descent. A calmness came over him. His knees drew in toward his chest, on their own, as if seeking the lost comfort of the womb.

It should have been easy to let go, to breathe in a big gulp of sea water and end it, but his instincts wouldn't cooperate. With a reluctant yet overpowering sense of purpose he accentuated his fetal position as tight as possible and worked his cuffed wrists from behind his back by slipping them around his butt. He pushed off the bottom of the harbor, his hands in front of him now, and broke the surface without a sound. He sucked in air with a quiet gasp and tried to get a fix on his position. Unseen voices bounced back and forth across the water.

He had to keep moving to stay afloat. He found if he crossed his wrists, one over the other, he could widen the gap between his elbows and pull off a modified breaststroke. He hid among the moored boats, grabbing a mooring line here and there when he needed to catch his breath, and continued working his way south with the tide.

The fireboat came into view from behind a medium-sized ketch. The deputies on board cut the motor and drifted up not more than ten yards from him and rode the current in silence. A searchlight swept the forward starboard quadrant. Marshall had just enough time to tread behind a tethered dinghy before the beam swung toward his position on the port side. He prayed that his chattering teeth wouldn't give him away.

His boat was still within sight. It looked like any number of forty-four foot sloops moored in the harbor but for the ancient skiff secured to the stern.

He held tight to the line tethering the dinghy to its mother ship, a cabin cruiser of thirty feet or so, and stared hard and long at the innocuous little skiff across the way. With it still secured to the stern, how did Debra get off the boat? Did she jump? Was she thrown overboard? Maybe she wasn't discovered yet, lying dead in one of the cabins.

Images of carnage, both imagined and real, threatened to bring on another panic attack. He couldn't close his eyes without seeing his daughter's lifeless body staring back at him. He had no idea when or how she had come aboard.

If only he could find a safe place to concentrate . . . or to remember. How long had he been unconscious? An hour? A day? Thinking it might have been longer spiked his runaway heart rate. He let go of the line and brushed his jowls with the palms of his hands. Not much beard stubble. It was too dark to make out the date on his watch next to the steel cuff biting into his wrist, but the luminous hands on the dial indicated one-thirty.

A blinding light lit up the water around him. Helicopter rotors roared overhead and Marshall dove for cover. He stayed underwater and worked his way toward the mooring buoy securing the cabin cruiser. He found the anchor line and followed it up close to the surface. He held his breath for as long a possible, then came up for air next to the buoy. He ducked back underwater and repeated the process until the chopper moved on.

He changed tactics and swam against the tide. The main thrust of the search seemed to be moving south, toward the harbor entrance. That would give them over a mile of congested waterways and docks to search before they reached open water.

A degree of peacefulness settled over the bay as the chopper widened its search pattern. It was an eerie prelude to the anger Marshall felt welling up inside of him. He directed it at his pursuers. It provided him with the fuel and motivation to keep moving. If they caught him, it was over. There'd be no chance of the DA or local law enforcement looking for anyone else. They had already demonstrated their unwillingness to go the extra mile the last time, giving up on Kathleen's death. And now this . . . happening all over again. How was it possible? How could his immediate family, the two people he loved most, cease to exist within two years?

He couldn't allow himself to think about it. Not yet. He focused on his breathing, on his stroke, on pacing himself. With a little luck, he should be able to make it to the east shore.

He was halfway across the bay when the police helicopter returned. He pushed on, already winded from the effort. He had to exert twice the energy for a fraction of the distance a normal swimming stroke would have covered.

The chopper slowed to a hover overhead. Marshall rolled over and looked up, exhausted. He had nowhere to hide in the middle of the channel.

FOUR

CHRISTINE BLAKE picked up the phone after the third ring. The voice on the other end didn't give her a chance to say hello.

"Where have you been? Do you know what's happened?"

"Calm down, Debra. I've been right here, asleep. What's going on?"

"Wes has just killed his daughter."

"What?" Wide awake now. "How did it happen? Some kind of accident—"

"It was no accident. The police are here, crawling all over the place." Debra paused to let out a long, exasperated breath. "I thought you were watching him."

"I was. There wasn't much happening, so I came home."

"Where did you last see him?"

"On his boat. He took a small skiff out to its mooring. I watched him climb aboard."

"Was Jennifer with him?"

"Yeah."

"What time?"

"A little after dark. I'd have to check my notes for the exact time."

Silence. No breathing, no background sounds. Christine wondered if the line had gone dead. When Debra finally spoke, she sounded calmer.

"I want you to cooperate with the police. They'll want a statement from you."

"Are you sure that's how you want to handle it? You're protected by confidentiality. We don't have to rush into anything."

"Give them whatever they want," Debra said. "Tell them everything."

"I don't know everything. How was Jennifer killed? Do they have Wes in custody?"

"I'm not sure of all the details. Just tell them what you do know."

Debra hung up.

Christine replaced the receiver on the nightstand. She tossed back the covers and didn't hit a light switch until entering the bathroom.

No sense going back to bed. She threw on some clothes and paced back and forth between the bedroom and living room, her apartment becoming more confining and less cozy with each step. She finally settled in at the kitchen table after microwaving a cup of water for herbal tea. She had a legal-sized pad and a pen in front of her.

She thumbed trough the pad's first few pages. She didn't know Marshall had a daughter until two days ago. Hardly seemed worth noting at the time. But Christine reviewed each page, anticipating a thorough line of questioning by the police and recognizing the need to be prepared. She flipped the used pages to a blank sheet for writing down more details, trying to think clearly but still stunned by the news, unable to concentrate on anything but Debra's abrupt behavior over the phone.

* * *

They didn't see him. The chopper hovered overhead, yet they didn't see him. The rotor blades were too high to disturb the water's surface, and Marshall struggled to stay as submerged as possible without creating any tell-tale ripples. He counted on his dark hair not to stand out and risked a glance up at the searchlight mounted on the chopper's belly as it swept the east shore, the crew on board obviously concentrating on the nooks and crannies illuminated along the docks.

After what seemed like forever, the chopper moved on, heading north, then turned west for another pass. The searchlight kept to the shoreline, with only occasional sweeps across the deeper water.

Marshall swam back the way he'd come, happy to see most of the police cruisers pulling out of the nearby lot. He spent a long two hours in the water next to the dinghy, watching the proceedings from his old hiding place. The fireboat, or another one just like it, had returned to the side of his boat. Nothing much happened until they transferred Jennifer's body and motored off at a somber pace in the direction of the harbor patrol station. Only the one-man patrol boat remained.

He tried to stay low in the water as he worked his way to the docks in front of a familiar boatyard. His hands were raw from clutching mooring lines and scraping against barnacles. He was chilled to the bone, and his skin felt greasy from what he hoped were pollutants in the water rather than the blood. All he could smell were the brackish odors of the bay.

He came in close enough to look over the boatyard's surroundings, straining his senses for any movement or noise around Walter Jenkins's shop. There was side door at the far end of the north wall, just beyond a narrow flower bed bordered with river rock. One of the rocks was a fake that screwed apart to reveal a hollow space for hiding a key. Most of the boat owners knew about it and were allowed access if Walter wasn't around.

Shivering from the cold and hunched low under the glare of security lights, Marshall darted to the side of the shop. The shivering made it difficult to fit the key into the lock. He finally shoved it in and opened the door. His eyes adjusted to the dark interior, helped by the ambient light coming in through the windows from an outside lamppost. He'd never used the shop for himself, but he knew his way around from helping Walter with the restoration of an old Chris Craft.

He needed to get the cuffs off. Walter had a grinding wheel bolted to the workbench, but using it meant drawing attention—the machine sounded like a sex-starved alley cat on steroids. Before he started it up, he searched for anything else he might need. A denim jumpsuit hanging on a post caught his eye.

"Yes!" he said, flinching from the sound of his outburst. He ran over and claimed his prize. He climbed into the pants portion and pulled up the zipper as far as he could, letting the long sleeves hang loose.

More comfortable now, he continued the search, finding a long-billed fishing cap and over five dollars in coin from one of the workbench drawers.

Despite the warmth of the coveralls, he began shivering again as soon as he switched on the grinding wheel. A metallic screech sang out over the whine of the motor when he started cutting. The fatigued muscles along his shoulders and wrenched arm tightened, threatening to cramp up as he held the chain against the wheel. He fought to maintain steady pressure and not lose the groove. Under a shower of sparks, the center link glowed red hot, spreading heat to the cuffs, burning his wrists. The first sense of relief he'd felt all night washed over him when the scorched, cut loop of hardened steel fell to the floor.

The individual cuffs were still warm and secured around his wrists, but his hands were now free of each other. He slipped them through the sleeves, zipped the coveralls closed, and locked up, replacing the key.

He stalked among the shadows of the restaurant next door and found a gap in the lattice-work screening the foundation. He squeezed under the floor and crawled into a maze of pilings, looking for a place to hide. It brought back memories of a day years ago when his dog broke her leg. She couldn't walk on the leg at all, and he watched her crawl off into the shrubs next to the house. Maybe she wanted a safe place to be alone and heal, but it seemed to him as if she had been looking for a place to die. She was a big German shepherd, and even with the useless back leg she managed to burrow into those bushes with a pitiful surge of determination. Like right now, the way he was scratching through the dirt and sand.

Another scream gathered in his chest but he only had the strength to let out a wet sob and sprawl onto the ground. A numbness closed in around him and entered his limbs. It worked its way deep inside, searching for his soul. Maybe he'd been right about the dog. Maybe there was a time to quit. Just find a place to crawl off and die.

* * *

Dawn came. He was still alive, but the numbness remained. He wormed his way up the crawlspace to the front of the building, where he had a good view of Pacific Coast Highway through the lattice. A bus stop stood next to the parking lot entrance. He concentrated on it with everything he had, trying to distract himself from thinking about Jennifer. Or her mother. He needed Kathleen now more than ever, aching for her touch, for her soft, reassuring whispers. But there was only silence, until the sound of a labored engine came out of the gloom. An ancient Toyota pick-up truck finally appeared and pulled over and deposited two uniformed Latinas at the curb. They were there for the first bus of the day. Probably cleaned houses in Emerald Bay or worked at one of the Laguna Beach hotels.

He crawled back to the rear of the building, found the gap where he'd entered, and exited by the same route. He looked out at the water. The patrol boats were back. Two uniformed officers stood on the dock not more than a hundred yards away, the one facing him referring to a small notebook. Marshall ducked down a narrow sidewalk before the cop glanced up. The sidewalk ran between the restaurant and a fence alongside the boatyard next door. Marshall followed it to the parking lot and hoped he didn't look as conspicuous as he felt on his way over to bus stop.

He had to wait about five minutes for the southbound bus. After a polite nod to the two women, he filed in behind them and picked out enough quarters out if his front pocket to cover the bus fare and tossed them into the hopper. He sat at the rear of the bus, unable to contain a quiet sigh as it pulled away from the curb. He gained control of his breathing, trying to relax. He slouched in the seat to lay his head against the backrest. A stab of pain at the base of his skull brought him upright in a hurry. He reached back and felt a mushy lump behind his right ear. It was the epicenter of the nagging headache he'd been ignoring all night. He probed and prodded with exploratory fingers, finding the most tender spot and pressing harder. The pain felt better than the numbness he'd been experiencing, like the soreness of a repaired tooth coming alive after the Novocain starts to wear off. Then, without warning, the tears came. He leaned forward and buried his face in his hands.

The bus downshifted for the climb up the hill next to El Moro. Marshall had only a few more minutes to compose himself before they reached the intersection of Broadway and Pacific Coast Highway in Laguna Beach, as safe a place as any for getting off the bus. He was waiting at the door when they rolled up to the stop. A few more passengers had come aboard on the way through town, but they didn't give him a second glance. A barefoot man in a faded jumpsuit didn't attract much attention around here—just another member of an eccentric homeless population that had been prowling Laguna's streets for decades.

He walked over to Forest Avenue. The bakery was still there. It had been remodeled during the years since his last visit. The coffee and pastry were more expensive, the clientele looked more affluent. When he paid for his coffee, he scrunched in his arms to keep the sleeves over the steel cuffs. The occasional jingle of the remaining link attached to each cuff mixed with the sound of coins hitting the counter. He made it out of the bakery without incident and turned down the sidewalk. He found an empty bench half a block farther. Someone had left a morning paper folded on the seat. Marshall sat down and sipped his coffee for a moment before picking it up.

He winced at the headline.

CORONA DEL MAR DEVELOPER SOUGHT IN DAUGHTER'S MURDER

It got worse:

Wes Marshall, a prominent Corona del Mar land developer, is being sought in connection with the murder of his daughter, Jennifer Marshall. Her body was found last night on Mr. Marshall's boat by Harbor Patrol Officers assisting in a 911 call received by Newport Beach Police. Marshall was apparently at the crime scene when officers arrived, but disappeared shortly after. A coordinated search by Orange County Sheriff's Deputies and the Newport Beach Police Department is currently underway. No official statement has been made at this time.

Wes Marshall is the former husband of Kathleen Marshall, whose body was found last year near their Corona del Mar home. Asked if there was a connection between the two deaths, a spokesman for the District Attorney's Office refused to speculate, other than to mention that the case remains open—

Marshall had read enough. He stifled an acidic belch from the coffee churning in his stomach and felt the caffeine go to work on his frayed nerves. He was about to get up from the bench when a voice out of the past called his name.

"Wes . . . is that you?"

Marshall looked over at the approaching man. He hadn't seen Marty Sheldon since Kathleen's funeral.

"Goddamn, Wes, how long has it been, a couple of years?" Marty stepped up to the bench, ready to shake hands or come up closer for some kind of embrace. Left hanging, a concerned look clouded his face. "What's with the get-up, anyway? You okay?"

Marshall kept his arms crossed, tucked in tight to his chest, afraid the cuffs would show. He couldn't reach for the paper refolded on the bench between them for the same reason. Marty absently picked it up and sat down next to him.

"The guys at the club are always asking about you. I hope you haven't let your membership lapse."

"I've been doing a lot of sailing," Marshall said, trying to control the quiver in his voice. It was like learning to talk all over again.

"I heard something about that. So you got a boat, huh?"

"Yeah, awhile back. Since I saw you last."

The cloud lifted, but Marty's stare held steady. "Must be a lot of work, keeping her in shape, and all."

Marshall snuck a self-conscious glance at his coveralls. "It's not that bad. Mostly fiberglass and teak, and she's still pretty new. Had a problem with the bilge pump, though. Been working on it since first light. Thought I'd come down here and find a day laborer to clean up the mess and polish some brass."

"What's the matter, the local swabs too uppity for that sort of thing?"

"You know how it is. Hard to find decent help. Then I remembered some of the places from the old days where I could pick up good workers for a little cash under the table."

Marty nodded in agreement, looked away at the storefront windows, and relaxed against the wood slats that made up the bench's backrest. "It's not like it used to be. They ran off most of the Mexicans years ago." He turned toward Marshall, more casual now. "That old motel on PCH? It's history. Not many places left they can afford, even with a bunch of 'em sharing a unit. Best place to look is the Circle K parking lot north of town, but by this time of the morning the local contractors have probably picked it clean. I don't think you'll find anyone looking for work hanging around here."

"The lot was empty when I drove by," Marshall said. "I came down to the bakery for coffee. I remember it used to be pretty good." Leaving the coffee cup where he'd set it on the bench, he stood up and drove his hands into the bottom of the coverall's front pockets. He kept his distance to avoid a parting handshake. "I was just about to head back home."

"Where are you parked? I'll walk with you."

As Marty rose to his feet, Marshall backed down the sidewalk. "That's okay, I'm just over on Broadway and I'm already running late. I was hoping to have this done before work. Be sure to say hi to the guys for me."

He turned with a little half-skip and almost broke into a run. Pacific Coast Highway was half a block away. He stared straight ahead at the intersection and concentrated on holding his gait at a reasonable pace. It was all he could do to keep from looking back.

FIVE

CHRISTINE BLAKE sat in her Camry in front of the Newport Beach Police Station. The sun was still low enough to cast shadows across the exterior concrete steps leading to the entrance. They stood empty, only fifteen of them every time she counted, but they appeared steeper and more foreboding the longer she waited. She distracted herself with another glance at the name she'd written on a page torn from her memo pad.

It read, Del Hallstrom—Lieutenant, just like he'd said it over the phone. First and last name, in a friendly sort of way, followed by the weight of his title lest she forget this was official business.

She picked up a manila envelope beneath the memo and rechecked and rearranged the contents one more time. She'd need them to help her recall every detail of her surveillance. She knew how the police were about details.

The last few days were the most important, starting with the afternoon she'd found out about Jennifer Marshall.

* * *

Christine remembered how calm the water had looked that day, out beyond Marshall's office, down the hill and across Pacific Coast Highway, past the harbor and the Balboa Peninsula. She was parked between Anacapa Way and Farallon Drive, on an unmarked access road that snaked its way among the parking lots on the west slope of the Newport Center Corporate Plaza.

The copper roof of Marshall's two story office building stood below her on a terraced ledge facing the coastline.

She passed the time trying to think of a graceful way to back out of her deal with Debra. Spending her lunch hours staking out the office was getting old, as was how foolish she felt. She unwrapped what she hoped would be her last on-the-run deli sandwich and waited once again for Marshall to make a move.

He appeared from the rear door of his office just as she bit into her sandwich. She made a haphazard attempt to rewrap the sandwich and then tossed it on the passenger seat while Marshall climbed into his Suburban. She started her car but didn't move until she saw which direction he took after pulling out of the lot. They were on separate terraces and had to wind through a maze of access roads leading to Newport Center Drive, the only way out of the plaza. She didn't see a posted speed limit but was sure she broke it in an effort to get to the street first. She waited through an extra sequence of traffic lights at the intersection for Marshall to show up. When he pulled onto the road a block below her, she let him make his turn and dropped in behind him after he passed by. She followed him up the hill to Fashion Island, where he parked near an outdoor escalator.

She parked a few aisles over and followed him on foot, up the escalator and across a courtyard, to one of the cafés. She found a place to sit out on the courtyard between the shops and department stores. It was a perfect day to take advantage of the café's outdoor seating, and Marshall didn't disappoint her. A few minutes after he was seated, a good-looking blonde joined him at his table.

Christine pulled out her digital camera. The patrons in the restaurant and the shoppers milling about the courtyard gave her plenty of cover to snap some good shots. After Marshall and his companion finished lunch, Christine abandoned Marshall and followed the blonde to her car.

An hour later Christine sat at her desk, staring at a faxed printout from the Department of Motor Vehicles. She picked up the phone and called Debra.

"Why didn't you tell me Wes has a daughter?"

"Christine . . . hello to you, too."

"Sorry, I guess I'm not in the mood for chitchat. I've been doing some unnecessary running around and squandering favors over at the DMV just to find out what I should already know."

"You must be talking about Jennifer."

"No kidding. It would have helped if you had said something about her. Is there anything else I should know? Friends he might visit? Anything like that?"

"You really are mad at me, aren't you?"

"Don't sound so hurt. I'm not mad. After drawing blanks all week I thought I'd finally stumbled onto something, that's all. I'm just a little frustrated."

"Okay. I forgive you."

She forgives me. Christine let it pass.

"Let's see," Debra said. "The only other person I can think of—someone he might spend some time with—is the old guy he sails with. Other than those little jaunts he takes after dinner, that's where he spends his extra time."

"Maybe that's where he'd been going after dinner, to work on his boat or to hang out with his sailing buddies."

"I don't think so," Debra said, "not the way he dresses. That's probably the reason he comes home first—to clean up and change clothes. Just be patient. It's been almost a week since he's gone out. He's overdue. Stay with him for a few more days."

Christine watched the house again that night. The windows were dark, the lights out now for some time. She was parked down the street, under a gnarled and twisted monster of a ficus tree that had won its battle with the sidewalk decades ago. Salt air drifted in through the open driver's door window. Distant surf beyond the cul-de-sac sounded like the rustling leaves in the high branches above her. The wide trunk and thick lower branches of the ficus were too sturdy to show any movement, but the tall palm trees lining PCH a few blocks away swayed in the breeze freshening out of the northwest. Christine checked her watch one last time, then started her car and pulled away from the curb before all the nocturnal whispers could lull her to sleep.

Debra called her with a heads-up the next evening. Marshall was on the move, and Christine arrived at her observation post in time to watch him pull out of his driveway.

Marshall's Suburban was easy to follow, riding high on beefed-up suspension. The custom lumber rack and vanity license plate made it all but impossible for Christine to lose track. She maintained a comfortable distance behind it on the northbound 405 as Marshall cruised alongside the carpool lane at the freeway's unofficial speed limit of eighty miles per hour. She experienced a few tense moments when he transitioned to the Marina del Rey Freeway, but she managed to stay with him without being too obvious, or so she hoped. A quick mile later the freeway ended. Christine let Marshall stray a few more car lengths ahead as he made his way from Lincoln Boulevard to Bali Way. He turned left at the Ritz-Carlton. A red Ferrari shot in behind him from the opposite direction before Christine could follow him in, and they all rolled up single file to the hotel entrance. It was valet parking only. Christine had to wait for the Ferrari's owner to be served before she could follow Marshall into the lobby.

She lost him. Not even a fleeting glimpse when she walked in. The front desk was quiet. A young man wearing a dark suit, white shirt and dark tie, and a rose boutonnière shading his brass nametag, looked up from what he was doing behind the counter as Christine approached. He smiled a greeting.

"Hi," Christine said. "I'm just here to meet someone. Can you tell me if Wes Marshall has checked in?"

The desk clerk punched a keyboard and looked down at a monitor somewhere out of Christine's sight. He shook his head. "Sorry, he hasn't checked in." A few more keystrokes. "And I'm not showing a reservation for Wes Marshall."

Christine looked around, stalling, trying to think. She didn't want to waste the trip to the Marina. There were still no guests at the desk, and the clerk seemed reasonable enough. She finally said, "I'm sure he said the Ritz." She paused another moment. "You know, I think I have a picture of him."

She said it as soon as she remembered them—the photos she'd taken the day before of Marshall and his daughter. She had held one of them aside before filing the others away and now pulled it out of her shoulder bag, continuing to talk as she passed it over the counter.

"Maybe you've seen him. I suppose he could be staying at another hotel. We're just meeting here."

The clerk raised an eyebrow. With a knowing smile, faint, but unmistakably there, he handed the photo back to Christine.

"Sorry, I don't recognize the gentleman, the clerk said, nodding at the photo, "but I've seen the woman. She checked in about an hour ago."

"Are you sure?"

"Absolutely," the clerk said. "I checked her in myself." The knowing smile was turning stale. "I really can't answer anymore questions. We have a strict policy regarding the privacy and safety of our guests, and I'm afraid I've already overstepped my bounds."

"But if I ask you about a specific guest, by name, you're allowed to tell me if he or she has checked in, aren't you?"

A reluctant nod.

"Has Jennifer Marshall checked in?"

After a moment, another nod, even less enthusiastic.

Christine knew better than to ask more questions. She wasn't going to get a room number or anything like that. She returned the photo to her shoulder bag and thanked the clerk for his help. He acknowledged her with a poor imitation of his initial smile.

She cruised the lobby, wandered the corridors on the first floor, and ended up at an inconspicuous table in the lounge after strolling past the open-air portion of the restaurant for a close look inside. She nursed an iced tea and stared at the dormant cell phone she had just placed on the table. She decided not to call Debra and went home.

* * *

I wonder if calling her would have made a difference, Christine thought, now counting the concrete steps again. She gathered up the memo and the envelope and stuffed them into her shoulder bag and climbed out of the car.

The hum of fluorescent lights accentuated the early-morning silence inside the station. A desk sergeant manned his post facing the front door. He sat at the far end of a narrow foyer that offered no chance of entering the building unnoticed.

"Quiet in here," Christine said.

The desk sergeant maintained a bored expression, as if not really watching her approach. "That's how we like it."

"I'm here to see Lieutenant Hallstrom."

"Ms. Blake?"

Christine nodded.

"He's expecting you."

The desk sergeant indicated the door to his left. Christine entered a hallway and followed his directions to Hallstrom's office. The door stood ajar, and she peered inside.

"Lieutenant Hallstrom?"

A crew-cut man, all steel and flint, glanced up from his desk. He had the look of a military type who appeared better suited for a forced march rather than seated on a padded chair.

"My name's Christine Blake. We talked on the phone."

"Of course." Hallstrom unfolded his lanky frame and came up head and shoulders above her. "Please come in."

He reached over to shake Christine's hand and offered her a seat facing the desk. He dropped back into his chair and said, "Have you seen the morning paper?"

"No, but I turned on the TV before I came over. The local newscasts are having a field day."

Hallstrom settled in, pushing back from the desk. "That's why I wanted to get your statement right away. Before things have a chance to get . . . distorted." He paused, making eye contact for an extra beat. "Don't get me wrong. We've got the guy. That is, we know Marshall did it, but you never know how things might turn out later if this goes to court."

"If?"

"We still haven't found him. Chances are his body's somewhere in the harbor, pinned under a mooring buoy or on its way out to sea." The springs in Hallstrom's chair squeaked as he abruptly returned to an upright position. He leaned forward and rested his arms on the desktop. "Sorry. I'm getting ahead of myself. Some of this stuff we've kept from the press."

"But he could be at large."

"That's a possibility. If he is, any ideas where he might like to hide out?"

Christine shook her head. "Don't know that much about him. Like I said on the phone, I watched him board his boat with his daughter. That's about it. After a while they turned on an interior light. When they turned it off, I waited around for maybe half an hour, then left. I didn't know anything was wrong until Debra called in the middle of the night. She said you'd be wanting to talk to me and that I should cooperate fully."

"Right now I can use all the help I can get. I understand from Mrs. Marshall that you've had her husband under surveillance for the last few days. You probably know more about him than you think. If he turns up alive and this goes the distance, it could help us line all the ducks in a row for the DA. We aren't always fortunate to have a professional such as yourself witness a murder."

"A professional? What did Debra say about me?"

"Not much. Just that she hired you to watch her husband. I assumed you're a PI."

"Not exactly. Though sometimes I feel like one."

Christine fished a business card out of her bag and flicked it like a poker dealer onto the papers cluttering Hallstrom's desktop. He picked it up for a quick look.

He glanced back at her. "Confidential Advocate?"

"More like a children's advocate. Among other things, I provide legal assistance to underage kids who don't have much of a voice concerning the decisions other people make for them."

"So you're a lawyer."

"Just a one-woman operation. I handle everything from adoption issues to parental abuse. A lot of the time I'm out in the field, looking for lost runaways, tracking down deadbeat dads, that sort of thing."

"Do much divorce work?"

"I try to stay away from it."

"How successful are you?"

"At staying away from it?"

Hallstrom waited for an answer.

Christine relaxed deeper into her chair and shrugged. "Not successful enough. This was my first case, if you want to call it that."

"Why don't we go over it, from the beginning."

"Best I can do is tell you where I entered the picture. Who knows where all this began. I'm having a hard enough time believing it actually happened."

"Take your time," Hallstrom said, leaning back again.

Christine sat up and leaned toward him, as if sitting on the opposite end of a seesaw. "First of all, Debra and I are friends.

Not close, but I've known her for a few months now. She's been having problems with her husband. They're still newlyweds, yet she asked me to follow him."

Hallstrom remained quiet, urging her on with a barely perceptible nod.

"She wanted to find out if he was cheating on her, and if so, with whom. I turned her down. About a week ago she offered to pay me. It was a generous offer."

"Is that when you started watching him?"

"I worked him into my schedule, swinging by his office at lunch, seeing if he left the house at night, that sort of thing. I was about ready to give up when last Tuesday he met someone for lunch. I learned later that it was his daughter, Jennifer, from his first marriage. I wasn't aware of who she was at the time and snapped a few photos of them together. After they finished lunch, I followed her to her car and used the plate number to get a line on her ID."

Christine produced the manila envelope, pulled out a stack of photographs, and handed a few off the top to Hallstrom.

"Once I knew who she was, I forgot about her . . . until I tailed Marshall from his house to the Ritz Carlton in Marina del Rey. I lost Marshall somewhere between the parking lot and the lobby, but a desk clerk recognized Jennifer from one of the photographs. He told me she had checked in an hour earlier.

"That should be easy to verify," Hallstrom said. He picked up a pen and jotted a quick note. "If the daughter checked in, we can find out."

"Not that it matters," Christine said.

Hallstrom looked up from his writing. "Oh, it matters. It could help establish the kind of relationship Marshall had with his daughter. Give us a motive. It might even shed some light on what happened to his first wife." He put down his pen. "What happened next?"

"At the Ritz? I ended up at the lounge wondering what to do. I came close to calling Debra right then."

"Why didn't you?"

"I don't know, something held me back. I didn't want to tell her anything until I knew what was going on. There could have been a perfectly innocent reason why Marshall went to the hotel, despite the look on the desk clerk's face when I showed him the photo. The clerk didn't really know anything. He recognized Jennifer in the photo, but so what? It didn't mean Marshall was out of line. Maybe Jennifer checked in at the hotel to get away from an abusive husband or boyfriend or something like that. Maybe she wanted to talk to her dad about it."

"Or maybe you didn't want to believe the alternative."

"That's a valid point. I don't think I did. But I stayed around for a while, and when nothing happened, I went home. Then yesterday morning, bright and early, Debra called. She asked me what was going on, told me her husband hadn't come home yet. She said it was the first time he'd stayed out all night. I told her I'd followed him to the Ritz-Carlton."

"Did you bring up Jennifer?"

"No, I still didn't know his daughter's story, so I didn't say anything about her. I told Debra that I wasn't able to see who he met, but that I had a lead and would get back to her.

"We left it at that. Then Debra called back shortly after, more upset than ever. Marshall had just come and gone. He told her he had a golf date with her father and that he wouldn't be home for dinner. They argued when Debra confronted him about the Ritz. Rather than give her a straight answer, Marshall stormed out of the house, telling her not to wait up, that he'd be spending the night on his boat."

"So you knew where he'd be," Hallstrom said.

"Not really. That's just what he'd told Debra. For all I knew he had another meeting set up at the Ritz or some other place. I asked Debra when and where he was going to play golf. She said she'd find out and called me later with the tee time at her father's club in LA.

"She made arrangements for me to get in. I arrived a little after four o'clock, about an hour before they finished their round. I was sipping iced tea on a veranda overlooking the eighteenth green when Marshall's group walked off. Marshall was in a hurry, only taking a moment to talk to the older of the other three men before rushing off. I made it to the parking lot in time to follow him out. He was upset about something."

"Did he go directly to his boat?"

"Turned out I could have waited for him there. He pulled into a driveway off PCH that led back to the docks. I used the parking lot for the bar next door. I'd been there before and was familiar with the narrow deck out back. It's elevated, about ten feet above the water. From the south corner you have a view of where he usually parks.

"I made it through the bar and out onto the deck just before Jennifer's BMW pulled in next to his Suburban. I watched them climb out of their vehicles. Jennifer walked over and wrapped him up in a big hug. It wasn't the kind of hug normally exchanged between father and daughter. I lost sight of them when they walked down toward the boats secured along the wharf. A few minutes later they came into view aboard a rowboat powered by a small outboard motor, heading out to his boat."

Hallstrom was taking notes again. "And what time was this?"

"Close to seven thirty."

"Any more pictures?"

"Just of Jennifer's car. It was pretty dark and I was too far away for the other shots to be of much use."

Christine handed Hallstrom more photos.

After a quick glance he set them aside. "And you were only there for half an hour?"

"No, I didn't leave until nine o'clock. What I said earlier was that I left half an hour after they turned out the lights. I hung out for a while, biding my time on a barstool by one of the windows with a clear view of the boat. When it became obvious they weren't going anywhere, I left. I had what I needed."

"Wasn't it about time to inform Mrs. Marshall?"

Christine said nothing.

"I don't get it," Hallstrom said. "Here you've amassed all this evidence pointing to what can only be described as disturbing behavior between Marshall and his daughter, and you don't say anything? Wasn't that what you were hired to do? To find out who Marshall was seeing?"

Christine looked down at random spot between the front of Hallstrom's desk and the floor. "I didn't want to be responsible for creating a scene." She brought up her eyes and stared back at Hallstrom. "Can you believe it? I was afraid Debra might come down and do something stupid, make a fool of herself, or worse. She can be pretty headstrong. I thought it would be better if I broke it to her in the cold light of morning, in person, with a typed report and prints of all the photos."

"And you didn't see anyone else come or go from the boat?"

"No, I didn't."

Hallstrom rolled back and opened drawers and rummaged through their contents. Christine looked around the frugal office. More like a large cubicle with a ceiling, devoid of personality. No framed pictures sitting on the desktop or awards hanging on the walls. Her mouth was dry from nerves and too much talking and tasted like stale paste. Despite the open door, the atmosphere inside the room was close. Her antiperspirant had broken down when she first entered the building, and as she returned her gaze to Hallstrom, she could only hope that the air was a little fresher on his side of the desk.

Hallstrom found what he was searching for. "Hope you don't mind going over this again, for the record."

"Not at all. I know the drill."

Hallstrom looked at her with a question in his eyes. It remained unasked as he turned his attention to finding and loading a fresh cassette into the pocket-sized recorder he'd just placed on the desk.

Christine asked for a glass of water. After gulping it down, she repeated her story for the recorder. She waited for them to transcribe her statement and signed it before she left.

SIX

CHRISTINE LET out a deep breath when she settled in behind the wheel of her Camry. She sat there for a quiet minute to shed the tension, then fired the ignition and pulled out of the station's parking lot.

She had been curious about Debra's enthusiasm to help the police. But when Christine looked at it from her point of view, at how Debra must have felt when they woke her up with the news, well, her response was understandable.

Understanding Wes Marshall was a little tougher. Christine was familiar with incestuous behavior, but nothing like this. Not two adults hiding their affair from the man's wife, appearing like any other father-daughter out at lunch, then sneaking off at night to secret rendezvous at out-of-the-way hotels and dimly-lit boats. How long had it been going on? And if it was long term, why marry Debra? Jennifer could have stayed at home and lived with her father. Nothing unusual about that. They could have kept it all a secret in their own house. Was marrying Debra an attempt to get out of it, to start leading a normal life that he ultimately couldn't live? Is that why he killed Jennifer? Did he just loose it somehow and in a fit of rage and guilt go completely berserk?

And what about the death of his first wife? Hallstrom had made a good point about a possible connection. On the other hand, maybe Marshall's grief over the loss of his first wife somehow drove him closer to his daughter, and one thing led to another.

Slow down. Why all the speculation? It doesn't matter now.

Still, Christine couldn't get all the thoughts and images out of her head. The two of them out at lunch the other day, appearing so *normal.* If she hadn't actually seen them last night at the boatyard, the way Jennifer came up and smothered Marshall with her body, Christine wouldn't have believed it.

She approached PCH, a few blocks away from the police station, and looked over at the surrounding cars herding up to the red stoplight. She tried to get her mind on something else. She focused on the cars rather than their occupants, not wanting to make eye contact as they all came to a stop. As usual around here, she was surrounded by German cars. She took a good look at the black BMW in the lane next to her, a car-length ahead. It was just like Jennifer's . . . except for the color . . .

It all came back in a flash—Jennifer's gray BMW with the black convertible top parked in Marshall's driveway the night she followed him to the Ritz. The headlights of his Suburban had shined on it like a spotlight when he backed out and swung onto the street.

How did that get by me?

Christine waited for the light to change, unable to do anything for the moment. Earlier, while they had been waiting for an admin to transcribe her taped statement, Hallstrom received word that Jennifer had, in fact, checked in at the Ritz-Carlton Wednesday night. The hotel's credit card records confirmed the desk clerk's recollection. So Jennifer had been there, no question. And yet her car had remained at Marshall's house.

How did she get to the hotel ahead of Marshall? She couldn't have driven over with him. Christine would have noticed her sitting in the Suburban while following him, and he was the only one to get out at the valet station at the entrance to the hotel.

Of course, it could have been a different BMW belonging to someone else. Christine looked around again at all the German cars. Plenty of people own BMWs. But what were the odds of a friend or visitor parking the exact same model and color in Marshall's driveway that night?

The light changed. Christine turned right on PCH, but her mind was still back at Marshall's driveway. She couldn't remember seeing a license plate on the BMW, or even looking for it, but she had been familiar with the car. She'd run its plates the day she followed Jennifer from the restaurant. She knew the year, make, model, and color. She recognized it as Jennifer's when she saw it again. No reason to be suspicious about it at the time.

But now it bothered her. She rejected her first impulse to go back and share her thoughts with Hallstrom. He'd be too busy with his own agenda, which was apprehending Marshall or finding his body. If there were any details to sort out, he'd want to take care of them later.

* * *

Christine drove past her office and continued up PCH to the bar from where she'd watched Marshall and Jennifer. She told herself she wasn't going to get involved or interfere with the police investigation—she just wanted to look around and gain a fresh perspective now that she knew what had happened last night.

She pulled into one of the empty parking spaces in front of the bar. It wasn't open yet and she had to go around to the side walkway and work her way the rear deck.

She stood there for a few minutes, then went down the gangplank leading to the docks. She walked in the same direction she had seen Marshall and Jennifer take last night, eventually coming to a stop at a roped-off section of the dock that was under repair. Unable to go farther, Christine turned around, almost making it back to the gangplank before an older man caught her attention. He stood beyond a set of vertical sliding doors, half open from floor to ceiling, at the entrance to the workshop next door to the bar.

She had almost missed him, back in the shadows, wearing an untucked tee shirt over baggy Bermuda shorts. He was working on the wooden hull of a small boat. A short flight of concrete steps led from the dock to a paved landing in front of the shop. A boom and tackle rig was bolted nearby for hoisting boats in and out of the yard. Christine climbed the steps and made her way past a few empty cradles and over to the open doors.

"Hi there," she said, just outside the threshold.

The old man glanced up, preoccupied with his work "Something I can do for you?"

The graveled edge of the old man's voice fit well with his large, raw-boned frame. She could tell he was a sailor by the way he stood over his work, his knees habitually flexed and ready for the next roll of a pitching deck. His shaggy white hair and bristly beard added an air of independence to his gruff manner.

"I hope I'm not bothering you," she said, walking toward him. "My name's Christine Blake." The boat he was working on came into view and distracted her train thought. "Is that an old Chris Craft? It's beautiful."

"Thank you," the old man replied, keeping his eyes on the hull. "It's a Chris Craft, all right. A 1951 Riviera."

"Must be an antique," Christine said.

"Just a classic. Not quite old enough for antique status."

"I love these old speedboats," Christine said, walking up closer, brushing her hand along flawless mahogany. "Looks like it's ready for varnish."

"That's just what I was getting ready to do," the old man said, "I hope you're not interested. She's not for sale."

"Don't worry. I'm not in the market for a boat. It's just that I've acquired an appreciation for old things. My boyfriend is into surfboards, the older, the better. He does a great job restoring them to their original condition."

She studied the boat for an extra beat, then looked at the old man. "I recognize that gleam in your eye. You're a lot like my friend. The value of this boat has nothing to do with money."

"Sounds like my kind of lad," he said, using a dry brush to sweep away any remaining dust from the last sanding. Then he straightened up and tossed the brush onto the deck, staring right at her. "But why do I have the feeling you didn't come here to talk about classic boats or your surfing buddies?"

"No, she stammered, "that's not why I'm here. I thought—"

"You're blushing," the old man interrupted.

That only made it worse. Her cheeks started to burn. She tried to smile and said, "I just wanted to ask you a few questions."

"About Wes Marshall? I've been answering questions from the police and avoiding reporters all morning."

Her smile now felt out of place, frozen by the old man's statement. She let it thaw to an appropriate expression to match the changing atmosphere. She handed him one of her cards.

"I'm not with the police, and I'm not a reporter. I have my own law practice. I had an investigation going on before the events of last night took place."

"The events? You sound like a lawyer, all right." The old man kept his eyes on the card for an extra moment, then looked her in the eye. "You mean the murder."

"Yes," she said. "The murder. I was here last night, before, and for all I know, when it happened."

They talked about it. Christine didn't say who she worked for, but acknowledged that she'd had Marshall under surveillance. The old man seemed surprised by that, despite his casual shrug. He answered a few routine questions, then asked one of his own.

"What are you looking for now?"

"I don't know," she said. "All this happened before I could finish my investigation. I just found out about it this morning, and now it's out of my hands. I guess I need to get a handle on it, for my own peace of mind. My office is just a couple of blocks away. I thought I'd come over and look around, see what it's like during the day, that's all. I appreciate your time."

She started to move away, then stopped and said, "I hope you don't think I was stroking you, I really do like your boat."

"I figured you were sincere. I just like to give people a hard time, even a nice lass such as yourself." He paused for a moment, as if making a quick decision. "You know, there was something a little unusual that happened here yesterday afternoon. Did you happen to see that big hole in the dock?"

He gestured with a southward nod, referring to the roped-off section of the wharf that had impeded Christine's earlier progress.

"There used to be a couple of slips there until the other day, when a big sport fisher ran aground and took them out. Totally destroyed 'em, along with million dollar sloop. They're still picking through the wreckage."

"Where is it now, the sport fisher?"

"They managed to haul it away. That's not the problem. What's bothering me, other than the fact that I've never seen anything like this happen in the fifty-some years I've been here, is that one of those slips is the one Wes Marshall uses."

"How many boats does he keep here?"

"Just the one."

"But that's where they found him, wasn't it? On his boat?"

"It wasn't his boat that got run over. He was out sailing when the sport fisher plowed into his slip. That means he's got to keep her moored offshore until the slip's rebuilt, on account of there's nothing else available. The next thing you know, they find him out there with his dead daughter."

"So you think there's a connection?"

The old man shrugged. "The police don't think so. Or they don't care. For now they're okay with it being a coincidence."

"Who owns the sport fisher?"

"Whoever piloted the boat ran off in the confusion. There was no paperwork on board. The numbers on the bow were useless. Not even a name on the stern. The harbor patrol couldn't come up with anything. I told the police about it later, after the murder."

The old man picked up the brush for a few more half-hearted sweeps, then gave up. He turned his attention to Christine, pointing with the brush for emphasis. "What really bothers me, the unusual part, was seeing his daughter out here the day after the accident, by herself. I watched her climb into the skiff I'd loaned him for boarding his boat."

"You're sure it was her, Marshall's daughter?"

"I'm sure. I'd seen her once awhile back, with Marshall. He introduced us. She was a good-looking lass, a lot like her mother, from what I've been told. The thing is, I've never seen her out here before, by herself I mean, messin' around with her dad's stuff."

"What happened? Did you see her go aboard his boat?"

"No, not really. I was kinda busy and didn't pay that much attention. But I saw her on the wharf later on, almost ran into her on my way to the bar. She walked right on by, like I wasn't there."

"Do you remember what time it was?"

"I don't know . . . three or four, maybe. Right after I'd left my office."

The old man traded the brush for a tack cloth, then scanned the interior of the shop as if he'd lost something.

Christine could see her time was up. The old man nodded when she thanked him again for his help. Before she walked off, she said, "You know, here we've been talking all this time and I don't even know your name.

"My name's Walter Jenkins," the old man said politely, but still appeared anxious to get back to work.

"Nice to meet you, Mr. Jenkins."

He paused as soon as he heard his last name—or maybe it was the Mister. His preoccupied frown smoothed out. His eyes brightened. Under his beard lurked a benevolent smile or a smirk full of mischief, she couldn't tell which.

"You can call me Wally, all my friends do."

"Okay, Wally. See you later."

* * *

Walter watched her leave, then turned back and stared beyond the Chris Craft to a large nail buried halfway into a post, a convenient hook on which to hang his coveralls. He stood there a moment and slowly looked around again before walking toward his workbench, where something shiny had attracted his eye. As he came closer, he saw it was a severed chain link lying in a small pile of metal filings beneath the electric grinding wheel.

"I didn't think I was going senile," he muttered to himself, "not yet, anyway."

SEVEN

MR. MARSHALL!"

His name came through the phone's receiver as a terse whisper. He pictured Miss Phelps on the other end of the line, clutching the phone, her desk chair wheeling toward the credenza behind her desk after she sprang to her feet. She was like that. Not high strung, not overly excitable. More like hyper-alive. She'd been that way for as long as Marshall could remember.

If he didn't count the subcontractors and helpers from the early days, Miss Phelps was Marshall Development's first full-time employee. She had replaced Kathleen, his unofficial secretary when he started the business.

His wife had never received a paycheck, but she maintained accounts receivable and payable, scheduled the work, and handled all other aspects of the business that wasn't directly involved with building and remodeling houses. She was unofficially retired when Marshall hired Miss Phelps.

There was no one he trusted more. He figured Miss Phelps would be the one answering his private line. Its back-up extension was connected to the phone on her desk.

Relieved to hear her voice, he said, "Are you in your office?"

"Yes." The terse whisper again.

"I don't know what you've heard, but you've got to believe me—there's no way I killed Jennifer . . . I don't know what happened or what to do. I just need to talk to someone to keep from going out of my mind."

"I don't know what to say, Mr. Marshall. Of course I believe you.

Still Mr. Marshall. After all these years. And he still called her Miss Phelps, not Elizabeth, her given name. He'd never thought it proper for some reason, and the formal designation had quickly become habit. Now, in spite of the circumstances, he felt a smile crease his face.

"Thank God for that," he said. Now *he* was whispering.

After a brief silence, Miss Phelps said, "I think you should know that Mrs. Marshall is here."

"Debra?"

"Yes. She's snooping around the place with a man I don't like the look of. He's wearing an expensive suit and has the oily charm of a slick financial advisor or some kind of lawyer."

"She's there? Right now? You've seen her?"

"Yes, They just now went up to your office and closed the door. Is there something—"

"How did she look? Her hair—what color was her hair?"

"I'm not sure I understand . . ."

"I'm sorry," Marshall said, making an effort to slow down. "I know this doesn't make much sense to you, but as crazy as it sounds, I need you to describe Debra to me. Specifically, when you just saw her, what color was her hair?"

"Why, it's the same color as always—jet black."

At a loss for words, Marshall stood mute until a plan of action began to surface, as if on its own. When he found his voice, he didn't recognize it.

"I know I shouldn't be asking you this. It could get you into a lot of trouble, but I need you to do something for me."

He waited for a reply, and after another long moment, Miss Phelps said, "You'll have to tell me what it is before I can answer you."

"All right, see if you can round up some cash. Don't write a check or do anything that directly connects you with an unusual withdrawal. I also need clothes, and if possible, a car."

"The money and clothes shouldn't be a problem, Miss Phelps said. "I'm not sure about the car."

"Yeah, we need to be careful, I don't want your name on a rental agreement or anything."

"I'll see what I can do. Where will I find you?"

Marshall told her to meet him at the Laguna Bakery on Forest Avenue. He gave her his shoe size and said he'd need a presentable pair of slacks and a shirt.

"Oh, one more thing. I need a key for a pair of handcuffs. Go to a gun shop, a place like Grants over on Newport Boulevard. They probably sell just the keys, but if you have to, or if you think it would be less conspicuous, buy a set of cuffs. Just make sure they're standard issue Smith & Wesson, the type cops use.

After a moment, Miss Phelps said, "Is this the only way? Have you thought about turning yourself in?"

"It'll come to that, one way or the other. But not yet. I need to straighten a few things out first or I'll be on my way to death row. What's more important is finding out who did this. I'm not going to let them get away with it."

They said their good-byes, Miss Phelps sounding tentative. Marshall stayed on the line after she hung up. No reason, really, other than to hold on to his only link with something positive. He stood at a phone booth near the main beach at Broadway and PCH. Just as he was about to hang up, he heard the distinct click of another extension breaking its connection with what he thought had been a dead phone line.

* * *

Marshall found a quiet stretch of sand among the rocks between St. Ann's Drive and Thalia Street. He sat close to the lapping tide and focused on the horizon to avoid eye contact with anyone passing by. He watched the progress of a boat under sail, reminding him of the other morning—was it really only two days ago?—when the most pressing thing on his mind had been whether or not to risk taking out his boat.

Then he thought about Debra. Wherever his mind wandered, it always circled back to her. Who *was* she? It was hard to admit that he hadn't a clue, even harder to face the possibility that she'd been playing him all along. And her uncanny resemblance to Jennifer . . . he didn't know *what* to think about that.

Nothing had seemed out of the ordinary when he first met her. She had just moved down to Newport Beach from LA and by pure happenstance had hired Jennifer to decorate her condo at Promontory Point. The two women became friends; it was only a matter of time before Marshall ran into her. It wasn't love at first sight, but there was something going on, that déjà vu thing he used to convince himself that the attraction was real, at least for him.

He wasn't looking for a trophy wife, but he liked the attention he was getting, and he somehow let his ego convince him that Debra was into him for who he was, despite the twenty years that stood between them. But what did she really want? She didn't object to the prenuptial agreement. The only way she'd gain a share of his estate was to be legally married to him at the time of his death. If she wanted his money, why was he still alive? If she had been behind this, why squander the perfect opportunity to finish him off after killing the only other heir to his estate?

They never talked much about her past. She'd had modest success as a model and quit while she was ahead rather than compete with the younger competition. If she had needed it, Marshall figured her father supplemented her income. He looked like he could afford the expense, and Marshall saw nothing wrong with it. He'd financed his own daughter's interior design business and was proud of how well she'd done. A few tears would usually sneak up on him whenever he thought of the day she'd insisted on paying him back and handed him the envelope containing her first payment.

He felt the tears welling up again as he pictured Jennifer's face as he'd last seen it. His mind came round to Debra again, right on cue, and he tried to push her back into a dark corner but the images of both women began to merge into something all its own, smiling at him with a cold, malevolent grin.

He tried to refocus on the horizon, his teary eyes stinging from the salt and glare. He resisted the urge to close them by rising to his feet. He checked his watch. If he used a circuitous route to wander back to Forrest Avenue, he could pace himself to arrive at the bakery right at noon.

* * *

The unmarked police car was easy to spot: the usual off-white-no-frills, cheap hubcaps, and chrome spotlights tucked in front of the exterior rear-view mirrors. There was an obvious radio antenna mounted on the trunk, below which the government license plate confirmed any lingering suspicions.

Marshall watched the car ease into the painted left turn lane down from where he was standing and turn onto Forest Avenue. It parked in a loading zone near the corner. Two beefy plainclothes officers climbed out, failing to look casual as they scanned the early lunch hour crowd milling around on the sidewalks.

The two cops slowed down as they neared the bakery from across the street, showing an increased interest in the people near the entrance. Marshall stayed on the far side of PCH, shielded by a group of pedestrians waiting at the intersection for the light to change. He moved on toward Broadway, a block to the north, and crossed PCH when he got there. He still had some time to kill and hoped he was just being paranoid about what he'd seen at the bakery . . .

"Mr. Marshall."

That terse whisper again. Marshall spun around just as Miss Phelps was reaching for his shoulder.

"What are you doing here?" he said, keeping his voice down. They had stopped in the middle of the sidewalk, disrupting the foot traffic. "I thought maybe you'd called the police."

"Shhh . . ." Miss Phelps held a finger to her lips, then grabbed his sleeve and led him to the curb. "Let's cross the street and walk up to Cliff Drive. I parked my car there. It was the closest place I could find."

They crossed Broadway, walked through a liquor store parking lot, then up a concrete staircase leading to Cliff Drive. Miss Phelps nodded toward her silver Lexus parked across the street. Once they were safely inside the car, she said, "Your disguise is very effective. I barely recognized you."

"You should have seen what I was wearing a few hours ago." Marshall glanced out the windows, then back at Miss Phelps. "I thought the police were on to me. I had to ditch the plan to meet at the bakery. How did you find me?"

"I was able to get here early. I saw you cross the highway and turn away from Forest Avenue. I followed you."

"It looked like the cops were waiting for me. I thought you'd turned me in—"

Miss Phelps tried to say something, but Marshall talked over her words.

"—It's all right. I wasn't mad. At the worst, I knew you were only trying to do what you thought was right."

Miss Phelps shook her head. "It wasn't me."

Marshall believed her, remembering the click on the line after they had finished their phone conversation.

"It must have been Debra. Didn't you say she was in my office when we were on the phone?"

"You think she was listening in on your extension?"

"Can you come up with better explanation? It's either that, or the cops are psychic."

"Why would she turn you in?"

"I'm not sure, but I have other things to worry about right now. Were you able to get everything?"

She had him retrieve a nylon gym bag sitting on the back seat. He set it on his lap to examine the contents: a couple of polo shirts, chinos, and a pair of deck shoes. She reached into her purse and pulled out a roll of twenty-dollar bills.

"Here's three hundred dollars," she said, handing Marshall the money. "Sorry about the car. I'm afraid I couldn't come up with anything on such short notice."

Marshall stuffed the money into a front pocket. "Were you able to find the key I asked for?"

Miss Phelps started the car, a faint smile on her lips. "I received a most peculiar expression from the young man waiting on me at Grants."

Marshall tried to imagine the scene in the gun store when this slender, well-dressed older woman walked up to inquire, in her most professional and precise manner, about the availability of a specific pair of handcuffs.

They turned right on Pacific Coast Highway. Marshall settled back against the seat, which reminded him once again of the sore spot behind his ear and the constant, dull ache that encompassed his head, neck and shoulders. They passed Emerald Bay and began the gentle descent down to El Moro.

Miss Phelps spoke into the rearview mirror. "I wish that car would get off my tail."

Marshall looked back. The steel grille-guard of a large SUV filled the rear window.

"Looks like a goddamned Hummer," he said, "and it's right on our ass."

It backed off. Marshall looked at Miss Phelps. "What was that all about?"

She didn't respond, her eyes still on the mirror. Marshall was about to look back when a violent jolt from behind knocked them askew. The Lexus slued into a skid, the rear end trying to catch up with the front, drifting toward the shoulder of the road coming up on Marshall's side of the car. It seemed like the worse might be over, until he felt the trailing tires leave the ground. It was a familiar sensation, as if in a small airplane about to take off. Without wings.

The car came over on its side and continued sliding, then rolled onto its roof. It kept sliding. Marshall had failed to strap in. He had his arm braced against the headliner and could feel the asphalt and gravel trying to grind through the thin skin of the roof. The car finally came to rest.

"You okay?"

"I think so," Miss Phelps said, "but I'm having a hard time with the seatbelt."

Marshall untangled himself from the straps of the gym bag and brushed away some of the safety-glass granules that used to be the passenger side window. He crawled toward the opening and peered through the deflating side-door airbags "Shit, we're hanging halfway over a ditch. How does it look on your side?"

"It looks all right. I'm still having trouble with the belt, though."

Marshall squeezed between a headrest and the roof and surveyed the situation on the other side of the car from the backseat, the glass in the door still intact, the airbags undeployed. "You're right. This should be okay. If I can just get the door open . . ."

It wouldn't budge. He crawled back to the front seat. Miss Phelps was hanging by her seatbelt, the release mechanism jammed between the seat and center console.

"I think we're going to have to cut the belt," he said. "How are you, otherwise?"

"You mean other than hanging here like a trussed chicken?"

He interpreted her attitude as a good sign. He dug into the gym bag and pulled out the shoes. "I'll have to break the side window behind your seat. Too dangerous trying to get out on my side. Even if we managed to drop out the window without hurting ourselves, there's a chance the car could slide down on top of us before we could get out of the way. We're teetering right over the edge."

"Do you have something to cut the belt?"

"Not on me. How about the glove box?"

"There's a tool box in the trunk, next to the spare tire. It came with the car."

The momentary shadow of a vehicle darkened her window as it pulled off the road. It stopped somewhere in front of them. Doors opened and slammed shut and footsteps headed their way. Marshall didn't waste time looking out the windshield to see if it was the police. He hurried with the shoes and crawled over to the backseat. He tried the door again. The electric window button was useless. He positioned himself as best he could, his back against the opposite door, and broke out the window with an adrenalin-laced kick. He spun around on all fours so he could crawl out head first.

It was one move too many. Without warning, the car tipped over and slid into the ditch.

* * *

Marshall looked up through the broken window. A large, moon-faced head stared down at him, backlit by blue sky.

"Are you hurt?"

"No, I think I'm okay," Marshall said, his back against the rear passenger-side door.

"Take my hand," the moon-face said.

It was more like a huge paw. Marshall grasped it in a brother handshake, his fingers wrapping around the hilt of the man's thumb, and was hauled out of the wreckage. If the man had noticed the steel bracelet, he didn't show it.

The Lexus had spun one-eighty degrees, now facing the direction from which it had been traveling. The busted-out window frame was level with the road, the ditch no deeper than the width of the car. A younger and smaller version of the moon-faced man had managed to open the driver's door. Miss Phelps was still strapped in but supported now by the center console.

"I suppose this is an improvement," she said. "but I'd really like to get out of here."

Marshall's rescuer took charge. "Get me something to cut this belt with, Charlie."

"Sure thing, Dad."

Charlie ran up to their SUV and popped the rear hatch. He came back with a box cutter.

"I'm too big to squeeze in beneath her," his father said, "but if you could crawl into the passenger seat and hold the tension off the belt, I'll cut her free." He winked at Miss Phelps. "Just don't drop her when it goes slack."

With Marshall's help, the man cut the belt and pulled Miss Phelps out of the car without too much damage to her dignity. There were close to a dozen samaritans standing around or rushing over from hastily parked vehicles alongside the road.

The moon-faced man helped his son out of the car. He obviously wasn't ready to relinquish control of the situation. "Anybody see what happened?"

The bystanders moved in closer, murmuring among themselves. Someone spoke out.

"I came over the hill, and the Lexus was already sideways, kicking up a cloud of dust along the shoulder. I didn't see a collision, or anything."

A chorus of voices joined in, each one trying to be heard. Marshall distanced himself, blending in with the rear portion of the crowd, while Miss Phelps had Charlie go back for her purse still inside the car. No one seemed to pay attention as she followed Marshall away from the group entirely.

"I think that's the Hummer," he said.

"Where? Was it those men who helped us out of the car?"

"No. Up there." Marshall pointed at the crest of the next hill, less than a quarter of a mile to the north. "It's the right size and shape, and it's just been sitting there. I haven't seen anyone come or go. Can't tell how many passengers from here."

"Who is it?"

"I have no idea."

"What shall we do? People have their cell phones out. The police will be here any minute."

Marshall looked around. They were at the bottom of the hill, where El Moro creek passed under the highway and fed into the ocean. No problem crossing over to the beach. "Maybe I can hike over to Crystal Cove, get lost in the crowd. Ought to be plenty of tourists and beach goers there on a day like this." He returned his gaze to Miss Phelps. "Where's the bag, anyway?"

"It must be in the car."

Marshall drifted toward the Lexus.

"Wait. You better take these."

She handed him two keys, one for the handcuffs, the other one attached to a plastic plaque with a number on it.

"They still give out keys like this?"

"Apparently so," Miss Phelps said. "I rented you a room at the La Quinta Inn."

"Over on Sand Canyon, by the old Irvine Store?"

"Yes. I paid cash for a couple of days. I used another name and told them I didn't have a credit card. I must have appeared trustworthy, and they agreed to a small deposit in case I made any toll calls. I was planning on dropping you there." She reached back into her purse. "You'd better take this as well."

"I don't want to get caught with your cell phone. It could look bad for you."

"Just say you stole it from me."

"After I took you hostage and hijacked your car?"

"Something like that. Better yet, don't get caught."

"Easier said than done. Here they come."

He dove into the Lexus for the gym bag as a siren wailed in the distance, drawing nearer. The crowd began to disperse.

Gym bag in hand, Marshall glanced at Miss Phelps for a parting nod, then crossed the highway at the first break in the traffic. He made it down an embankment and onto the beach before the patrol car arrived. He'd have to risk being exposed until he reached the headlands rising out of the sand a few hundred yards away, where he'd be screened from the highway all the way back to Corona del Mar. The last time he looked, the Hummer was still at the top of the hill. He lost sight of it when he reached the bluffs. He figured about a mile to the old colony of Crystal Cove.

Marshall kept a wary eye on the high ridge to his right and glanced over his shoulder occasionally for anyone following. He unlocked the cuffs and threw them into the ocean. He held on to the key. The few people he came across appeared to be regular beach types, showing up more frequently the closer he came to his destination.

He finally reached the first of the cottages nestled along the base of the bluff, a few yards from the water. Most of the dwellings terraced above them were boarded up or were in various stages of repair.

He crossed the shallow mouth of Los Trancos Creek, barely wetting the tops of his shoes, and came upon a hardpan trail that ended at the entrance to the Beachcomber Restaurant. It was the closest structure to the water, the size of a small diner inside, with twice the available seating outside on its wooden deck. A few long strides to his left and he'd be wadding in the Pacific. He turned right and headed for the public restroom behind the building.

He came out sporting a new look, leaving the gym bag, coveralls, and extra shirt in a trash container near the door. He flipped open the cell phone to call a cab while continuing along the trail. It led to a loading area for the shuttle service that hauled the less ambulatory visitors to and from the parking lot up the hill and across Pacific Coast Highway.

Marshall knew his way around. If he stayed on the trail, it would take him to the lot, a five minute hike if he walked briskly. The problem was the tunnel, the only sensible way cross PCH on foot. It was about a hundred yards long, and very narrow, designed for pedestrians only. A perfect place for anyone following him to set a trap.

The dispatcher on the phone interrupted his thoughts. He made arrangements for the cab to pick him up at the entrance to the parking lot off PCH. The shuttle arrived, but climbing aboard held no more appeal than entering the tunnel.

Marshall waved off the shuttle, then followed it on foot the long way to the parking lot. He crossed PCH at the stoplight at Los Trancos, then had to endure a stressful ten-minute wait for the cab to arrive. The cabbie was mercifully quiet during the drive, and he accepted payment with bored indifference at the front entrance to the La Quinta Inn.

EIGHT

CHRISTINE STARED across Pacific Coast Highway from her office window. It wasn't much of a view. She occupied one of the four upstairs suites of a two-story concrete and glass structure built in the late fifties. All she could see from the window was the highway itself, a portion of her parking lot, and a wide expanse of the Balboa Bay Club's five-story stucco walls across the way. It effectively blocked any glimpse of the harbor just on the other side.

But she could watch occasional pedestrians pass by and keep tabs on the cars as they entered and exited the parking lot she shared with the other tenants. She happened to be looking out in that direction when Debra Marshall's white Mercedes pulled in.

Debra had a knack for showing up like that, unannounced, whenever the situation suited her. Whenever she happened to be in the neighborhood. Christine shut down her computer and waited for the sound of Debra's stiletto heels climbing the outdoor steps.

The door opened without a knock.

Christine swiveled around in her chair as Debra entered the room. The woman looked too damn good, considering the circumstances. Not so much as a frown marred her waxed brow. Her assertive posture enhanced perfectly proportioned features wrapped nicely in a St. John knit that must have set her back at least three thousand dollars. Christine tried to keep the irony out of her voice.

"How are you holding up?"

Debra ignored the question, her eyes scanning the room. She grabbed a chair and dragged it closer to the desk and sat down.

"Have you talked to the police yet?"

Christine nodded. "Earlier this morning."

"And?"

"And what? I told them what I saw."

"Which was . . ."

"Pretty much what I told you over the phone."

Debra broke eye contact. She turned to look outside the window in front of Christine's desk.

Is she smiling?

I must be seeing things, Christine thought, studying Debra's profile as she looked toward the Bay Club across PCH.

Debra turned back. No hint of a smile now. "Do they have any idea what happened to him?"

"If they did, they didn't let me in on it. As far as I can tell, they're still looking for him."

For the first time since she'd entered the office, Debra appeared agitated. She stood up and started pacing.

"The sooner they find him and get this over with, the better. I don't know how much more of this I can take."

"There's a good chance he didn't make it, Debra. You better prepare yourself for the worst."

"The worst? The man killed his daughter. And the way they found her . . . how could it possibly get any worse? How am I supposed to explain this to my family?"

Christine felt as if she had been watching a performance rather than an outpouring of genuine emotions. And that faint smile. It was back again. Was it really there, or was it Debra's way of hiding how she must be feeling?

"Where are you off to?" Christine said, attempting to change the subject. "You're a little overdressed for this neck of the woods."

"Oh . . ." Debra stopped pacing. "I'm on my way to see my attorney. He has an office in Century City. I'll be staying in town for dinner." She returned to the chair but remained standing behind it, her well-manicured hands resting casually over the back. "I guess our business is over. I just wanted to come by and tell you how sorry I am . . . for dragging you into this."

"I'm sorry, too. But what's done is done. No matter what, it would have happened anyway. It's not your fault."

"Maybe not. But it's my fault that you were involved."

No argument there. Not at first blush. Not until Christine admitted to herself that her own greed had led her down this path.

It was the money, plain and simple.

Debra collected herself and headed for the door. Christine accompanied her outside, self conscious of the vague uneasiness she felt whenever they stood close or walked together. Debra had to be over six feet tall in those heels.

Christine watched her walk the short length of hallway to the head of the steps. She had never noticed the strut before, the restrained yet suggestive sway of the hips. It was something you had to work at, Christine thought, wondering why Debra made the effort. It only tarnished the otherwise polished image she presented to the world.

Christine's phone rang. She hurried back into her office, then slowed down when she recognized the East Coast number on the caller ID display. She waited for the answering machine to take the message.

"Hi, Christine. I'm at Dad's house. He's at Mass General, undergoing cancer treatment. It looks pretty bad."

The line went quiet. It was her brother, Matt, on the line, probably waiting for her to pick up. After a long moment, he said, "I know you guys haven't talked for a while. I'm not sure what that's all about, but whatever it is, why don't you give the guy a break and give him a call. It would be better if you came out. I know you'll regret it later if you don't. If nothing else, call me back."

After another pause, Matt recited his cell phone number and hung up.

Christine waited for the machine to switch off, then sat down in her chair behind the desk.

* * *

Marshall figured room 207 was on the second floor and walked down to a stairway at the far end to avoid passing by La Quinta's office. He climbed the stairs to an outdoor corridor and found his room halfway back the way he'd come.

He beelined for the bed after bolting the door, too tired to even think about eating. He stretched out, fully clothed in the chinos, polo shirt, and deck shoes that Miss Phelps had purchased for him. It felt good having regular clothes on again. After going through hell to get them, he wasn't about to take them off now. He glanced around for a last look at his surroundings, saw that everything was in order, and gratefully settled his head onto the pillow, letting out an audible sigh.

He hadn't had his eyes closed for more than thirty seconds when a loud knock rattled the door. A coarse voice behind it said, "Hey Marshall, open up. We want to talk to you."

Marshall flew off the bed, his pulse pounding against his eardrums as he rushed to the window facing the back lot. He opened it quickly, tearing off the screen in the process, and climbed out feet first so he could hang from the sill before letting go. Just before he dropped, he looked over his shoulder and saw a man staring up at him, waiting.

What the hell . . .

He was big. Easy to recognize. Marshall had only seen him once before, but the man had made an impression. Hard to forget only a day later. And Marshall had a pretty good idea who was making all the noise on the other side of the front door—a bigger and scarier version of the guy waiting below.

"Come on down, Marshall."

The man on the ground was smiling. Even from twelve feet above he appeared large and menacing. But Marshall was committed to jump. It was no use climbing back into the room. The front door was about to be torn off it's hinges.

"Fuck it," Marshall said, pushing off the wall, hoping to fall on his antagonist.

The move caught the big man by surprise. Marshall saw it in his face just before impact. He landed on a meaty shoulder and felt something crack underneath the flesh.

They both tumbled to the ground. Marshall scrambled to his feet. The big man stayed down, grimacing in pain as they locked eyes.

"Luke!" he howled. "The motherfucker jumped."

Marshall couldn't look away from that laser stare, paralyzed by conflicting doses of fear and fascination. A shout from above broke the spell. Luke had busted through the door and was looking out the window, about to jump. Marshall spun around and ran as fast as he could.

The La Quinta Inn took up only a portion of an old refurbished warehouse that stretched out for a good city block. Marshall kept up a steady sprint to the far end of the structure. He ran alongside the adjacent railroad tracks. On the other side of the tracks lay open fields. His only chance for cover was the parking lot on the east side of the building.

He risked a glance over his shoulder as he turned the south corner. No one in sight. He came around to the front of the building. An old fashioned, covered boardwalk ran along partial sections of the frontage. He worked his way north and climbed the steps to the entrance of a restaurant. He looked for the Hummer in the parking lot.

It was a big lot, taking up the entire length of the old warehouse. There were a lot of cars. Then again, the Hummer was a big vehicle. Marshall couldn't find it. He came down off the steps, wishing he knew how to hot-wire a car.

He walked across the lot. It bordered an abandoned onramp for the Santa Ana Freeway. There was a row of free-standing, single-story buildings lined up on the north corner of the lot. They looked like retired houses converted into retail shops and small offices. They stood between him and the La Quinta Inn when he reached the intersection of the old ramp and Sand Canyon Avenue.

Then the Hummer roared into view. It pulled onto Sand Canyon from behind the warehouse, a cloud of dust trailing in its wake. It sped off away from him, in the opposite direction of the freeway.

Marshall watched it disappear down the road. Instead of relieved, he felt alone and stranded at the quiet intersection. He couldn't go back to the room at the inn or stay anywhere near it.

He decided to check out the restaurant down the block. Maybe he'd call a cab and grab a bite while he waited. He ought to be able to find a place to sit and watch the road. He was halfway there when he caught sight of the Prime Time van parked at the inn.

The driver was behind the wheel, referring to a clipboard. There were a couple of passengers occupying the middle row of seats behind him. Marshall came up to driver's window.

"Going to the airport?"

The driver looked up from the clipboard. "Mr. Sanchez?"

"No, I'm not on the roster. I'm just wondering if you could fit me in."

"I don't know. I'm pretty full, and there's a good chance they'll call me en route with more pick-ups."

"How much is the fare?"

"Thirty-five dollars."

"To John Wayne?"

"I'm going to LAX."

"Even better," Marshall said, not thinking, but knowing, as though he'd just recognized the guiding hand of fate. He peeled off three twenties from his roll. "I'll tell you what, here's sixty. The change is yours. If you don't want to call it in, well . . ."

The driver looked him over. "You got any luggage?"

Marshall shook his head.

The driver jerked a thumb at the front seat next to him.

* * *

Marshall had the driver drop him off at the first terminal at Los Angeles International Airport. He approached a waiting line of taxicabs and climbed into the one in front.

"Let's head to Mulholland Drive. I don't know the address, but I'll recognize it when we get there."

He'd been to Paul Cappannelli's house only once, the day before he married Debra. It had been an uncomfortable evening. Debra didn't get along well with her parents, and it showed. All the more reason the golf match had come as such a surprise.

"When we get there, which way on Mulholland?" the cabbie asked.

"Head toward Encino."

"How far?"

"About a mile or so," Marshall said, eying the traffic bunching up around them. The cab slowed to a crawl.

The cabbie swiveled his head halfway around. "Hope you're not in a hurry. Must be a wreck up ahead. We shouldn't be running into any traffic this time of day."

"Don't sweat it," Marshall said.

The cab came to a complete stop. A few weak horn blasts sounded here and there, as if expressing shared frustration rather than directing anger at each other. Marshall settled back into his seat, mindful of his aches and pains.

They spent the next twenty minutes traveling the last two miles to the Mulholland exit at the top of the hill, then left the traffic behind. The cabbie pulled over in front of a house Marshall chose at random near Calneva Drive.

After the cab drove away, Marshall strolled down Calneva looking for a key street sign or landmark that might unlock his memory. Nothing looked familiar, until a turned corner revealed the rugged hillside overlooking Cappannelli's back yard.

Marshall found a place to wait it out under the outdoor deck in back of one of the houses on the ridge. He worked his way up close to the structure's foundation, confident that anyone who happened to look up from across the way wouldn't be able to see him hidden within the dark, permanent shade of the overhang. The hillside below him was too steep for further property development, and he had an unobstructed view of the shimmering pool in Cappannelli's back yard. The driveway running out from the far side of the roofline lay empty.

He explored the dank recesses of his shelter. He wouldn't be able to hold out here for very long. He needed water and food, and he needed to stay awake. He knew he was suffering the effects of dehydration and tried not to think about the water. Staring down at the pool didn't help. He saw no signs of life around the house.

NINE

CHRISTINE PADDLED hard to make it over the six-foot swell before it broke. On the far side of the peak, Joel Spencer wheeled his longboard around to catch the wave. She dug deeper and scratched harder when he dropped in and carved a turn in her direction. He walked up to the nose of his board, casual, as if unaware of their impending collision, yet somehow avoided her as she punched through the cresting lip.

Damn, he makes it look so easy, she thought, tossing her wet hair out of her eyes as she turned toward shore and watched his ride. The fluid silhouette of his body remained visible through the back of the wave, his head and shoulders occasionally bobbing into full view as he worked his way along, then disappearing where the last inside section bowled up near the shore.

Too far away to see the expression on his face, Christine could only imagine the grin he was wearing when he pulled out, unscathed. He was probably sneaking a glance her way right now, just to make sure she was watching. He was still just a boy, showing off, trapped in a man's body ten years older than she was.

They were surfing at Church, her favorite place, named after the wood-framed structure that had once stood near the high tide line. No public access via the old frontage road. The only way in was on foot, either the long haul from San Clemente or the shorter walk from San Onofre State Beach, a half mile or so to the south. They had hiked in well before dawn, hoping to catch a few waves for themselves before the crowd arrived. To her amazement, they were still the only ones out.

Joel had caught the last wave of the set. The sea was now calm, almost still. Christine waited out the lull, impatient, eyes scanning the open water. He finally drifted up beside her after the long paddle back to the lineup.

"This is good stuff," he said. "The swell is hitting the point just right . . ."

She kept looking for waves, too caught up in her search to hear him. The early gray light distorted her depth perception and played tricks with her visual sense of the horizon. Ocean and sky blended together without so much as a vanishing point for reference. She could see for miles, or maybe her visual range was only a few hundred yards. There was no way to tell until the next set of swells appeared and gave her something to focus on.

The sight of the forming waves brought her out of her daydream. Joel nudged her on, told her to take her pick. She paddled out a little farther to position herself for the second wave. It was a clone of the wave Joel had just caught, and he let out a whoop of encouragement as she came to her feet.

She rode the wave a long way, reluctant to pull out even as it merged with the shorebreak rolling in over the shallow rocks. She paddled back out at full speed, juices flowing and spiked with energy from the waves breaking around her.

Joel was waiting for her. When she came within earshot, he said, "I guess it had to happen."

She looked over her left shoulder to follow the direction of Joel's nod. Off toward San Onofre a small band of surfers trudged across the wet sand near the water, the surfboards under their arms appearing in the distance as primitive shields carried by a lost tribe of nomadic warriors.

"It was fun while it lasted," she said, up close now, their boards almost touching. "How long do you think we have?"

"It'll be a while before they get here, maybe another hour or so before there's enough of 'em in the water to get in our way. Our arms will probably turn into noodles before then."

"Maybe so, but right now I don't want this to end."

She caught his elusive smile this time, a quick glimpse as he turned his board and started paddling for a better take-off position.

"Then what are you waiting for?" he said, facing the open water, his voice rising to be heard as he pulled away. "We can't let any of these waves go to waste."

* * *

"I can't believe how good you're getting," Joel said. He rubbed his face with a towel, then paused before he started on his hair. "It's only been what . . . two years?"

She sat on the sand and looked out at the water. It was turning bluer as the sun rose above the hills behind them.

"All that windsurfing in Massachusetts gave me a head start," she said, keeping her eyes on the water, the crowd already at critical mass. "Besides, how can anyone look bad on a day like this? All you have to do is stand up, turn, and hold on. The wave will do the rest."

"Don't be so modest. I saw you out there. You were ripping the place up. Very impressive, for an Ivy Leaguer."

He spread his towel next to her and stretched out, leaning back on his elbows. "So what's bothering you? I haven't heard more than a mouthful of words out of you all morning."

"It shows, huh?"

"Just a little."

"I should have told you what I was up to, but at the time it didn't seem like a big deal."

"And now it is?"

"Yeah." Christine squinted from the sunlight coming over Joel's shoulder. "You hear about that murder the other night, the woman out on the boat?"

"Sure, it's been all over the news. What's that got to do with—"

"The guy who did it? Wes Marshall? I was following him that night."

"You're kidding," Joel said, sitting up.

"I wish I were. It started about a week ago, when you went up to Santa Barbara. Marshall's wife talked me into following him."

"What for?"

"To see if he was cheating on her, what else?"

"Since when did you take on that kind of work?"

"I didn't. That is, I normally don't, but she was very persuasive. And then there's the eight thousand dollars."

Joel fell back on his elbows again. "This is getting better all the time."

Christine sidled up next to him. They were both wearing short-sleeved wetsuits, legs bare from mid-thigh down. She absently rubbed her closest leg against Joel's to brush off the sand that had dried on her skin. She kept her eyes out on the water to avoid the direct sunlight while she talked.

"It didn't start out like that. She was casual about it at first—hinting about her marital problems, asking me, in offhand ways, what she should do about it. That sort of thing."

"You already knew her," Joel said, "and never bothered to tell me about her?"

"Not much to talk about. I met her at a fundraised for our children's foundation. I'd just given a speech, the one where I'm begging for money, and she came up and handed me a check. It was a huge donation. After that, she started attending meetings. We're about the same age, so we naturally gravitated and became friends. Sort of. I really don't know her that well."

"What about her husband? I read in the paper that his first wife was the woman who fell off that cliff last year. You must have known about it."

"Not at first. I didn't know who her husband was until later."

"Eight thousand dollars seems like a lot of money for just following a guy around," Joel said. "Is that the going rate?"

"I seriously doubt it. But I'm sure she thought it gave her enough leverage to micromanage me. It probably belonged to her husband, anyway.

"She showed up at my office the day you left for Santa Barbara. She stood in the doorway and asked me how much I made an hour. When I told her I didn't charge a flat fee, that it depended on the client and the circumstances, she waved me off and pulled out her trusty checkbook. She walked over to my desk and wrote out the check as if she was paying for groceries. Said I should be making at least a hundred an hour and was willing to double it if I spent the week working for her."

"Well," Joel said. "considering how you got stiffed last month . . ."

"There's that," Christine said. "And all of a sudden I'm staring at a big, fat advance. I couldn't help it. I grabbed the check. I didn't have much experience with surveillance, but how hard could it be? I didn't know her husband. No chance of him recognizing me."

"You never met the man? And you're friends with his wife?"

Christine brought up a hand to shade her eyes from the sun. "What's so strange about that? Don't you have friends whose spouses you haven't met?"

"I suppose. But they're probably not very good friends."

She thought about it for a moment, then said, "You're probably right. Maybe that's why I didn't feel so bad about taking her money."

"There's more, isn't there?" Joel said.

"What do you mean?"

"I know you, Christine. There's still something bothering you."

"It's just that I've just got a lot on my mind right now. I need this weekend to sort it out." The look on Joel's face gave him away. It made her smile. "Don't worry. It's not about us."

"Do I look concerned?"

Before she could answer, Joel grabbed her by the waist and pulled her on top of him, then kissed her on the neck, just above the collar of her wetsuit. They rolled off the small sand berm they had been sitting on and ran down to the water to rinse off the sand. Christine beat Joel back to the towels and started drying off.

A wave broke in the distance. It sounded big and far away. They both turned toward the horizon. Joel slowed to a stop for a better look, still down by the water's edge, his fresh tracks pooling water in the hard, wet sand behind him. He shouted up to Christine, "I knew the swell would pick up again."

Christine turned back and watched him climb up the berm, the sun still punishing her eyes.

He said, "You sure you want to leave?"

"It's getting late. My regular work's been piling up and I've got a lot of catching up to do. I really have to go." She glanced at her diver's watch, the Rolex her father had given her a lifetime ago, reminding her of Matt's call "I can still make it to my office before noon."

After another long look at the water, Joel said, "All right. If we're leavin', let's get goin'."

Christine carried her surfboard down to the water to rinse the sand off the board's waxed deck. She waded out to her knees, stepping gingerly over the slick, round rocks that covered the shallows. She let the board float for a while, fin up, and kept a hand on its belly so it wouldn't get away. Another big wave broke outside. It didn't look quite so inviting. It rolled in without a rider, unconcerned about all the surfers it had caught inside and who now scrambled to get over, around, or through its thick face and crashing white water. A few of them made it out far enough to catch the next wave, and when one of them stood up, Christine could see how much bigger it was getting.

She pulled her board out of the water just as the soup from the first wave came up to hit the shore. She went back for her towel, draped it around her neck, and hurried off to catch up with Joel. He was about twenty paces ahead of her, heading for his van parked at San Onofre.

* * *

They pulled over and stopped beside the on-ramp before taking the freeway. They had a good view of Lower Trestles. The waves continued to grow larger.

"Look at that," Joel said. "Some of the sets are closing out. Trestles needs a south swell if it's gonna get *this* big."

"Can you believe how fast it's changed?" Christine said. "It's like a different day."

She'd never ridden big surf, not like this, and as much as she'd like to take it on, especially with an experienced surfer like Joel around, she couldn't deny the relief she felt when he pulled onto the road.

A mile down the freeway they exited at the El Camino Real off ramp in San Clemente. Joel's house was another five minutes away and he didn't waste any time unloading Christine's surfboard when they had arrived. She'd been keeping her board in his garage since trading her VW Bus for a new Camry. It was parked at the curb in front of his house.

She was barely out of his van, collecting her wetsuit and the fanny pack she had stashed under the passenger seat, when Joel reappeared from the garage with his big-wave board.

"Aha," she said. "So this is what it's all about. No wonder I didn't get an argument about leaving so early."

"Just thought I'd make the best of the situation," Joel said, "and there's no time to waste. The glassy conditions back at

Church won't last. There's another high pressure system building up off the coast up north. I don't think it'll get as windy as the last few days, but it'll be strong enough to blow everything out."

He pulled down the rear hatch and came around to give Christine a quick kiss.

"Gotta go," he said.

Christine smiled a farewell. Joel climbed in behind the wheel and answered her little wave with a lopsided grin as he turned his head and backed out of the driveway. He was halfway up the street when she reached her Camry.

She drove back to the freeway. Near San Juan Capistrano she transitioned to Pacific Coast Highway and followed it up the coast. She passed through Dana Point, South Laguna, and Laguna Beach, ignoring the ocean views that had once dazzled her when she was new to the area.

TEN

CHRISTINE JOGGED along Pacific Coast Highway, on her way to her office. It was about a mile from her apartment, more or less, depending on which route she followed. She'd take the long way home after she turned around at the parking lot.

She had gone straight to her place from Joel's house. The lap to the office and back was strictly therapeutic. She didn't plan on working for the rest of the weekend. She hadn't lied about the work itself; it really was pilling up. A good excuse to give Joel for leaving early.

The surfing had been a welcome distraction, and she felt better after talking with Joel, but now she needed time alone. She wasn't ready to share *all* her problems with him.

The call from Matt still ran through her mind, repeating itself over and over, like the recorded loop on her answering machine. It forced her to think about her father, something she had been trying not to do for the last two years.

She picked up the pace, sprinting the rest of the way to the office, as if it would help purge the past out of her system. She jammed a quick one-eighty turn at the parking lot and was back to speed within the next few strides. She didn't slow down until halfway up the hill on Tustin Avenue.

Her running partner, Tuco, seemed to be enjoying himself. He was built more for endurance than speed, but Christine couldn't come close to keeping up with him in either category. She had to grind it out to reach the top of the hill, too winded to say a word. Tuco trotted alongside, as silent as ever. That was the best thing about Rottweilers; they couldn't talk.

* * *

Even Tuco showed signs of wear by the time they arrived home. He dashed straight for his water dish under the wooden staircase that climbed to the front door of Christine's apartment over the garage.

She didn't know why she got along so well with the Tuco. He belonged to George and Marla Khazanovich, Christine's landlords. Christine never had a dog as a kid, never wanted one or thought much about it. George Khazanovich had once said that Tuco wasn't so much a pet as a companion. The thing was, Tuco picked his companions, not the other way around.

It had started with the running. The Khazanoviches were reaching retirement age when Tuco was a puppy, sort of a substitute for their children when the last of them had left home. Tuco was full grown by the time Christine moved into the apartment out back, and George wasn't getting any younger. He had welcomed her offer to take him out for exercise when she went jogging.

As their bond strengthened, she sometimes let him run free along the shoreline down on the Peninsula. She'd couldn't help but smile to herself whenever she noticed the reactions from passers by. There was a wild look about Tuco, scrappy and dangerous and unpredictable. Just like his namesake, the Eli Wallach character in *The Good, the Bad, and the Ugly*. Not only was there an uncanny resemblance, the dog played the part like he'd read the script.

Christine left him at the water dish and climbed the steps to her apartment. Once inside, she opened up the place. The breeze felt good coming in through the living room window facing the ocean. A portion of the horizon was visible over the rooftops below her, Catalina Island appearing closer than usual.

The answering machine for her cordless home phone sat on a small vanity desk under the window. She had also parked her cell phone to charge there last night. No messages on the machine, but there was a voicemail from Walter Jenkins on her cell:

"Hello Christine. Wally here. Something's come up. I'd like to talk to you about it as soon as possible. I'll be at my shop or at my office next door. Please give me a call." He signed off after repeating his phone numbers.

She punched in his office number. Walter was answering before she had the phone to her ear.

"Good to hear from you," he said. I hope it's all right that I called."

"Not a problem. What can I do for you?"

"If you don't mind, I'd rather not talk about it on the phone."

"Damn it, Wally, I'm a sucker for that old line. Does that mean we have to meet?"

"Can you come to my office?"

"I'm not sure I know where it is."

"It's next door to my shop, second story facing the water. It's the only office door without a number."

"Give me half an hour."

* * *

Walter Jenkins was waiting in the doorway when she reached the top of the steps. He showed her in, offered a seat on the couch, and wheeled out an old wooden chair from behind his desk toward a more conversational position in front.

"Thanks for coming," he said, adjusting a worn cushion that had slipped halfway off the polished seat.

"Don't mention it," Christine said, leaning back comfortably on the couch, fresh from her shower, her hair still damp. She scanned the view through the window, then let her gaze drift across the room. When it reached the bookcase, she stood up and strolled over for a closer look.

The shelves were lined with hundreds of books. She caught the names of Conrad, Hemmingway, and Twain. Scattered among them was a haphazard collection figurines ranging from third-world fertility fetishes to refined miniature renditions by M I Hummel. The shelves of honor near the top displayed extensive volumes by Patrick O'Brian and Wilbur Smith. All of the books were hardbound, many of them appearing quite old.

There was nautical paraphernalia strewn about like leftover debris after a rummage sale, as if no one wanted the ancient brass telescope mounted on a tripod, or the carved female figurehead propped in a corner. The faint, rhythmic clicking of a worn ceiling fan whispered above her. The fan was out of balance and had a slight wobble, its lazy revolutions barely keeping up with the swinging pendulum of an old railway clock mounted on the far wall.

"Nice office," Christine said.

Walter's eyes brightened, highlighting that enigmatic smile of his. "Mind if I ask you a few questions?"

"Sure," she said, still standing at the bookcase.

"Are you through with Wes Marshall?"

"Oh yeah. That goes without saying."

"Do you think he killed his daughter?"

"It looks that way."

"But what do you think?"

"Does it matter?"

"It might. Do you have any experience in law enforcement?"

"Yeah, I do. Until two years ago I lived in Boston, where I was an assistant district attorney."

"Now we're getting somewhere," Walter said, leaning back to stroke his beard, the ancient springs in is chair protesting with a tortured squeak. "I assume you're not doing that here. I mean, you're no longer with the DA or anything."

"No, I work for myself. Why all the questions?

"Well . . . in light of your past experience, maybe you could offer me an opinion on something."

Before she could respond, he leaned forward and said, "Remember the boating accident I told you about? Down there?"

He nodded toward the window, and Christine walked over for an elevated view of the barricaded section of the wharf she'd seen the other day.

"It seemed to me all along there was a connection between the accident and the murder," Walter said, "but I had no idea what it could be. Then I came across this."

He rose from his chair to pick up a framed black-and-white photograph that had been sitting on his desk. He handed it to Christine, and eight by ten that looked as if it had been taken a long time ago given the hair style worn by the man posing next to a large fish hanging by its tailfin.

"What, exactly, am I looking at?" Christine asked.

Walter stubbed at the picture with his forefinger. "See that boat in the background?"

Christine nodded.

"That's the boat that ran over my dock."

Christine examined the image closer.

"I have breakfast at the Pavilion every now and then," Walter said. "This morning, on my way to the men's room, I ran into a friend of mine. He was standing in front of a wall full of pictures. That photo you're looking was hanging next to his shoulder when we stopped to talk next to the entrance to Davy Jones' Deep-Sea Fishing Charters. The restaurant, bar, and charter outfit are all under the same roof. I must have passed by those wall-to-wall pictures a million times, and as dumb luck would have it, today I actually looked at 'em." He pointed to the boat in the photograph again. "You see the structure above the cabin? That's called a tuna tower."

Walter produced a few Polaroid photos of his damaged dock taken on the day of the accident. He spread them across his desktop. They had been shot from various angles to the sport fisher. Although the hull was badly damaged, its upper structure remained intact.

"See there, that offset angle they had to use to keep the auxiliary steering section centered? It's the same setup they'd used here." He picked up a Polaroid and held it next to the photo Christine was holding. "When I thought I recognized it, I grabbed a handful of the pictures off the wall and brought them over here to compare side-by-side with my Polaroids."

Christine had to agree, the similarities were unmistakable. "Who owns the boat?

"I'm not sure, but if I had to guess, I'd say it belonged to the charter outfit. At least it did back then."

"Anyway we can find out?"

Another smile lit up Walter's face. He dug through the framed pictures on his desk until he found the one he was looking for. He set it before Christine, who had just placed the original photo aside.

This one's taken from a better angle. You can't see much of the upper structure, but there's a good view of the stern."

Christine picked it up for a closer look. She read the name painted on the stern.

"Devil May Care."

She looked up at Walter. "You may have something here. I don't know what, but something." She set the picture back on the desk. "What do you want to do about it?"

"I don't know. But with you being a former DA and all, what do you think? Should I take it to the police, or just let the accident investigators have it? The thing is, I'd like to do the best thing for Marshall. Could this help him? It's obvious why they did it."

"Why they wrecked his slip?"

"Of course," Walter said. "Plain as the nose on your face—they had to force Marshall to moor his boat offshore. There would have been too many potential witnesses if it had been docked in its regular place, right under all those lights shining out of the restaurants and office suites. Anyone casually glancing out of a window or walking along the wharf might have been able to see or hear what was going on."

"I'll admit," Christine said. "this is all pretty fishy, but my guess is that the police will continue writing it off as a coincidence. They think they know who killed Jennifer, and that's all they'll focus on until they catch him."

"But what then?"

Christine remained silent.

Walter gave her a hard stare. "Like I said, there's no way he killed his daughter."

"Well, you might as well give the information to the investigators working on the accident. They'll move on it right away. If you're hoping to turn up something that connects the accident with the murder, that's probably your best shot."

"I guess it's the only shot," Walter said.

Christine lingered at the desk, handling a few of the other pictures. "Anything else of interest here?"

"Not really. Just a bunch of guys standing next to their catch. You've seen the best shots of—"

"I don't believe it."

"What?" Walter came around to Christine's side of the desk.

Christine had picked up one of the framed pictures. She handed it to Walter. "One coincidence, okay, it happens. But when the coincidences start pilling up—"

"What is it?" Walter said, staring at the picture.

"That guy closest to the fish? The one in the Hawaiian shirt? That's Wes Marshall's father-in-law."

"Are you sure? This picture could be thirty years old."

"I just saw him for the first time two days ago. The same day as the murder. I watched him walk off the eighteenth green with Marshall at a golf course in LA."

"And you're sure it's him."

"No question. He looks just like Tony Soprano, only with more hair."

"Tony Soprano?"

"Come on, Wally. Don't you watch cable?"

"Sure. The History channel once in a while, the Discovery channel—"

"Take my word for it. The man in the picture is a younger version of the man on the golf course. He's just grayer and heavier, that's all."

They both stood silent at the desk, the wobbly fan ticking away the seconds.

"The problem is, I don't know his name," Christine murmured.

"Huh?"

"Oh . . . it's nothing, I was just thinking out loud."

"Thinkin' about the father-in-law?"

Christine didn't answer right away. She looked back at the picture. She still couldn't come up with a logical explanation for Jennifer's car in the driveway. Now this. "Somebody should talk to him and find out what he knows about the boat. See how he reacts."

Walter looked her directly in the eye. "And who might that somebody be?"

"Don't look at me."

"But it's starting to bother you, isn't it?"

"It doesn't matter. This is police business." She set the picture back on the desk. "There's nothing I could do, anyway."

"How about if I hired you?"

"Hired me? For what?"

"You're still a lawyer, aren't you?"

"Yeah."

"Practicing law in California?"

She nodded.

"Well, I want to hire you. I want to sue the people responsible for damaging my property."

Christine returned Walter's stare. "That would require finding the responsible party."

"Exactly," Walter said, maintaining eye contact.

"Look, I don't have the time or resources or—"

"But you're already involved," Walter said.

Yes, she was involved, and it hadn't felt right from the start. She returned to the couch. She sat up straight near the edge of the seat and regarded Walter while she made up her mind. A wave of apprehension swept through her as soon as she spoke.

"Maybe we can work something out. But first I'd like to know what you're up to. Why are you so interested in helping Marshall? From what I understand, there's good chance that he drowned the other night."

Walter brought his chair up closer and sat down. "Like I said, I don't believe he did it." He leaned forward and lowered his voice. "And don't worry about him floating up onto shore anytime soon. He's alive."

The old guy knows more than he's telling me, Christine thought. But if there was any aiding and abetting going on, she didn't want to know about it. They were both on the edge of their seats now, facing each other like players on either side of a chessboard.

"I guess I could look into it," she said, "and Wes Marshall's father-in-law is the logical place to start."

* * *

Christine called Debra's cell as soon as she reached her office and had to leave a voicemail message. After spending a few minutes looking for a home phone number, she realized Debra had never given her one. She called information, but the number was unlisted. She was about to call in a favor at the phone company when Debra returned her call.

Debra asked about her husband.

"I haven't heard yet," Christine said. "But I just talked with Hallstrom. He had a few follow-up questions for me, wanted to know your father's name and address. I told him I'd check my notes and get back to him."

"Why would he want to know that?"

"Just filling in the blanks," Christine lied. "You know how cops are. When I told him about the golf match with your father, he wanted to know his name, that's all."

"You told him about my father?"

"Look, Debra, when you march into a police station with information regarding a murder, they're going to leave no stone unturned. They probe relentlessly for all the details. It's pointless to keep anything from them."

The line went quiet on Debra's end. Christine was taking a calculated risk involving Hallstrom. He knew nothing about Debra's father, at least not from Christine. She distinctly remembered skipping over that part of her surveillance when telling Hallstrom about the day of the murder. But Debra didn't know that, and Christine didn't think she'd want to talk to Hallstrom about it.

A moment later Debra said, "I don't want my father involved in this."

"He's not involved. I doubt they'll question him. They just want his name, for the record. I'll be glad to tell them the next time they ask—if they ask. I probably won't hear from them again. If I do, I'll save them the trouble of having to ask you about it."

"I guess that'll be all right. I've already talked with them enough." Another slight pause. "His name's Paul Cappannelli."

"He live around here?"

"No, he's in LA county. He has a house off Mulholland Drive."
Debra gave her the address.

"Okay, then. That should cover it.

Debra hung up without saying goodbye.

ELEVEN

ALL MARSHALL wanted to do was roll over and return to the dark and safe haven of a dreamless sleep. He might have succeeded if not for the annoying lumps and pokes that accompanied even the slightest movement. Then he tasted the dirt. He opened his eyes and bolted upright. He'd had his face pressed against the bare ground and now he brushed away the dirt and the small pebbles and the sharp twigs that had stuck to his skin and tangled in his hair. The hillside overlooking Paul Cappannelli's house came into focus.

There's the black Hummer.

He'd waited all night for this. For the outside chance that his prayers would be answered and that Luke and James and Cappannelli would all get together. And he'd almost blown it by falling asleep.

He checked his watch. How could he have slept until one-thirty? He looked back down the hill, just to be sure about the Hummer sitting in Cappannelli's driveway.

Marshall crept out from under the overhanging deck. The hillside was too steep to climb down directly to the house below. He worked his way back to Calneva Drive and found a gentler slope where he could cut over.

He came down off the hill and skirted the wall running along Cappannelli's corner of the cul-de-sac. Everything depended on making it around front. He tried to act like he belonged there when he reached the driveway.

He stood behind the Hummer, where he could reference the license number, and stared at the wrought iron numbers next to the front door of the house. He flipped open Miss Phelps's cell phone. As he was about to punch in 911, he froze.

He didn't know the name of the street.

How could I be so fucking stupid?

He spun around to look for a street sign. All he saw was the blur of a fist hurling toward his face.

Marshall didn't lose consciousness this time. Not quite. He could feel his heels against the driveway pavers as he was dragged toward the house. Someone picked him up from behind and shoved him onto a small chair. He was in a twilight, his vision unfocused, his face numb. He couldn't figure out why he was unable to explore it with his fingers. He couldn't move his hands.

Luke strode over and tossed a glassful of water in his face. "Can you believe this dumb fuck, just walking up to the front door? Luke grabbed a fistful of hair and jerked hard on it, forcing Marshall to look up at him. "Hey, dumb fuck. Didn't you realize we could see every move you made from down here?"

Marshall shook his head free and blinked away the water. Cappannelli, Luke, and James stood above him. James was the one with the elaborate cast encasing the right side of his upper body. His right arm protruded ninety degrees out, a slight bend at the elbow. It was supported by a rod attached to brace along his flank. Marshall tried not to look at his eyes.

Cappannelli stepped closer. He held Miss Phelps's cell phone where Marshall could see it.

"Calling someone?"

Marshall didn't respond.

Cappannelli turned away. "Luke, did he get a call off?"

"No sir. I checked. Last call he made was yesterday. A cab company."

Cappannelli tossed the phone onto a workbench nearby. "Okay, so who were you going to call?"

The words were gibberish to Marshall. He ignored Cappannelli and concentrated on more immediate problems. He tried to get his hands free, finally figuring out that they were tied behind him. He was secured to a folding card table chair, the extra clothesline balled up near his feet. Puzzled by the plastic sheet beneath him, he looked at the workbench where Cappannelli had thrown the phone and finally realized he was in the garage. The chair holding him captive had been placed on top of a large plastic drop cloth.

"It's amazing you lasted this long," Cappannelli said. "I couldn't believe it when Luke called from the hospital." He turned to James, who was now sitting on another folding chair against the wall. "Let me get this straight—the shoulder was dislocated and broken, is that right? And something about a fractured collar bone . . .?" Cappannelli directed his glare back to Marshall. "Luke had to drag James out of intensive care and bring him over here so I could see all the damage you inflicted for myself."

Marshall finally spoke. "Why are you doing this?"

"That's not important. What's important is how you happened to show up at my house, what you expected to accomplish, and who else, beside the three of us here in the garage, knows what you're up to."

"Go to hell."

Cappannelli bent down, right in Marshall's face, spraying it with flecks of spittle as he spat out, "Don't misunderstand me. You're dead. It's over—a forgone conclusion. The only thing you can possibly hope for is that I tell Luke to walk up behind you and put a bullet in your brain. If you don't want to cooperate, I'll just have to give in to James's wishes and let him talk to you in his own unique fashion. I think you'll find that he can still be pretty resourceful with his left hand."

Marshall looked at the tools on the workbench, imagining what they could do to flesh and bone.

Cappannelli backed away, assumed a more conversational tone. "So . . . now that you're coming around and have a better understanding of the situation, let's start over. Tell me about your secretary. I believe her name is Phelps, isn't it?"

Marshall stared straight ahead. Luke had moved out of his field of vision. Marshall pictured him screwing a silencer onto the barrel of a small caliber handgun, waiting for the nod from Cappannelli. James stood up and stumbled over to Cappannelli's side, wearing the same malevolent expression Marshall remembered from the day before. No one in the room said a word.

A knock on the rolled-down garage door broke the silence.

Cappannelli wasn't standing more than five feet away from the other side. He looked around, slowly shaking his head for everyone to remain quiet. Once again came the unmistakable rap of bare knuckles on hard wood.

A woman's voice called out. "Hello . . . Mr. Cappannelli. Are you in there?"

Without a word, Cappannelli slammed his fist into his open left palm, miming a message for Luke to take Marshall out. Marshall didn't have time to flinch before something hard collided with the back of his head, almost directly on top of the tender lump already there. He fell onto his left side, taking the chair with him.

It was quiet for a moment, then James whispered, "How 'bout I wait in the living room; I'm feeling lousy."

Marshall kept his eyes closed. He heard footsteps shuffle across the garage floor, followed by the sound of the side door opening and closing and the bolt slamming home.

* * *

"Who the hell are *you*?"

The voice caught Christine by surprise. She half-jumped as she turned around next to the garage door. Her cheeks burned to the top of her temples. She talked and tried to compose herself all at the same time.

"Mr. Cappannelli? My name's Christine Blake. I'm sorry to disturb you. I rang the front doorbell but no one answered. I was a little concerned. The door was ajar. With no answer and all, I thought there might be a problem. Then I heard voices coming from the garage and realized you could be in there and not hear the doorbell."

Cappannelli stood on the driveway, a few feet away from her. "There's no problem here. Now what do you want?"

Christine studied Cappannelli's features. No question about it; he was the same man in the photo Walter had borrowed from the Pavilion. Other than his dark curly hair going gray and the addition of a few pounds, he hadn't changed much in the years since it had been shot. He just looked bigger and meaner in person.

She also had his friend to think about, the one standing in the doorway. He stood about six inches taller than Cappannelli and was built like a Russian weightlifter, without the stomach. Not the kind of people to mess with, she thought, but finding out too late to change tactics.

"I'm investigating a boating accident that happened a few days ago," she said. "It was on Wednesday, to be exact, in Newport Bay."

That spurred a reaction. Although he tried to hide it, the look of surprise was painted all over Cappannelli's face. She waited for him to say something. His expression soured.

"Let's talk about this inside, Ms. Blake. No reason to stand out here in the driveway."

Christine backpedaled. "Thanks, but I'd prefer to stay out here. I only have a couple more questions, and I'll be on my way."

"Nonsense," Cappannelli said, flashing a pale imitation of a smile, "I insist."

Cappannelli's hostile insincerity was scaring her. If that wasn't bad enough, the bigger man was walking toward her from the doorway.

She ran.

Cappannelli's driveway was close to a hundred feet long, with manicured Italian cypress trees spaced to create an effective wall of privacy. Christine broke into the clear. The wrought iron gate at the curb was still open, her car parked beyond it, next to the curb. Heavy footfalls pounded the pavement behind her.

A man across the street looked over, walking his dog, a plastic bag full of dog shit in one hand, the leash in the other. Christine slowed down, gave the man a casual wave, and trotted over to her car. The sound of the running footsteps had ceased.

Her heart didn't stop hammering until she reached the freeway on ramp off Mulholland.

* * *

Cappannelli fumed, ready for his pound of flesh. He stormed into the garage and saw the empty chair overturned on the tarp. Two lonely lengths of clothesline had been discarded nearby. The window over the workbench was open, allowing the outside breeze to slip through the broken screen and fan his smoldering face.

Luke said, "Sorry boss. I must be losing my touch."

Cappannelli glared at him. When he finally talked, it came out as a coarse whisper, as if daring Luke to come close so he could hear better.

"You're going to lose a lot more than your touch if you don't find that sorry sonofabitch, now, before the cops do." He tore his gaze from Luke and looked around the room, his eyes blinded by rage, his voice rising. "And what the fuck just happened out there. Where did the woman come from and how did she find out about the goddamned boat?"

"I don't know, Mr. Cappannelli. We were really careful. There's no way—"

"Don't talk. Drag James off the sofa and get the fuck out of here. Find Marshall."

* * *

Marshall fought an almost uncontrollable urge to lie down. His head ached. The initial burst of adrenaline was spent. He forced himself to keep running.

He'd taken a nasty hit back in Cappannelli's garage, but he'd been out for only a few seconds. He had kept his wits about him and stayed completely still. He barely breathed until the departing footsteps of Cappannelli and his men fell silent. When the side door to the garage slammed shut, he risked a glance to see if anyone had stayed behind. A flood of relief washed over him when he realized he was alone.

He had used every ounce of newfound energy to wriggle out of the clothesline that had loosened after his fall. He opened the window, tore through the screen, and flew across the back yard and scrambled over the wall. He cut through several more back yards before he found a street that headed downhill. He didn't stop to catch his breath until he'd made his way down an additional few blocks, then settled into a wobbly but steady jog and tried his best to look like a weekend jock out for some exercise.

He hoped no one would take a good look at his wardrobe. Chinos and deck shoes weren't exactly what the well-heeled runner was wearing these days, not to mention his beat-up face. The few people he'd come across had driven by without a glance.

Helped by his downhill momentum, he was able to keep his speed up. He passed scores of well tended expensive homes, all of them ensconced behind an invisible wall of silence, as if all who lived there were off somewhere else or sequestered inside.

He soon felt less conspicuous, almost invisible, and he thought of Cappannelli and the two guys in the garage. He'd almost forgotten about the police, but now he started to entertain thoughts of surrendering to the first patrol car that came along. If it came down to it, jail would be a better option than what Cappannelli had planned for him.

Weighing his limited options kept his mind busy and helped him manage the pain. But as time wore on, thinking about his problems became too distracting. He had to start concentrating on the important things, like putting one foot in front of the other without falling down. He was somewhere around Encino or Sherman Oaks. If he kept moving downhill, he'd eventually run into Ventura Boulevard.

* * *

James couldn't take much more. They'd driven across Mulholland, as far as the freeway on ramps, then back to Cappannelli's neighborhood in a desperate rush to find Marshall. The problem was Marshall had too many streets at his disposal.

After thirty minutes had passed it was obvious that he'd slipped away. James kept his mouth shut but his clenched teeth couldn't mute the groans. He was sitting shotgun in Luke's Hummer. The suspension felt like it was hardwired to his shoulder, transmitting jolts of pain with every bump in the road. He had his seat all the way back, but it didn't give him enough room to find a comfortable sitting position. The way his right arm stuck out, he had a hard time keeping it from knocking against the door when Luke turned or applied the brakes. With nothing to hang on to, James tried to use his left hand as a brace, pushing it against the ceiling in an effort to stay upright when he felt himself tipping or leaning too far.

He winced in pain every time he had to move, and he saw Luke watching him sweat out every sway and bump. Now and then he let out a howl when Luke turned too fast or sped through a dip in the road. Luke finally pounded on the steering wheel in frustration before easing off the gas.

"Okay . . . where do you want to go, back to the hospital or over to your place?"

"Are you kiddin'? I couldn't handle the drive back to Irvine. Take me home. And try not to hit every goddamned pothole on the way there."

Luke shook his head, mindful now of the speed.

"Too bad we weren't driving a couple of cars and linked up on our cell phones. We probably could have boxed him in on one of these cul-de-sacs."

"I don't think so," James said. "There's too many streets, too many back yards, and too much landscape to hide in. He's long gone." He eased back in his seat as best he could. The chase was over, and he wiped the sweat and tears off his face with his good hand. He had his head turned toward his window and he talked to the rows of houses rolling by. "What does Cappannelli want with this guy, anyway?"

"Beats me," Luke said. "This sure isn't one of our usual collections. It's more like something personal."

"You can bet your ass it's personal," James said. "The guy's married to his daughter."

Luke said nothing.

"Weird, isn't it? One day we're playing golf with the guy, the next day Cappannelli wants him dead."

"Now I suppose the boss will have to wait his turn."

James twisted away from the window and managed to point his head halfway at Luke. "I might have felt like killing him, when those doctors were rearranging my shoulder. All I could think about was how much pain I was going to inflict on that asshole for fucking up my shoulder."

"What . . . you've changed your mind?"

"I don't know. I've had time to think."

"About what?"

"About Cappannelli."

"What about him?"

"C'mon, Luke. That whole thing out at his golf club. Kinda strange, wasn't it? I mean, when's the last time he had us out there to play golf?" James waited half a beat for an answer, then said, "It's not like it was social. I didn't hear him say, 'Would you boys like to join me and my son-in-law for a quick round of golf?'"

"I'll admit," Luke said. "It was a little weird."

James nodded in agreement. It turned into a flinch. He steadied himself, gave up trying to move his head at all and had to keep looking at Luke out the corner of his eye. "It was strange, all right. And that was no casual invitation. We were on the job." He watched Luke take his eyes off the road and glance his way. "What are you not telling me?"

"I guess you didn't know about the boat."

"So you've been in on this from the beginning?"

Luke answered with a silent nod.

"And the thing at the golf course—hanging around afterwards, playing gin, drinking at the bar, Cappannelli making sure to talk to the night shift guy out at the guardhouse on the way out—I guess that was all part of our alibi."

Luke didn't nod this time. He just held on to the wheel tighter, his beefy knuckles turning white.

James faced forward and let out a sigh. "Well that's just fucking great. I don't mind busting up the usual bunch of deadbeats and losers he sends us after—to hell with 'em. They deserve everything they get. But this personal beef with Marshall—"

"So what?", Luke said. "Personal, business, whatever—we get paid just the same."

"No, it's not just the same. Guys act different when it's personal, and when guys start doing things different, they fuck up. That's the rat hole Cappannelli's dragging us into. We've been working for the guy how long? Shit . . . I can't even count the years. But you know what? He's always been professional. A quick call, a name, an address, whatever. We get what we need and go out and do the job. No fuss, no muss. But this business with Marshall . . . I don't like it."

"This really bothers you, doesn't it?"

"Yeah, and I'd feel better if it bothered you a little."

"I don't really give a fuck."

"Listen to me, Luke. Sometimes you don't pay enough attention . . . you know, to the details."

"That's not what they pay me for. I kick ass and take names, that's it. I don't sweat the small shit."

"Well, my friend," James said, "that small shit can surprise you sometimes, spinning right alongside of you on the way down the toilet."

"You think I'm stupid?"

"Fuck no. You're damn good, Luke. You know that. For Christ's sake, you've pulled my bacon out of the fire more than once. Remember that crazy homeboy pulling the shotgun on me? Man, when he turned around, there they were. The bore of those goddamned double barrels ten times bigger than anything I'd ever seen, at least when they were pointed at my chest. If you hadn't made it through the back window when you did, I'd of had one helluva hole in me.

"Yeah," Luke laughed. "I put a pretty good move on that ol' boy, didn't I?"

"I'll never forget it. Even now, when I shut my eyes and listen, I'll swear that my ears are still ringing from the sound of those two barrels going off just after I ducked."

"We were lucky that time," Luke said.

"We have been lucky," James agreed, then lowered his eyes to survey his cast. "Until now."

"Now Marshall's got all the luck," Luke said. "He's one charmed sonofabitch, I'll say that much for him. He's gotten away from us twice—three times if you count the cluster-fuck on PCH."

"You're right," James said, slowly positioning his head back toward the window. "And it's not a good sign."

"Now you're just trying to make me nervous"

"No, I'm trying to tell you to be careful. I'm going to be out of action for a while. I can't do much until I get this cast off, and it'll probably take months of physical therapy before I'm back to full strength. In the meantime, you're Cappannelli's main man. Watch out. If he starts to unravel, steer clear of him."

James stared blankly out the window. They didn't say another word until Luke dropped him off.

TWELVE

Christine drove nonstop to Joel's house. She let herself in through the side door and walked into the kitchen and came up behind Joel and put her arms around him. She didn't feel like talking. He was chopping vegetables on the cutting board. He turned around inside of her embrace.

"Hey, it's good to see you, too."

Christine held him tighter, pressing her face into that special niche she liked between his neck and shoulder.

They might have made it to the bedroom if they hadn't stumbled onto the living room couch, where they made love and she clung to Joel for a long time afterward. She still didn't feel like talking. When Joel got up she reached for the throw draped over the back of the couch and curled up under it. She had her eyes closed but could hear Joel pulling on his pants.

"Are you all right?" he asked.

"I don't know. I can't seem to catch my breath."

Joel sat down next to her on the edge of the cushion. "Is there something I can do? Do you need to see a doctor?"

"It's not a medical problem. I just had the shit scared out of me and had to drive the goddamned freeway with my eyes glued to the rearview mirror not knowing what kind of car to look for or who—"

"Shhh . . . slow down," Joel said, gently stroking her shoulder. "You're okay now. There's nobody after you."

"You have no idea what you're talking about."

"Why don't you clue me in?"

Christine pushed herself up to a sitting position. She smiled sheepishly at her discarded clothes. "What the hell just happened?"

"Don't change the subject."

"Give me a minute."

She gathered up her clothes and walked into Joel's bedroom. She stripped off the blouse she was still wearing and kicked off the one shoe and jumped into the shower in the adjoining bathroom.

She came into the kitchen ten minutes later wearing one of Joel's shirts and a pair of sweatpants that she liked to keep at his house.

"Feeling better?" Joel asked, sitting at the table while his marinara sauce simmered on the stove.

"Still a little shaky."

"You want to tell me about it?"

"God, Joel, I don't even know where to begin."

"Why don't you start with what happened before you got here. I know you don't remember what happened on the couch."

"Come on, that was a joke. I was just being facetious"

"You're changing the subject again."

"I don't want to drag you into this."

"You already have. You were scared, and you came here. That's a good start. Now why don't you tell me what's going on?"

Christine sat down across from him and reached over and clutched his hand. "Thanks for being here. It really helps."

"I'd like to do a lot more than just be here."

"There's nothing more you can do."

"Just tell me who you were running from."

Christine finally gave in. "It was Wes Marshall's father-in-law."

"How'd you get mixed up with him? What—"

"First I'd better tell you about Walter Jenkins."

* * *

Christine brought Joel up to speed. She told him about Walter Jenkins and his discovery of Paul Cappannelli's possible involvement with Jennifer Marshall's murder. She told him about the inconsistencies already bothering her before she'd first met Walter at his shop.

The marinara sauce was still bubbling away, untouched, when she finished talking. Joel had his chair tipped back against the wall, his arms folded in front.

"So you decided to drop in on this Mr. Cappannelli," he said, "without knowing a thing about him. What were you thinking? If the guy was up to something, wouldn't it be a little dangerous to confront him? By yourself? That's a job for the police."

"I know. Kinda stupid, huh?"

"Did you actually find out anything?"

"No. But the guy's dirty."

"How can you tell?"

"It was obvious. I've had experience with guys like him."

"In Boston?"

"Yeah, that's why I ran. Looking back on it, maybe I overreacted. But at the time . . . Christine looked down at the table. "I don't know. I've never really stopped running."

Joel brought his chair back down on all four legs and sat up to the table. He said nothing. Just looked at her.

Christine met his gaze and tried to smile "I once read that until a person learns from his mistakes and makes the right corrections, he'll be trapped in a cycle of repetition, that the same circumstances will repeat themselves, over and over again, until he gets it right. I'm starting to believe it.

"This whole thing—Debra, the murder on the boat, her husband, my suspicions—it's part of a repeating cycle that I seem to fall into. I mean, what are the odds of me getting mixed up in something like this?"

"You mean this has happened before," Joel asked.

"Not exactly, but close enough.

"Back home, when I first joined the Suffolk District Attorney's Office, my colleagues were after a local mobster named Ed Thacker. Debra's father reminds me of him. Anyway, we had a long sheet on him. Everyone knew he was well connected, and not just with the mob. He had powerful friends on the other side of the street as well. That was the only explanation for his uncanny ability to stay out of jail. It got to the point—at least it seemed to me—where he was thumbing his nose at us. He was that blatant. And being the gung-ho rookie on the staff, I was determined to be the one who convicted him. I was going to make a difference. I didn't care how hard I had to work or how much of my own time I had to burn."

"How'd it turn out?"

"Not well. But by now I'd been working for the DA for just a few months, which had made my dad very happy. He's a Superior Court Judge, third generation. I have two older brothers who chose not to follow in his footsteps. I'll give you three guesses who was chosen to carry on the family tradition. Things like that can be very important to someone with blue-blooded roots in New England. My dad made that clear to me early on. He expected . . . no, he demanded to hand down his sacred judicial robes to one of his offspring, and I was his last hope.

"I bought into it. I applied myself, earned good grades, and made it into Harvard Law School—with a little help from Dad and his alma mater buddies. I graduated with honors and turned down the recruiters from some decent law firms. I was headed for the DA's office, the fastest track to the bench. Dad didn't think I'd be with the DA very long—just a stepping stone along my career path.

"Things went pretty well for the next couple of years. I never got Thacker to court, but my conviction record for the cases that did go the distance was perfect. Then I was assigned a child molestation case.

"We had a suspect in custody—a recently paroled sex offender. All we had on him was his arrest sheet and some weak circumstantial evidence. Too weak, in my opinion, to take to trial. I hadn't lost a case yet, and I wasn't about to start now by taking on a lost cause. Dad had always stressed the importance of a good trial record, and that was my only concern. I argued with the DA to drop the case and got my way. Not more than twenty-four hours after we'd released the suspect, he sodomized and killed an eight year-old boy.

"I'm not going to dredge up all of the details. All you need to hear is that I knew he was guilty. Maybe I couldn't have proven it, but I knew it was him. I observed his interrogation, talked with the arresting officers, and interviewed the child and his parents. And I ignored what my instincts were telling me—this man was dangerous and he should be kept off the streets, at any cost. He couldn't have hurt anyone while in custody and tied up in the legal system. It devastated me when I heard the news . . . and that I was responsible for the second boy's death."

Joel rose quietly to tend to the stove. Christine watched him stir the sauce as she continued.

"I needed someone to talk to. The only person I could think of was my dad. He agreed to meet me that night at his house and I got there early. I let myself in and went into his study to wait for him. For no other reason than restless boredom, I sat at his desk, like countless times before when I was a kid. Sitting there brought back fond memories of my childhood, when all I wanted was my dad's approval. I'd daydream of how proud he'd be of me when I was a big success.

"I was feeling better, with all those pleasant memories drifting through my mind, when I looked down at the lower right hand drawer of his desk. For as long as I could remember, the drawer had always been locked, and with the idle curiosity of a little girl who used to play there, I gave it a tug.

"The damn thing slid open. I never looked past the manila envelope. It was sitting on top of a stack of folders in the front of the drawer. You couldn't miss it. I picked it up to take a closer look, wondering what was inside. I mean, it was bulging, looking so strange in there with all those neatly ordered files. It wasn't sealed, and when I picked it up all this cash starts spilling out. I didn't bother to count it—one hundred dollar bills banded together in ten thousand dollar stacks. The note scrawled on the inside flap of the envelope got my attention. It read, "Don't forget the 15th." The handwriting was as easy to recognize as Ben Franklin's grinning face. Ed Thacker wrote the note. During my investigation, I'd seen plenty of samples of his writing. It was very distinctive."

"Your dad was on the take?", Joel said, dropping the wooden spoon into the saucepan. He came back to the table. "He'd been helping Thacker all that time?"

"Do the math," Christine said. "I'd seen enough. I placed the envelope back where I'd found it and closed the drawer. I ran out of the house, praying I wouldn't run into my dad, got in my car and drove off. Before I was a block away, I'd made up my mind. I decided to leave Boston. I knew I was running away from it, but I didn't know what else to do. I was already feeling physically sick from learning about that boy's death, and I knew I was in for a rough time. The press, the boy's parents, my superiors . . . I was going to have to deal with them. It was a lousy time for finding Thacker's payoff in dad's drawer. By then I was running the Thacker investigation. I was still on his case and no closer to an indictment. No matter how I handled dad's involvement, it was going to ruin my deteriorating credibility. And if I didn't come forward at all, if I just closed my eyes and forgot what I'd seen in his desk, I'd be as guilty as he was and even a worse hypocrite for keeping my job at the DA's office. So I quit. I left the state."

Joel stared at her, wide eyed. "Why California?"

"I always wanted to be a real surfer, you know that."

"Oh yeah," Joel said, "the frustrated windsurfer from Massachusetts."

"Don't laugh, there's a few decent spots along the coast. It just gets too damn cold back there. Anyway, it was more than just the surfing. I'd had enough of living my life the way I was told. I found a realtor to list my house, sold my car, and kept the VW Bus. I got rid of anything that I couldn't cram into it and took off."

"I guess that explains the children's foundation," Joel said, "and the kind of work you do."

"That's part of it. I can't change the past, but maybe I can make a difference in a child's future. I'll never be a crusading DA up to my eyeballs in criminal investigations, or a Superior Court Judge handing down momentous decisions, but every now and then I might be able to give a kid a break. I thought about that a lot while I was on the road. After I arrived in California I spent a couple of weeks looking around. I had a pretty good idea of what I wanted to do and where I wanted to stay—somewhere south of LA and north of San Diego. I stopped looking when I reached Newport Beach. I found a great place to live and pretty decent office space on PCH. You know the rest."

"Yeah," Joel said, "and here you are, up to your eyeballs in a criminal investigation."

Christine shrugged. "Like I said earlier, maybe it's for a reason. This time I'm not going to ignore my instincts."

"But you need to be realistic. Maybe the past is trying to tell you something, maybe not. It doesn't really matter. I still think you should take this to the police and be done with it."

"You're missing the point. The police detectives and the DA's office are staring at a slam dunk. All they have to do is find Marshall, and they're done with it. They're not going to appreciate me butting into the investigation, not without concrete evidence to give them."

"So what are you going to do?"

"I don't know yet."

* * *

Christine felt like eating by the time Joel had boiled the pasta. They ate quietly at the kitchen table while the dusk lit the window over the sink with a pale, tangerine hue.

"We missed the sunset," Joel said, "but I'd still like to sit out on the porch for a while."

"That would be nice," Christine said.

"Go ahead, I'll be right out after I clean up."

Christine stood up to pick up the plates. Joel crowded over and took them away from her.

"Go on, I've got this."

"Okay . . .I'll see you outside."

She kissed him while handing off the plates. "Thanks for listening to my tale of woe. I've had it bottled up for too long."

She walked out to the porch and sat in Joel's favorite chair. She planned on staying close to him all night. She looked down the street toward the ocean, a block away at the bottom of the hill, where the last traces of dusk had faded into darkness. A marine layer covered the moon and was working its way inland. No light reflected off the water's surface. Waves broke and rolled onto shore, their phosphorescence hidden behind the rooftops at the end of the street, their presence sounding very near.

* * *

By the next morning, the marine layer had thickened into a blanket of fog that covered the coastline. The haze didn't make it to the 405 freeway, but it reached far enough up the hill to shroud Joel's house in a damp, gray mist. After taking quick glances out the bedroom window, Christine and Joel had no trouble going back to sleep.

Around seven thirty, Christine made a pot of coffee. She dashed out to the front porch, grabbed the delivered copy of the

Sunday Times, and brought two cups of coffee back to bed. An hour later, a layer of newspaper pages scattered the top of the sheets.

Christine was reading the *Book Review* when Joel handed her the *Orange County* section, folded over to highlight an article on the bottom of the first page. "I think you might be interested in this."

She tossed the Book Review aside and accepted the paper. Her eyes caught the small headline:

SERVICES ARRANGED FOR JENNIFER MARSHALL

The article stated that Jennifer Marshall's body had been released. It was to be buried Monday, next to her mother's, at Pacific View Cemetery.

THIRTEEN

MARSHALL WAS fully awake when the shopping cart pulled up. He remained still, his legs pulled up to his chest. He was huddled in a small space between the back of a Dumpster and a cinder block wall. Trash began to fall and it reverberated with muffled, drum-like sounds of soft objects hitting heavy sheet metal. It was over as quickly as it started, and he waited quietly for the sound of the cart to move on.

It had been a long night. He'd never experienced such a degree of thirst or hunger, unable to pay for a simple bottle of water. He pictured his remaining pocket change, sitting on Cappannelli's workbench with Miss Phelps's cell phone. He'd forgotten them during his rush to break out of the garage.

The sound of the cart faded away, leaving silence in its wake. Marshall sat there, his head resting on crossed arms, when the aroma in the alley began smelling better.

He jumped up to look into the Dumpster. He pulled himself up and over, careful not to squash anything when he landed inside. The trash had recently been emptied, and a new pile of old produce and stale bread now lay strewn about. Marshall didn't know where to start. He picked up an orange and bit into it, right through the skin, and savored the juices bursting into his mouth. If it was going bad, he didn't notice. There was a good selection to pick through: greens, fruit, and a few old loaves of bakery-style bread in paper wrappers. All I need now is a bottle of wine, he thought, gathering up what he could carry out.

"Quite a salad bar, don't you think?"

Marshall had taken off his shirt, with the idea of stuffing it with a few selected items, when the voice interrupted him. He raised his head, looked over the rim of the Dumpster, and locked eyes with the wary stare of a street veteran. The man's stout torso was covered with a tan threadbare blazer. He wore a floral print shirt tucked into nondescript gray trousers that were almost long enough to reach the top of his Mexican huaraches, the kind that have tire treads for soles. A Dodger's baseball cap perched on his head barely contained the springy mass of steel-gray curls bunched behind his ears and spilling over his collar. His beard was a whiter shade of gray, as thick and as close cropped as a young boy's crew-cut. No telling how old he was.

"I guess it was just a matter of time," the man muttered to himself, "before someone else found out about it."

Marshall was too stunned to talk. The man shuffled closer, a shopping cart trailing behind him. Not the usual supermarket type, but the smaller two-wheel variety normally associated with elderly ladies. Other than a broom sticking out of a plastic tube wired to a corner, a few folded paper bags lining the bottom, and a small knapsack hanging from the handle, the cart was empty.

Marshall found his voice and tried to sound cheerful. The last thing he needed was a confrontation with this guy over salvage rights. He didn't know anything about life on the street, but imagined it was pretty rough, with people getting beat up, or maybe even killed, over relatively petty issues. "Hey, there's plenty here. Why don't you let me help you load up your cart?"

"That would be kind of you," the man said, his wary eyes narrowing into a curious squint. "I don't think I've seen you around here before. Are you on the street?"

"I guess so," Marshall said.

The man was only an arm's length away. He opened one of his paper bags and filled it with the produce Marshall handed up to him. In a few minutes he had three full bags stuffed into his cart. Marshall passed him one last armload—the shirtful he was going to keep for himself—then jumped out of the Dumpster.

"Thanks a lot," he said, plucking the bundle out of the man's hands. He set it on the pavement and tore into it with the enthusiasm one would expect from a starving man.

"You're not from around here, are you?" the man asked.

"No, I'm not," Marshall said, between mouthfuls of bread and pulls on the orange. "I'm not even quite sure where I am."

"You're just inside the Encino city limits. I try to get here early, right after André culls out the old produce and bakery goods from his store." He gave Marshall a hard look. "It's the best kept secret in town. I'd suggest you move on down to at least the other side of Sepulveda. The cops around here'll run you in on a JDLR in a New York minute."

Marshall asked, "A JDLR?"

"Yeah, Just Don't Look Right.

"It's that obvious, huh?"

"Have you seen your face lately? What happened, if you don't mind my asking?"

"Let's just say I've had a bad experience."

"Experience is not what happens to a man. It is what a man does with what happens to him."

"Or maybe this world is another planet's hell."

The man regarded Marshall for a moment, and then, with a knowing wink, announced, "You'd better come with me," before walking out of the alley and turning right down Ventura Boulevard.

Marshall gathered up a few pieces of fruit and the remainder of the loaf of bread he was eating, shoved them into a paper bag the man had left for him, and put on his shirt. He hurried out to the street and caught up with the man half a block down.

They walked in silence, side by side, going east along Ventura Boulevard. When they passed a row of store front windows, Marshall was so startled by his own reflection that he had to stop and make sure it was really him. The stranger staring back at him was someone he'd never seen before. It wasn't the matted hair, the three-day beard, or the purple bruise highlighting his swollen cheekbone. That didn't bother him. It was his eyes. They had that spooked look of someone over the edge.

"Goddamn, I look worse than Charlie Manson."

That stopped the old man. He'd walked on while Marshall stood there in front of the window. "You haven't killed anybody, have you?"

This is all I need, Marshall thought. Here I am, looking guilty as hell and wandering around LA, home of the high-profile murder cases. He imagined newspaper photos of his own wild-eyed, deranged face taking a permanent place among the city's infamous rogue's gallery. It doesn't even matter if I'm innocent, he thought. I'm fucked for life. He tried to calm down, taking a few deep breaths before catching up with the man.

"No, I haven't killed anyone," Marshall said. "I've just had a very rough three days. If I could find a place to wash up it would help a lot."

"I might be able to arrange that for you," the man said. "Hang in there, we'll be there soon."

After half an hour of steady walking, the man slowed down. "Wait here a minute. I have to find Lydia. I'll need her permission to use the garden."

Marshall was left standing on a corner, several blocks past the 405 freeway. The area wasn't exactly run down, but there was definitely a less upscale feel to the place. He understood the man's recommendation to move east of Sepulveda. It ran alongside the freeway, and almost as soon as they had passed under it he started seeing street people about. Not many, just a man or two here, a woman there. He wouldn't have noticed them at all a few days ago, but now they were a welcome sight. Not only would their presence help him blend in, Marshall also felt a strange affinity for them. He realized the extreme condition he found himself in was just another day in the life for the unfortunate souls living on the street. He'd had a bad three days—they were living it, full time.

Marshall stood there, recalling the countless times he'd passed by a homeless transient or made a comment about a "bum on the corner with a cardboard sign". Now he was haunted by their pathetic faces, reflecting a world of unpleasant hardships and little hope. A world he'd have to deal with.

"Let's go," the man said.

Marshall followed him around a corner and down an alley to a solid wood fence separating the third and fourth buildings on the north side. The man pulled out a pocket knife, inserted it into one of the small spaces between the fence's cedar planks, and released a spring latch on a gate that was undetectable until that moment. After taking a quick look around, the man pulled the gate open, admitted Marshall, followed him in, and pulled it closed.

The man said, "Don't ask me why I'm doing this; for some reason I trust you. You're the first person we've had back here."

Marshall nodded. He didn't say a word. He was too surprised by his surroundings to talk. They were standing in an old alleyway. The dimensions of the space and the old asphalt made that clear. But it wasn't an alley anymore. Not with all those roses growing on makeshift trellises up against the sides of the buildings and on the high Stucco wall separating them from the front sidewalk.

He didn't notice the woman at first, hunched over the base of one of the plants and quietly tending the soil. She was wearing a blue work shirt, sleeves rolled up, and tan trousers. Her faded red hair was tied in a knot on the back of her head. Marshall couldn't see much of her face, but from what he could make out he'd have a harder a time guessing her age than he'd had with the man.

"That's Lydia," the man said. "You don't have to introduce yourself, I already did. She wouldn't have anything to say, anyway."

Marshall said, "Hello, Lydia," and got no response.

"See?" the man said. "I told you. It takes a while for Lydia to get comfortable with people. But don't take it personal. And don't worry, I put in a good word for you."

Marshall nodded his thanks, and the man pointed out a coiled water hose next to the rear wall of one of the buildings. Marshall enjoyed a long drink before directing the stream to his grimy face. He scrubbed it with his free hand.

"I can't believe this little hideaway that you two have managed to carve out."

"That's just what it is, a hideaway. We'd both appreciate it very much if you don't tell anyone about it."

"Your secret's safe with me."

The man squatted on his haunches, his back against the wall of the west building. Marshall sat down on an old produce crate and listened to him.

"A few years ago, they decided to wall up this old section of alley, you know, to keep people like us from hanging out here. They couldn't build anything. It's an access-way or something. You see that manhole cover? I'm sure that had something to do with it.

"Lydia and I were checking it out when they were putting up the fence along the alley. She had this crazy notion that we'd be able to sneak in here and fix it to grow flowers. She said it got plenty of sun and that she could work it, on the sly. As soon as they finished the fence and the wall in front, Lydia and I started to work. I'd boost her over the fence, then jump over myself. We knocked out chunks of asphalt along the walls and planted little bushes Lydia had gotten ahold of. That hose bib was working and we used a pail to carry the water."

Marshall looked over to where the man was sitting, noticing the door and walled-off window next to him.

"I figured whoever owns the place came out here once in a while to check it out," the man said, nodding toward the door. "They left everything alone, and I didn't think they would mind if I rigged up a gate so we wouldn't have to climb over. Anyway, it's been over a year now. Lydia comes every day to take care of her roses. When they're blooming, she'll always have a bunch with her on the street, and she has a few regular customers who'll toss her a couple of bucks for a long-stemmed rose, or more, for a rose bouquet."

"Do you guys sleep here?" Marshall asked.

"No, I think that would be pushing it too far. Besides, there's not any shelter back here. We usually spend the night in the Sepulveda basin. We've rigged a little spot where we can stash our things and stay dry."

Marshall didn't have time to get comfortable. Within a few minutes the man climbed to his feet and beckoned him to follow. They walked back out to Ventura Boulevard and entered a donut shop a few doors down from the corner.

"Hey, Lars," the man said, escorting Marshall to the counter and looking over the rows of pastries in front of them.

A balding man in a white T-shirt and a well used apron appeared from the recess of the kitchen, walked up behind the counter and said, "How you doin', Doc? You're late today. I was getting a little worried about you."

"Oh, I've been catching up on old times with my friend here—"

"Wes . . . Wes Brown," Marshall interjected, realizing that he hadn't exchanged names with the man yet.

"Nice to meet you . . . Wes," the man behind the counter said. "Any friend of Doc's . . ." and he just let it trail off, looking at Marshall suspiciously.

"Look, Lars," Doc said, "Wes, here, has run into a little bad luck. I'd sure appreciate it if you could give him my breakfast while I tidy up outside."

"Sure, Doc, if that's what you want."

"Wait a minute," Marshall said. "I didn't come in here to take anybody's breakfast."

Doc said, "It's just a donut and a cup of coffee, and besides, I'm not hungry." And with that, he went outside, pulled the broom from his cart and started sweeping the front sidewalk.

Before Marshall could go after him, the man behind the counter said, "It's okay, Wes. Doc comes in here every morning for his coffee and pastry. If he wants you to have it, that's fine with me. C'mon, take your pick."

"Well, I have to confess . . . I've been looking over those bearclaws; they look pretty good."

"Have a seat, and I'll heat one up for you."

Marshall took a seat at one of the tables by the front window. Other than the two of them, the place was empty. Lars sat down across from him after he delivered the bearclaw and cup of coffee.

"Doc isn't very good at introductions, is he? My name's Larson Sweeney; everybody calls me Lars."

"Glad to meet you," Marshall said, extending his hand across the table. "And thanks." He took a sip of coffee before continuing. "You're right about his introductions. I didn't even know his name until I heard you call him Doc."

"So you two just met, huh?"

"That's right."

"That surprises me," Lars said. "Doc don't usually take up with strangers. He likes to keep to himself. Once you get to know him, he's okay, but that can take a while. And he don't let too many folks into his little circle of friends."

Marshall ignored Lars's inference. "Why do you call him Doc? Was he once a doctor? He seems pretty well-educated."

"It was something like that," Lars said. "He was a psychologist or psychiatrist; I'm not sure which. Some kind of headshrinker. That was years ago—fifties, early sixties."

"What happened to him?"

"I guess there's no harm in telling you," Lars said. "Hell, everybody along the boulevard knows his story. From what I understand, when Doc was first getting started at being a shrink, he got into experimenting with drugs. He wasn't doing it for fun or anything. He was really experimenting."

"Are you talking about LSD, that kind of stuff?"

"Yeah, LSD, that's what did him in. From what I gather, his experiments weren't very well-organized. Whatever it was, it knocked him for a loop, permanently. I guess they didn't know much about it back then. All they could do was lock him in the loony bin and see what happened. He wound up staying there for years, until Reagan took office and kicked everybody out. Doc's been on the boulevard ever since."

"I can't believe he's that old," Marshall said. "He doesn't seem that messed up, either."

"That's cause he thinks he's cured himself. Right after he was released, he came across a book: *The Doors of Perception*. Well, that straightened him all out. He claims that if he had read that book before he tried his experiments, things would have been different. He went on to read everything Aldous Huxley wrote— that's the guy who wrote the book. I know all about it. Doc's told me and everyone else around here all about Huxley. I'll bet you can't come up with a problem that Doc can't solve with a quote from one of his books."

"That explains it," Marshall said

"Explains what?"

"Why Doc's taken me under his wing. I'm a kindred spirit."

"How's that?"

"I've read a little Huxley, myself," Marshall said. "And I recognized the lines when Doc threw me one of his quotations. I answered him with a Huxley quote of my own."

"That would impress Doc, all right," Lars said. Then he moved closer to Marshall and lowered his voice. "Now let me give you a little free advice, it comes with the coffee and pastry. Doc's got some good friends around here. Not just his buddies on the street. I'm talking about the merchants along the boulevard. We've all known him a long time. He comes around every morning, sweeping up in front of our stores and maybe washing a window here and there. And we all like to help him out. You see Elsner's Laundry, down the street? They'll do a load of clothes for him every week. I'll see that he gets a cup of coffee anytime he wants, and both him and Lydia are in here most mornings for something to eat. You'll see roses from Lydia's little garden in everybody's shop. Even if it's just a lone rose in a jar by the cash register, there'll be a fresh one there every day. What I'm gettin' at, is that we all like Doc and his lady-friend. We wouldn't want to see anything bad happen to them. Or see somebody come by and take advantage of 'em. You get my drift?"

"Loud and clear, Lars. And I couldn't agree with you more. I like Doc, too. As for my situation, it's a little more temporary. I'll be gone before you know it."

FOURTEEN

THE ETERNAL residents of Pacific View Memorial Park occupied a gentle green slope rising behind downtown Corona del Mar. Their headstones lay flat, many of them scattered alongside concrete paths winding their way up the incline in lazy switchbacks converging at the front of a mausoleum crowning the hill. The paths were built for automobiles but were narrow and could only accommodate one-way traffic. Cars traveled at a snail's pace, whether in a long procession, or alone to allow occupants to search out a loved one's grave site.

Christine Blake sat in her Camry, up the hill from the Marshalls' family plot, a couple hundred yards away from the nearest car parked for Jennifer's service. Nothing fancy, just family and a few close friends. Christine was jotting down license plate numbers and looking over the participants with a pair of compact field glasses, not sure what she hoped to accomplish. Flat headstones hugging the grass didn't offer much cover, and she felt conspicuous out in the open, without a wall, hedge, or even a bush for cover. Just a few cypress trees spread out near the bottom of the hill, where they didn't interfere with the view.

At the last minute, Debra Marshall made her entrance. The morning sunlight danced along the polished flanks of her white Mercedes as it sped past the front gateposts and leaned into the first turn. It slowed down for the clump of parked cars blocking the path halfway up the slope and pulled in behind an old restored Jaguar. Paul Cappannelli stepped out of a black Cadillac parked a few spaces ahead, catching Christine by surprise. He walked briskly to the passenger side of the Mercedes and climbed in.

What are those two up to, Christine wondered, training her binoculars on the gesturing figures behind Debra's windshield, wishing she could hear them.

* * *

"What the hell are you doing here?"

"Is that any way to talk to your dear old dad, who's come all this way to be with his daughter in her time of grief?" Cappannelli shot Debra a benevolent smile, which quickly dissolved. "Where the fuck have you been? I've been trying to get ahold of you for three days."

"I've been kinda busy."

"You've been busy? No . . . I've been busy, trying to figure out why the fuck Marshall's still walking around. I must have been crazy to go along with your goddamned scheme. Now what the hell happened?"

"There was a slight change in plans," Debra said.

All he could manage to say was, "A slight change of plans?"

"Look," she said. "Marshall wasn't supposed to get away from the police. When they catch him, everything will fall back into place."

"You crossed me Debra, and I don't like it. If you were anybody else, you'd be history. The deal was Marshall dies, remember? It was supposed to be a boating accident, if I remember correctly. 'Just leave the details to me.' Isn't that what you said?"

"You wouldn't have gone along with me if I let you in on everything. But trust me, the outcome would've turned out the way you wanted . . . it still will. It might even be better this way. Maybe he'll get killed out there."

"He will if I have anything to do with it," Cappannelli said. "And by the way, a woman came by the other day, asking about a certain boat. Her name's Christine Blake. I don't suppose you know her."

"No . . . no, I'm afraid not," Debra said, shaking her head slowly, then taking an obvious glance out the window. "We better get over to the grave before the service starts. Do you think you can manage your role as a sympathetic father?"

Cappannelli stared at her, still pissed. He wasn't through with her. "The next time I send Wolcott on an errand you'd better be more helpful."

"I don't know enough about Wes's business to be giving your attorney the grand tour through his books—not yet. I couldn't even find them."

"As far as the jerks in Marshall's office are concerned, Wolcott *is* your attorney, and you have access to anything you want. And one more thing. What was that I heard about his secretary, Phelps. Wolcott told me she was talking to Marshall when you two were going through his office. If you hadn't been using the speaker phone on his desk to listen in, Wolcott would have never known—and neither would I. I sure as hell didn't hear a word about it from you."

Cappannelli's voice had been steadily rising; now he was shouting. He caught himself, waited for the echoes of his voice to stop ringing off the inside walls of the car, and then injected as much menace as he could into his soft whisper. "Now I'm just going to say this once: stay in touch. Whatever you know, I want to know. You clear on that?"

Debra nodded, the smooth skin over the arteries in her neck quivering with every quick heartbeat. Satisfied, Cappannelli opened the door.

* * *

Christine panned her glasses back and forth between the two of them as they climbed out on either side of the Mercedes. Debra walked around the front of the car, where Cappannelli waited, standing on the grass. She grabbed his arm and they walked toward the group of people milling around the small awning that had been set up at the freshly dug grave.

That woman is a piece of work, Christine thought, watching Debra's hips struggle to maintain their distinctive sway as she hurried across the grass down the hill. Something about the way she held on to Cappannelli was familiar. Maybe it was the tilt of her shoulders as she leaned next to him, or how she quickly cocked her head when she turned to say something. Christine started to feel a little disoriented. Seeing Debra with Cappannelli was like watching a re-run. She'd seen this before, and as soon as she realized when and where, she almost dropped the binoculars. It was Thursday night all over again—Wes Marshall and his daughter, arm in arm, walking down to the docks.

"I'll be damned," Christine said aloud, putting it together as she refocused on Debra. "That was you the other night."

Christine stared at Debra through the glasses, then unconsciously lowered them, not needing the magnification to see the truth. Not to recognize how well Debra had played her.

She had me pegged from the start, Christine thought, the last couple of months flashing through her mind like fast-forwarded scenes on an old VCR. Her stomach clenched as she thought of how she had worn her heart on her sleeve, talking about growing up with her father and brothers and never having any girlfriends, giving Debra the opportunity to be a real friend. Christine berated herself further for being the perfect patsy: self-centered, looking for someone to understand her, maybe even to feel as sorry for her as she felt for herself, oblivious to Debra's ulterior motives.

She looked down at the funeral service getting underway. Guilt coiled inside her. She was part of the reason they were lowering an innocent woman into the ground.

She thought about what she'd told Joel, about the past repeating itself until you get it right. And she saw what needed changing wasn't the way she handled things but the way she handled herself. Her mistake had been caring about what others thought about her, or worrying about how they might respond to her actions. It was time to do what she thought was right, the rest of the world be damned. She planned her next move as she waited for the service to end. It was the only way she could calm down.

The collection of mourners eventually broke into small groups and made their way back up the slope to their parked cars. They moved slowly, as if reluctant to leave Jennifer behind. Debra was one of the first to reach her car. With no room to turn around on the narrow path, she had to drive by Christine's Camry to reach the road. Christine saw her coming and ducked below the dashboard until she passed by. When Debra was far enough away, Christine started the car and followed her to PCH.

* * *

Christine kept several cars between them as they drove over the bridge crossing Newport Bay. They made a right on Dover and turned up a hill leading to the residential streets of Newport Heights. Debra parked outside a house on Clay Street. Christine turned down a street half a block farther down, pulled into a driveway to turn around, and slowly rolled back toward Clay. She stopped behind an oleander hedge growing near the corner, close enough to the edge to see past it. Debra had entered the front door of the house and in less than five minutes reemerged with an elderly woman in tow. They got in the Mercedes and drove off.

Christine wrote down the home's address and followed her. Debra led her to a new-looking building near Hoag Hospital on the other side of Newport Boulevard. A sign near the entrance read: LIFE CARE OF NEWPORT BEACH. Christine watched from a safe distance as Debra and the old woman walked across the parking lot and through the front door. She didn't see any reason to wait around.

As Christine pulled away, her cell phone rang. It was Walter Jenkins.

"I took that picture over to the Harbor Patrol office."

"The picture of Cappannelli in front of the boat?"

"Yeah, I didn't say anything about him, though. I just told them that the boat was a lot like the one that ran over my wharf. They looked it over, compared it with my Polaroids and agreed with me. They did some checking and confirmed that the boat belonged to Tony Anselmo. He used to own that charter outfit I told you about."

"Where is he now?"

"Dead."

"Are there any records of the boat being sold? Any new names on the registration documents?"

"Nope. Tony was the last person to own it. No way to tell where it's been since he died. No registration renewal payments or anything like that."

Christine thought it over for a minute, then said, "Look, Wally, I think there's something you can do to help out here. Just a little leg work. Would you mind?"

"Name it. But I'll have to deduct my time and expenses from your fee."

"Very funny," Christine said. "First of all, did you ever know the guy?"

"Tony Anselmo? Not really. I'd seen him around. That's about it."

"Okay," Christine said. "Then why don't you ask around. Go down to the Pavilion. You're bound to find some folks that knew him pretty well. See if you can find out if there was anything suspicious about his death, what kind of financial shape he was in, and what happened to his boat."

"Is that all?"

"Hey, you can handle it. Besides, everyone knows you around there. They'll be glad to talk to you. I'm sure you'll get results a lot faster than I could. Now I gotta go. I'm losing my battery."

Christine hung up, started her car, and headed home.

FIFTEEN

ARE YOU all right? I called a couple of times earlier and didn't get an answer. I felt bad about leaving you on the highway like that."

"I'm fine, Mr. Marshall. I actually rode with the tow truck driver to the body shop the Lexus dealer recommended."

"How did it go with the police?"

"That situation turned out very well for you. All the witnesses left before the police could question them. The large man who helped us collected his son and was among the first to leave."

"People don't want to get involved," Marshall said.

"That's true. And best of all, I was able to keep you out of it. I told the officer taking the report what happened—that I was hit from behind and lost control of the car, unable to identify the other vehicle as it drove away. By now there was only the officer and myself standing along the road. I suppose it didn't occur to him to ask if I had a passenger."

"That's perfect. I'm glad you didn't have to lie. How are things at the office? Everybody still working?"

"Yes, Mr. Marshall, everyone's here, doing their job. I've locked your office and left instructions not to answer your extension, not that anyone would come in and make themselves at home at my desk. I've made it clear that the corporation is solid, no matter the president's current status, and that their paychecks will keep coming, at least for the time being."

"Thank you," he said. "I should have known that you'd be on top of it. I was going to ask you to hold a meeting with Taylor and Davenport, have you tell them that you've talked to me and that I'm going to do my best to get this mess cleared up. But more important, I want them to know that the company will stay afloat as long as they continue to do their jobs."

"I think they already understand that. But I'll be sure to relay your message. You can count on us." Miss Phelps paused for a few moments before continuing. "I don't know if you're aware of it, but they buried Jennifer today. That's where I've been this morning."

A long silence, then Marshall said, "No, I didn't know that. Did they bury her next to her mother?"

"Yes, and they had a service, just a few words over the grave. I don't think anyone could have taken much more than that. It was very sad."

The tears came without warning, as if a faucet had been turned. They flowed down both cheeks and down the arm he used to hold the phone receiver to his ear. He let it drop to his side but maintained a tight grip, squeezing it for all he was worth. He looked down the street from the payphone at an uncaring world. When he brought the receive back to his ear, the shared silence from the other end was somehow comforting.

"It had to be tough on everyone there," Marshall finally said. I'm afraid to imagine what they must think of me. Was my mother there? How did she seem to be holding up?"

"Your mother was there, as was Kathleen's family. None of them said much, and to be honest, I couldn't say what they were thinking. It was obvious, though, that they were under a lot of strain. Old folks shouldn't have to bury their young."

"Thank you for being there," Marshall said. "You've already done so much . . . I want you to know that I appreciate it. And I'm afraid I've already screwed up your best efforts. I've lost the cell phone and the money."

"Oh, Mr. Marshall—"

"What ever happens from here on out, I want you to know what's going on. Debra's father has a stake in this. I don't know why, but he has it in for me. Make sure you remember his name—Paul Cappannelli. He wants to kill me. I know it sounds crazy, but believe me, I'm lucky to be alive. I've found a place to hide out for a while. Maybe I can last another day and figure something out.

"What do you want me to do?"

"I don't know yet. I need some time to think. I'll call you tomorrow."

* * *

"Come on in," Walter called out. When Christine came through the doorway, he said, "Don't mind me if I don't get up. This detective business can wear a guy out."

"That's why we pay you the big bucks," Christine said. She looked around, then sat down on the old wooden chair behind the desk, the only available place left to sit. "So what have you been up to?"

"I took your advice. I went over to the Pavilion, and after nosing around a little, I came across a lad who used to work for Tony Anselmo. He stayed on with the new owners after they took over the business. Calls himself Buck. I never did get his last name."

"That's good. What did he have to say?"

"At first he wasn't very helpful, but I guess I couldn't blame him. He was still on the clock, trying to do his job: cleaning up the rental boats, seining the dead anchovies out of the bait tanks, stuff like that. I offered to buy him a beer after he got off work. Told him that I knew Tony from the old days and wondered what had happened to him. Thought maybe he could fill in some blanks for me. Well, let me tell you, he met me at the bar next door to their shop about an hour later and loosened up considerably. In fact, after three or four beers, I didn't think he was ever going to shut up."

"I'm impressed, Wally. You seem to have a natural talent for this. However, there's just one thing you have to look out for when you use that technique. Make sure you don't get as drunk, or drunker, than your informant. Makes it hard to remember all the little details that might come out in the conversation."

"No worries," Walter said. "I was pretty careful, made sure ol' Buck drank at least two beers for every one of mine. I also jotted down a few things as soon as we parted company to make sure I wouldn't forget anything once you started grilling me."

With that, Walter swung his legs off the couch and onto the floor, sat up straight, and pulled a folded piece of paper out of his shirt pocket. He glanced at it, then tossed it aside. He'd had his share of beers, maybe enough to coax him into a little nap, but not enough to impair his memory. He recalled everything Buck had told him and gave Christine a lucid account of their conversation.

"First off," he said, "I got the answers to those questions you asked. Tony died of natural causes; he died broke; and I think it's safe to assume that the new owners of the charter business wound up with his boats. At one time he had quite a few of them. He had a larger vessel for deep sea fishing charters, the kind that go out all day with a big crowd crammed on board, and he also had a bunch of rental boats that stayed in the bay: rowboats with an outboard motor and a bait tank; small, single masted sailboats; some vintage Chris Craft cruisers with governors on the engines to keep them at a safe speed in the bay; the usual marina attractions."

"How'd he die?" Christine asked.

"Heart attack, about four or five years ago."

"Did he leave a family? A wife?"

"There was a wife, but they'd been divorced for a long time. According to Buck, Tony liked to gamble. It was bad enough to break up his marriage. I don't know about kids. That subject never came up. I'll tell you what did come up though, a lad by the name of Paul Cappannelli."

Walter couldn't help pausing long enough to throw Christine an I-told-you-so look, then continued with his story.

"Turns out Cappannelli's a loan shark. Over the years Tony got in pretty deep, borrowing money from Cappannelli to pay off his bookie, using his boats as collateral. Business was good enough for him to keep up with the interest, but Tony never did pay off the principle. If he ever won anything, he'd try to parlay it, lose it all, and wind up worse than before.

"By the time I learned this, the bartender had joined in on our conversation. He'd overheard us talking about Tony and came over to throw in his two cent's worth. Told us that Tony had always been a regular customer, and that near the end he was really putting away the bourbon. Buck confirmed it. Said that it got to the point where Tony was never sober after two or three in the afternoon. He wasn't a young man anymore, and I guess the stress and booze did him in."

"What about the boat," Christine said. "Does Buck know what happened to the *Devil May Care?*"

"Nope, he couldn't help me with that. He was out of work for a while, until the new owners got established and hired him back. When he returned, the sport fisher was gone, although the big deep sea boat and most of the rentals were still around."

"I'll bet Cappannelli felt he had the boat coming," Christine said. "Of course, his dealings with Tony weren't exactly legal, so he'd have to take possession any way he could. Believe me, he's not the kind of guy who'd have a problem with that."

"You sound like you already know him," Walter said, then took a long look at her. "Say . . . you haven't already been out to see him, have you?"

"I guess I forgot to tell you about that."

She spent a few minutes filling Walter in on the details of her encounter with Cappannelli.

When she stopped talking, Walter said, "He sounds dangerous."

"He is dangerous," Christine said. "And so is his daughter. I watched the two of them at Jennifer's funeral today, and I'm convinced that they set up Wes Marshall for killing his daughter."

"Then what are we waiting for?" Walter jumped to his feet, ready to bolt out the door. "Let's go. No need to call first. We should just go down to the police station and talk to the people in charge and clear this up."

"Not yet, Wally. Were not ready. All we have are suspicions and wild speculations, nothing we can prove. That's how the police would see it. And they'd be very upset with me for interfering with their investigation. Who knows? They might even think I'm involved. I've already gone in and volunteered my eyewitness account of the night of the murder. I signed a legally binding statement that explained how I was hired by Debra to follow her husband and that I saw Marshall and his daughter board the boat within hours or minutes of the time she was killed. I'm not ready to go back now with a whole new story. Not until I'm sure of what happened and can prove it."

"I guess that makes sense," Walter said, pacing anxiously. "But isn't there something we can do?"

"C'mon, Wally, why don't you sit down? You're making me nervous."

Walter let out a reluctant sigh, and sat back on the sofa.

"I am doing something," Christine said. "I followed Debra after the funeral. It paid off with a new lead that I'll check out in the morning."

Christine rose from the chair and hurried to the door. Before she walked out, she turned back toward Walter. "I noticed something else at the funeral. Maybe you can help me out with it."

"What's that?" Walter said.

"Well, I wasn't really at the funeral. I was watching it from a distance. Anyway, I noticed an older woman who didn't seem to fit in. She set herself apart from the small groups of friends and family. She attracted my attention from time to time, looking lost and very sad. I was wondering if you might know who she was."

"Was she kind of wiry . . . not frail, but wiry?"

"Yeah, I guess you could describe her like that."

"Then it had to be Miss Phelps," Walter said.

"Miss Phelps?"

"That would be my guess."

"Who is she?"

"She works for Marshall, been with him from the beginning. He told me about her once or twice when we were out sailing. He said she was the reason he was able to take so much time off work and spend it on the boat. He thinks the world of her."

"Well, that could be a good thing," Christine said, and walked out the door.

* * *

Christine sat on the sand after her run, just beyond the water's edge, and stared out to sea. The stars were out, the ones close to the horizon hard to distinguish from the lights on the offshore drilling rigs and slow-moving boats.

She was still breathing hard from what had to be her quickest lap between the Balboa and the twenty-second street piers. Tuco sat next to her, his leash slack between them. When her breathing returned to normal she climbed to her feet and led him back to her car.

Her Camry was parked on Balboa Boulevard. Christine unhooked Tuco's leash and opened the back door. He didn't want to get in. He was like that sometimes, when he wasn't ready to go home.

"I know," Christine said. "We *are* having a lot of fun."

Tuco just stood there. The stare-down lasted about thirty seconds, then he climbed onto the back seat.

That was about as close to misbehaving as Tuco ever came. He might *look* mean, but Christine believed half of it was due to the reputation associated with the breed.

She wasn't sure about the other half.

Maybe it was the calm stare. He never barked or growled or looked like he might bite someone. She had never seen him in a dogfight, although she'd seen other dogs aggressively approach him, only to back down when they got within range of his alpha-wolf vibe, or whatever primal voodoo he gave off. Christine knew his calm demeanor wasn't the product of weakness or a lack of confidence. Even she could sense the predatory readiness beneath the surface.

He was stretched out across the back seat when she pulled up behind her garage. Now he didn't want to get out.

"OK, have it your way," Christine said. She rolled down a window and climbed out. "I'll leave the back gate open if you change your mind. Just don't run off."

She was halfway up he stairs when she remembered why she'd gone out in the first place—her office. After talking to Walter and her run on the beach, she had completely forgotten about it. She turned around and headed back to her car.

SIXTEEN

CHRISTINE WAS glad she'd made the effort when she turned into the empty parking lot. She left her car in the closest space and sprinted up the outdoor stairway leading to her door.

She put the key in the lock. It wasn't bolted. The door swung open. Something was wrong even as she reached inside for the light switch. It was a reflexive response to opening the door. Before she had time to think, a large hand caught her wrist and pulled her in. The back of another hand slapped her hard across the face. She hit the floor. The office door slammed shut. The hand grabbed her by the neck, as if she could be picked up off the floor like a disobedient kitten. The pain was almost paralyzing, but she managed to get her feet under her, afraid something would break if she didn't help herself up.

Out of the dark, near enough to smell its breath, an unpleasant voice said, "Thanks for showing up. You've saved me a lot of trouble."

Christine's senses hadn't come up to speed yet. All she could manage was, "What are you—"

The voice's owner shoved her across the room, hard enough to knock her head against the wall. She slid down onto the floor.

"I'm giving you a break here, letting you see my gentle side. Believe me, you don't want to piss me off. Right now, I just want to ask you few questions."

Christine's eyes were adjusting to the darkness. She didn't need much light to recognize the big guy from Cappannelli's house the other day. He walked over and picked her up by the neck again, led her to one of the chairs in front of her desk, and slammed her down.

"Now why don't you tell me how you found out about the boat?"

"The boat? What are you—"

It might have been an effortless flick of the wrist, but it knocked Christine back in her chair, almost toppling her over. She tasted blood running from her nose. She leaned her head back to stem the flow. She hoped she wasn't crying. If there were tears on her face she couldn't feel them.

"Let's try it again. How did you find out about the boat?"

"I don't know what—"

She never saw it coming. The big guy hit her fast and hard with a closed right fist. It landed on the left side of her face. She tumbled out of the chair and fell on her side. She tried to prop herself up but it was too much for her. She rolled onto her back, almost unconscious. He brought the chair over and picked her up by the front of her sweatshirt and threw her back down on the seat.

"When are you going to learn? When I ask a question, I want an answer."

Christine had trouble keeping her head up. It would roll off to one side or drop down toward her chest, then jerk back up. Like a driver who'd been on the road too long and was fighting to stay awake. Her words barely came out.

"Please . . . don't . . . don't hit me again."

"Then let's have it."

Christine closed her eyes, waiting for the punch. When it didn't come, she opened them just wide enough to see his face, inches from her own. She didn't let her eyes waver from his gaze when she said, "It was Debra. She told me about the boat."

He let go of her sweatshirt and stood up straight. He wore thin, tight fitting leather gloves. Christine didn't like his smile.

"So Debra told you, huh? Now why would she do that?"

Not knowing what to say, Christine acted a little more rummy than she actually was. She made it up as she went along, letting the words come out slow, buying as much time as she could.

"She talks a lot, and I pay attention."

"She talks a lot, does she? Why is she talking to you?"

"She wasn't exactly talking to me . . . I was eavesdropping."

"Keep going. Let's hear it all."

"Her husband hired me."

Christine kept her answers brief. It was a struggle just to talk. Her act wasn't that hard to pull off. The left side of her face had gone numb as soon as she was hit. Her left eye was already swollen shut and hurt like hell. She brought up a tentative finger to touch it, then used her hand to wipe away the blood on her face while she continued talking.

"He was suspicious. I found out things."

"What were you doing at Cappannelli's house the other day?"

Christine closed her good eye, leaned back in the chair and said, "I thought maybe I could make a few bucks."

"You thought you could shake him down? You gotta be shittin' me. I can't wait to tell him about this."

The big man seemed pleased with himself "Just one more thing," he said. "Who have you talked to?"

"No one," Christine said. No matter what, she couldn't turn this guy loose on Walter.

He came down close again. "You really shouldn't lie to me. That could piss me off."

He stayed there awhile, studying her face. Then surprised her when he asked, "What about the secretary, Phelps?"

"I don't know her," Christine said.

"C'mon, you know her." He straightened up. "You've been to Marshall's office, haven't you?"

"No. I've only seen him here. And over the phone."

"So you don't know anything about the secretary?"

"Why should I? What's she done?"

"We know she's been helping Marshall. We were watching her, and she led us right to him. It was just a fluke that he got away, not that it matters to you."

The finality of the man's statement scared her. Behind him, she noticed her CPU had been unplugged and was lying on its side, her back-up hard drive and assorted flash drives and disks stacked on top.

And she saw how this would look to the police: break-in gone bad. Victim killed after walking in on intruder. It was a real and terrifying possibility. The image of Jennifer's coffin being lowered into the ground flashed through her mind and reinforced her fear.

Christine searched for a target. She'd have to hurry. If she was lucky, she might get in a kick. The man stood close, taking his time, pausing for a last look around. Enjoying himself.

Her first choice, his groin, was too high. From her sitting position, she had no chance of delivering a quick kick that could do much damage. He'd see it coming from a mile away.

But his knee . . .

Christine leaned back to get her foot off the ground, pulled in her knee, and stomped her heel against the middle of the guy's leg as hard as she could. He fell to the floor. She was out of the chair and through the doorway and halfway down the stairs before his footsteps came after her.

"You fucking bitch!"

She kept going, the footsteps gaining on her.

Is he running? How can he even walk?

She didn't dare look back. She focused on her car and wished to God that she'd left the window down. She reached for the backseat door just as the big guy caught up with her.

The door opened and Tuco flew by her. The momentum of the dog's lunge pushed the big man back, and Tuco had his teeth around his neck before they hit the ground. Tuco made several violent tugs, setting his large fangs deep into flesh, gristle, and arteries, crushing the man's windpipe in the process. He didn't let go until Christine pulled him off.

They both stood over him and watched him die, the elapsed time measured in heartbeats. It seemed like forever.

When it was over, Christine slumped down by the rear tire of her car, half crying, half laughing, caught up in a semi-hysterical reflex. Tuco remained on guard, between her and the body. He'd look over at the man's body, then back to Christine, as if asking if he'd done the right thing. When her tears slowed down, she hugged him, ignoring the blood on her arms from his sticky fur.

She finally stood up, told Tuco to stay, and ran back up the stairs to retrieve her keys still hanging from the lock on her office door. She unlocked the tenants bathroom off the open hallway on the first floor of her building. She returned with wet paper towels to clean some of the blood off of Tuco. It was all over his muzzle, and she didn't want him looking like a mad dog when the police arrived. She cleaned up his paws so he wouldn't track any blood around, then threw the towels into the Dumpster behind the restaurant next door.

She found her cell phone and called 911. The battery lasted just long enough to make the call. She waited on the bottom steps leading up to her office.

* * *

Every vehicle in Newport Beach with a city emblem painted on the side and a light bar stuck on the roof must have showed up at the small parking lot in front of Christine's office. Crime scene tape and flashing lights and a crush of personnel surrounded Christine's Camry and the body next to it.

Christine sat on the top step in front of the hair salon that occupied the ground floor, holding the leash she'd put on Tuco. A paramedic attended to her. They wouldn't allow a dog in their van and Christine wasn't about to let him out of her sight, not since the Animal Control wagon had arrived. She hadn't fielded many questions yet, but she knew they were coming. A couple of guys in suits were looking her over from a few feet away, talking to each other in low tones while they waited for her medical attention to be completed.

The man's body hadn't been moved. It was the center of attention, getting its picture taken and having the contents of its pockets examined.

When the paramedics tending to Christine had finished, the two plainclothes detectives moved in. The taller and older of the pair spoke first.

"My name's Hodges. I'm a detective with the Newport Beach Police Department. "This is Dennis Ash." He nodded at his partner. "He'll be working with me."

Christine regarded the two men with her good eye. They both looked the part: clean cut in a wash and wear sort of way, from their haircuts to their crepe-soled shoes. Hodges had on a better suit, but not by much. She guessed they both shopped at the same factory outlet. It was obvious that Hodges was the senior man. He had that seasoned look about him, treating the dead body nearby as part of the normal landscape. Ash was a little greener, watched Hodges's every move, and probably tried to act like him when he had the chance. While they were together it was clear that Hodges treated him like something of a gofer.

When Christine didn't respond, Hodges continued. "If you're up for it, why don't you tell us what happened."

Christine had her story ready and told it like it happened, at least most of it. She left out the question-answer session she'd had with the man, making a snap decision to also keep quiet about their previous encounter at Cappannelli's house. It would require too much explaining, and she wasn't up for going over it countless times down at the station. When pressed, she claimed she didn't recognize man and didn't know what he was after, only that she was sure he was going to kill her.

Hodges drilled her with more questions, or more accurately, rephrased questions he'd already asked.

"Detective, I can't do this . . . I need to go home."

Hodges let out a reluctant sigh and gave in, packing up his little notebook. Excusing himself, he walked away to confer with a new arrival on the crime scene. That seemed to give Ash the green light.

"Okay Ms. Blake, if you'll just hand the leash over to one of the animal control people. They'll be taking the dog now."

"The hell they will," she said. "He's staying with me."

"I'm afraid that isn't possible. There are procedures to go through regarding animal attacks."

"This isn't a rabid dog attacking people," Christine said. "He's a highly trained guard dog who's just saved my life. Nobody's taking him anywhere."

"I'm sorry, Miss. I'm sure you'll get him back in a few days. Now if you'll—"

"Let's not worry about the dog, Ash," a voice said. The man who spoke had walked out of the shadows, where he'd been talking to Hodges. It was Del Hallstrom, the detective in charge of the Marshall murder investigation. "There are still few cars parked by the restaurant. Why don't you go over and assist the officers taking statements."

"But sir," Ash protested, "regulations state that . . ."

Hallstrom glared at Ash for a few extra seconds, then turned his attentions to Christine.

"Hello, Christine. Your name caught my attention when I heard what went down here. Pretty nasty business." He made a show of looking around, shaking his head slowly after he'd scanned the body. "Any connection with Marshall?"

Christine knew what he was thinking; she'd be thinking the same thing in his shoes. A coincidence was the least likely explanation of her proximity to two dead bodies in less than a week. But she'd started out with her own spin on things and now she had to stay with it.

"If there's a connection, I don't know what it is," she said, not really lying.

At best, Hallstrom might find a connection between the dead man and Cappannelli, and ultimately to Debra Marshall. But she didn't think Cappannelli would want to be involved in any of this. He'd try to distance himself from the body as much as possible and would have no reason to say anything about the confrontation on his driveway.

"Look, Lieutenant, my head's killing me. Could I come down later to make a statement? Like I told your detective, I need to go home and lie down."

"Sure. You've had a pretty rough night. What did the medics say? Are you going to be all right?"

"Yeah, they said it looks worse than it really is. Nothing's broken, but I'll have a doozy of a shiner."

Hallstrom looked her over with an air of genuine concern. "I'll have a unit take you home. Why don't you come by tomorrow sometime to make your statement."

"What about my car?"

"We need to look it over. Same with your computer. The guy was ready to walk out with everything when you barged in on him, including your storage devices. I think this was more than just a robbery. We'll check your computer records for possible motives. For all we know, this guy could have been hired help."

"How long?"

"We'll expedite your car. I don't know about your computer stuff. I like to practice due diligence, and if our dead friend over there was after something in your records, we need to find out what it was. You could still be in danger."

Christine felt a pang of guilt for being less than truthful with Hallstrom, but it was too late to change that. Trying to explain now would only complicate matters.

"Thanks for not taking my dog."

"Consider it a professional courtesy. I asked around about you and heard good things. You play it straight and you'll find that I can be pretty easy to get along with."

* * *

It was close to midnight by the time a patrolman dropped Christine at her apartment. The first order of business was getting Tuco into the tub for a thorough bath. Dried blood still caked the thick fur around his neck and down his chest. When she was finished drying him, he sprang away and headed for the front door. He bounded down the stairs and ran laps around the back yard, stopping now and then to shake off the remaining bath water and roll on the grass.

Christine called Joel. He transitioned from groggy to wide awake during the short course of their conversation. Forty-five minutes later he was walking up the flight of stairs to her apartment.

SEVENTEEN

I T WAS early, plenty of time before they would start rolling in, as Christine sat in Joel's van above the parking lot behind Marshall's office. She wanted to account for every vehicle before she visited Miss Phelps. The big man's comment last night about staking out Marshall's secretary concerned her, and she wanted to see if anyone else was interested. As for herself, Christine was confident no one had followed her, but she kept a close watch over her shoulder. She wasn't about to be caught off guard again.

Miss Phelps arrived at eight sharp. Christine waited an extra fifteen minutes for good measure. The lot was now about half full and all the cars seemed to belong there. The same held true for the traffic on the adjacent lots and side streets. She left the van where it was and climbed down a sidewalk staircase leading to the office parking lot.

She was greeted by a receptionist seated behind a high desk in the foyer. After asking for Miss Phelps and waiting for a couple of minutes, the woman she'd seen at the funeral entered through a doorway. She was dressed in a well-tailored pant suit ensemble that flattered her trim figure. Her body language was completely different from that of the lost soul she appeared to have been at the funeral. Here at the office she was in her element, in command of herself and her surroundings. She was obviously more than a secretary, and Christine dared to hope that she was finally getting somewhere. She offered her hand.

"My name's Christine Blake. If it's not too much trouble, I'd like to talk to you . . . privately."

"What's this about?" Miss Phelps asked, frowning at Christine's roughed-up face. The obligatory sunglasses could not cover all the damage.

"Please, is there somewhere else we could talk?"

Miss Phelps nodded, and ushered Christine back to her office. When they were inside she closed the door and adjusted the vertical blinds on an interior glass wall. She offered Christine a seat on one of the upholstered chairs in front of her desk and sat and the other herself.

"Now, what can I do for you?"

"Have you seen this yet?" Christine handed over a copy of the morning Times, folded to display the article describing the break-in at her office.

Miss Phelps reached for the paper and looked it over. Her frown went from perplexed to concerned. "I heard something about this on the news this morning." Then she looked up and said, "This is about you, isn't it?"

"Yes. Do you know Paul Cappannelli?"

Miss Phelps seemed to pale at the mention of the name.

"The man who attacked me? He worked for him."

Miss Phelps let the paper fall onto her lap. She removed her reading glasses and rubbed the bridge of her nose. "My God, it just keeps getting worse." She slipped her glasses back on and looked at Christine. "I've never met him, but I know who he is. He's Mr. Marshall's father-in-law. May I ask how this involves you?"

"Fair enough," Christine said. "Mr. Marshall's friend, the man who rents him dock space, hired me to look into an accident that destroyed his slip last Wednesday. He hopes an investigation will shed some light on what really happened on Marshall's boat the night his daughter was killed."

"And what have you found out?"

"I'm not completely sure yet, but I think your boss is innocent. I guess that's why I'm here. For your help."

"I don't see what I could do."

"Let's be honest, Miss Phelps. I know you're involved. I also know it's asking a lot for you to trust a stranger. That's why I brought the article along. I think it shows how close I came to being a victim myself. You could be in danger as well. Last night the man who broke into my office mentioned that they were watching you, and that you led them to your boss."

"I was afraid something like that must have happened."

"So you've been in touch with Wes Marshall . . ."

Rather than answer, Miss Phelps sat quietly.

Christine stuck to her well-practiced habit of remaining silent, an old trick salesmen use for closing the sale: when the time's right to ask for a commitment, ask for it, and then keep quiet. If the customer talks first, he usually buys. It was just a matter of patience, and Christine could wait it out with the best of them.

Miss Phelps blinked first. Once she started talking, she kept going, telling Christine everything—Marshall's first phone call and his suspicion that Debra had overheard their conversation from an extension phone in his office; about providing the money, the clothes, and the cell phone; about the room at the La Quinta Inn. She mentioned the phone call from yesterday, and that she was expecting another one this morning.

"I need to talk to him when he calls," Christine said. "I've found out some things he needs to know. I'm sure he can fill in some blanks for me as well. Maybe we can pool our resources and find him a way out of this."

The older woman agreed. They both knew that he couldn't hide forever and that action had to be initiated, even if it meant turning himself in. Once they were of the same mind, Miss Phelps fetched a couple of coffees and the two of them waited for the phone to ring.

"If you don't mind my asking," Christine said, "why did you help him? It sure looked like he did it."

"I never believed that for a second. Never entered my mind. I've known Mr. Marshall for a long time and I know he is totally incapable of harming his daughter in any way. They were always close, a healthy closeness you'd expect between a father and his only daughter. Not this perversion the media is portraying."

Miss Phelps set her coffee cup aside and leaned in closer. "I remember when she was born. Mr. Marshall brought her to the office as soon as she could leave the house. He was so proud of her. And Kathleen, his first wife, well, they were already the perfect couple. Now they were a perfect family. That never changed . . ."

"Until Kathleen died," Christine said, finishing Miss Phelps's train of thought.

"Yes. That was another tragedy in the poor man's life. It's so hard to understand why bad things happen to good people."

They don't just happen, Christine thought, keeping it to herself. She was too cynical to believe that a man's wife and daughter could die violently within two years of each other without a premeditated plan behind it.

"Could you tell me about her," Christine said. "Mr. Marshall's first wife?"

Miss Phelps retrieved her cup and sat back. "They really were the perfect couple. I wasn't just saying that. Mr. Marshall had known Kathleen since high school. I believe they were an item, even back then. Once they were married and their baby was old enough for a sitter, Kathleen worked as hard as he had, pulling double shifts waiting tables while he pieceworked his way through the housing tracts spreading across the county. When the two of them realized how much money was piling up, they invested it into what became all of this."

Miss Phelps made a small gesture with her arms, palms up, and Christine reflexively looked around the office.

"That was twenty-five years ago," Miss Phelps continued, "and the business took of right away. That's where I came in."

"Seems like a long time to know someone," Christine said, "much less work for them."

"Yes it is. And you can take my word for it. Mr. Marshall is a good man."

Christine left it there. She settled back and finished her coffee. She was about to ask for a refill when Marshall's extension lit up.

Miss Phelps nodded to Christine after answering, indicating Marshall was on the line. She didn't give him much room to speak, interrupting right away with, "I assume you're finding a way to keep up with the news. Are you aware of an incident that happened in Newport Beach last night, where a dog killed a man? The man worked for Mr. Cappannelli. He attacked a woman in her office. She's here with me now, and I think you should talk to her."

Miss Phelps handed the phone over to Christine.

"Hello, Mr. Marshall."

"Who are you?"

"Kind of a moot point after that introduction, isn't it? Nevertheless, I don't want to use my name over the phone. I'm an attorney. How I became involved is a long story. I think you'd be interested in the details, but it's probably not a good idea to spend a lot of time talking on this line."

"Do you think someone's listening in?"

"Not the authorities, or they would have caught you by now. However, I don't think we can be too careful. And it's not the police I'm worried about."

"I hear you."

"There's a couple of people who've believed in your innocence all along. One of them is a friend of yours—the man who hired me. You can now add my name to the list. I'll try to help, but you're going to have to make a leap of faith and meet me, in person."

The silence over the line didn't last as long as Christine had expected.

"For better or worse," Marshall said, "I'm willing to take a chance. I have to do something, and I trust Miss Phelps's judgment."

"Okay," Christine said, "all we have to do now is find a secure line we can use to make our arrangements. Let's assume the worst and figure someone's listening in on this one."

They spent a few minutes designing a plausible scheme, when Marshall said, "I've got an idea. Miss Phelps has a standing appointment on Friday afternoons. Get her over there as soon as you can and I'll call and ask for her in thirty minutes."

Before she hung up, Christine relayed the message to Miss Phelps, who nodded back with a wry smile.

* * *

Jerome's Hair Design was located on Pacific Coast Highway, not more than a block from Christine's office. Miss Phelps said she had been going there for years. Ending her work week early at the spa was just one of the liberal perks Marshall had insisted on.

Christine and Miss Phelps drove separately, arriving a few minutes apart. Miss Phelps was standing at the front desk, talking to the receptionist, when Wes Marshall's call came in. The receptionist pushed the hold button and directed her to a courtesy phone in the waiting area. Miss Phelps answered the call, confirmed it was Marshall, and handed the receiver to Christine.

"Nice work," Christine said. "Where are you?"

"I'm in the Valley—Sherman Oaks."

"What are you doing in Sherman Oaks?"

"I was able to make it out to Paul Cappannelli's house. He's mixed up in this, and I thought I'd be able to bring it to the attention of the police. The whole thing backfired on me. I was lucky to get out of there alive."

"Where shall we meet?"

There's a donut shop on Ventura Boulevard, a few blocks east of the 405. It's not the Starbucks. It's an older place down the street called Ventura Donuts, right out of the fifties. If you're coming east down Ventura, it'll be on the right hand side. Sit by one of the windows facing the street. I'll be able to see you from a safe distance and make sure everything looks all right. How will I recognize you?"

"That'll be easy," Christine said. "I'll be the blonde wearing sunglasses that don't quite cover her black eye."

EIGHTEEN

PAUL CAPPANNELLI'S initial anger had turned toxic as he drove across town. He didn't need this grief, not now. He'd worked too hard and too long to accept anything less than satisfaction for his efforts.

He had come a long way from his early days of lending money to gamblers and drug dealers. Respectable businessmen now demanded his services. Over the years he had amassed an investment portfolio substantial enough to assist the occasional CEO with a cash flow problem. More often, it would be a corporate VP who needed personal help. When commission and override checks went south because of cyclical dips in sales, Cappannelli was the go-to man.

Of course, he was always paid back on schedule, usually early. Taking advantage of quick turnarounds in business would allow his clients to pay off their debt before the high interest rates could do much damage. If business stayed sour, they'd scramble for a traditional loan to get them out of trouble. It wasn't so much the high interest rates that were a worry; it was knowing the penalty for falling behind in payments.

For Cappannelli, that was the rub. As long as he did business the way he did, he'd always feel like a second class citizen. It didn't matter that he could conduct meetings in his upscale office in Century City, call himself a venture capitalist, and preside over a cash-heavy corporation. Nor did it matter that he'd bailed out influential people who found themselves in "embarrassing" financial difficulties, thus ingratiating himself into select country clubs and trendy social circles. It wasn't enough. Money and a few perks thrown his way didn't cut it. He wanted to hold his head high and bask in the respect of the stuffed shirts and high society types that had always looked down their noses at him.

But respect was a tough nut for him to crack. It wasn't something he could beat out of someone. And now, just when he's finally getting close to breaking through, Luke goes and gets himself killed. That kind of negative attention could ruin everything.

When he pulled up to the small bungalow in Studio City, his anger threatened to boil over. It required all of his willpower to control himself as he spent the next ten minutes banging on the front door, calling out James's name.

* * *

All the racket woke James out of a deep, narcotic sleep. He had to figure out where he was and how to get out of bed without hurting himself. It wasn't going to be easy. His collar bone didn't like the idea and let him know it, but whoever was at the damn door wasn't going away. He finally made his way out of bed, more irritated with each step closer to the door. He was ready with a few choice words when he opened it. The words stuck in his throat at the sight of Cappannelli. He couldn't remember him ever coming by.

Cappannelli brushed by him, stood in the middle of the living room and waited for James to shut the door, then said, "Luke's dead."

"What did you say?"

"I said 'Luke's dead,' you dumb fuck. God, the two of you are enough to make me want to puke. Look at you, standing there like a reject from the emergency ward, and now your asshole partner's dead. You guys are doing a great job of fucking me over."

James couldn't believe what he was hearing. He wasn't sure what bothered him more, the news about Luke or the way it was delivered. Cappannelli had never talked to him like that before, and he didn't like it. If he had been healthy, or even able to move, he might have done something about it. But as it was, all he could do was painfully lower himself into a stuffed chair and take whatever Cappannelli wanted to dish out.

After he'd settled into a semi-comfortable position, James asked, "What happened?"

"I don't know all the details," Cappannelli said, "just what I heard on the morning news. I wasn't aware of what Luke was up to, but evidently he thought he'd go and hassle the bitch that was out at the house the other day. Turns out she's a lawyer. That's all I need, isn't it? A goddamned lawyer crawling up my ass. Where the fuck did she come from? And how did she find out about the boat?"

Cappannelli stopped for a moment to glare at James. He didn't say anything. The eye contact was enough to get his message across.

"Why would she show up at the house like that? And the way she just blurted out her name—it makes me think she's either real stupid, or she just blundered on to something and was checking it out, not really knowing what she was getting into."

"You still haven't told me what happened to Luke."

"Like I said, Luke thought he'd track down this bitch. Her name's Christine Blake. She has an office in Newport Beach. I guess he found it. He went over there after business hours to toss the place, and was interrupted by Blake. The short version is she had a goddamned Rottweiler with her. He tore Luke's fuckin' throat out."

"Damn." It was all James could say, the last conversation he'd had with Luke still fresh in his mind. Now he was dead.

A full minute passed before anyone spoke.

More composed, Cappannelli finally said, "Now I want to make sure we're clear on a few things before anyone starts asking questions."

"Who, the police?"

"I mean anyone: cops, lawyers, anybody we don't know—hell, even people we know—I don't want any of 'em finding out about my connection to Luke. I don't want 'em finding out about you, either. Sure, everybody knows about you guys, but not in the way I'm talking about. We don't have a direct link, not on paper. That's why I pay you through a dummy corporation."

"What about the woman, Blake? She was at your place and saw Luke there. By now she could have told the police everything she knows."

"Maybe, maybe not; that depends on her agenda and who she's working for."

"Got anyone in mind?"

"Let me put it this way: there's not too many people playing this game. Now that Luke's gone, there's just you, me, and Marshall. And a wild card—my so-called daughter."

"You've got a lot of nerve, coming over here to blame me and Luke for your troubles." James had taken enough shit. He couldn't hold back his anger any longer. "Now you tell me that Debra's out there, unleashed. If I'd known about her in the beginning, I never would have gotten involved."

"But you are involved," Cappannelli said. "Luke drove that boat over Marshall's berth to set things up. The next day his daughter is dead. Those two little details are connected, all part of a plan. You're in this deep, and if there are any more fuck-ups on your part, I'll show you what real trouble is."

James regretted his outburst; it wasn't a smart move. All it did was alienate him further from a very dangerous man. "Look, Mr. Cappannelli, I won't even pretend to know what's going on. I was sacked out on your sofa when Blake came around. Luke had said something about it, but not much. I don't know anything about

Marshall, other than what you've told us, and that ain't much either. But if Blake knows about the boat, or even thinks she does, other people might know about it too. That's where your problems are going to come from, not from me."

Cappannelli stood there for a moment, nodding his head slightly. "You just keep your shit together, James, and I'll try not to burden you with any more of my problems." He stepped toward the door and opened it. Before he walked out, he looked back at James. "Just make sure you don't add to them."

Cappannelli closed the door behind him, leaving James to stew over what had just happened. He'd seen Cappannelli mad before, but never like this. And as he sat there, thinking, his own anger resurfaced. He didn't like the way Cappannelli had barged in, full of piss and vinegar. Not a word of condolence for Luke, who was only trying to do the right thing. Hell, it was obvious that Cappannelli didn't care if the two to them lived or died. Now James could worry about getting flushed down the very toilet he'd warned Luke about. If Cappannelli went down, James was certain he'd be dragged down with him.

After an hour of sitting and thinking, James made up his mind. He rose from the chair and slowly worked his way across the living room to an old roll-top desk in an adjoining room. He retrieved a battered address book from its place in one of the pigeonholes, found the number he wanted, and made a call.

NINETEEN

CHRISTINE AND Joel missed the donut shop on the first pass. They backtracked the last few blocks of Ventura Boulevard and finally saw the place wedged in among the storefront windows on the left side of the street. They wheeled into an open parking space along the curb and Christine climbed out and jaywalked across the four-lane boulevard to the front entrance.

The tables were empty, save for a bald man in a T-shirt nursing a cup of coffee and reading a discarded portion of the Times. He was sitting at a window table, the farthest from the front door. When Christine walked up to the counter, he stood up and asked her what he could get for her as he made his way along the back wall. He rounded the donut cases and came up behind the counters and coffee pots on the other side. She ordered a cup of coffee and a cinnamon roll, paid the man, and found a seat at one of the window tables. She was about halfway through the roll when a middle-aged man walked in off the street.

He stood in front of her. "Christine Blake, I presume?"

Christine worked on a mouthful of cinnamon roll. She chewed slowly, looking him over before saying anything. He didn't look as bad as expected. She had geared herself to be ready for a character out of an old black-and-white movie on the late show, an escaped convict who'd been running through the backwoods and swamps for days. He'd be wearing filthy clothes, have an unwashed, stubbly beard, and probably wouldn't smell good. His ravenous stomach would force him to snatch the uneaten portion of Christine's roll off its plate and wolf it down without bothering to chew, all the while looking around with a wild-eyed nervousness.

A faint smile crept up on her lips, despite the circumstances and her efforts to keep a straight face. "Excuse my staring. Sometimes I let my imagination get the best of me."

Marshall grabbed a seat on the other side of the table. "Am I supposed to know what that means?"

Christine looked closer, seeing how the angry bruise on the left side of his face stood out. His eyes bore a troubled expression that didn't match the determined set of his jaw, and his hands clenched into tight fists on top of the table. He turned his head for a glance at the bald man who had returned to his paper and cup of coffee, then back at Christine. "I don't think we should stay here too long."

"I've got a van across the street," Christine said, gathering up the remains of her roll.

* * *

Marshall followed Christine out of the bakery. They cut across the sidewalk, She motioned toward the other side of the street, leading the way in a half-run to beat the oncoming traffic. Arriving at a van, Marshall opened the passenger door, then froze.

"What's going on? I thought it was just going to be you."

"It's okay. He's my boyfriend. He wouldn't let me meet you by myself."

"I guess I can understand that," Marshall said, hoisting himself into the front seat.

Christine slid open the side door, climbed in back, and introduced the two men.

Marshall reached over and shook Joel's hand. "The Joel Spencer? The surfer? You used to be famous."

"Yeah . . . that was a long time ago."

"I didn't mean it like that. It wasn't that long ago. I'll bet they still recognize you in the water. You still making boards?"

"Oh yeah."

"Well, it's a pleasure to meet you. For about five seconds I forgot why we're here."

Marshall turned back to look at Christine. "I found a copy of the times and read the article about the break-in. That's were I saw your name."

Christine shook his hand. "Sorry, I guess I forgot to properly introduce myself."

"Do you know how lucky you are? How'd you get involved with Cappannelli and his boys, anyway?"

"You're wife hired me."

Marshall felt the blood drain out of his face, leaving him lightheaded and nauseous. He opened the door, but Joel had already pulled away from the curb and the door slammed shut from the impact with a parked car.

"What the fuck—" Joel shouted, his head swiveling back and forth between Marshall and the road. He turned right at the first available street and sped away from the boulevard, his eyes now fixed on the rearview mirror.

Christine's hands found Marshall's shoulder. "Hey, take it easy."

Marshall spun around in his seat. He'd have to stay in the van until it slowed down. Christine pulled back her hands, showing him her palms.

"We're only trying to help you. Let's not get crazy."

"Pull over, before I do get crazy."

"You got it, man," Joel said. He braked hard, bringing the van to a stop in the middle of the street.

Marshall leapt from the front seat. The sound of the side door sliding open was followed by footsteps running up behind him.

"We know Debra set you up," Christine called out. "She was impersonating Jennifer, wasn't she?"

Marshall stopped running. He bent over, hands on knees, fighting back tears. He didn't care anymore. They could do to him what they will.

Christine stayed back a few paces. When Marshall didn't go anywhere, she motioned toward Joel to find a place to park. She waited for Marshall to pull himself together.

He finally straightened up, still looking away, and said. "So you're working for Debra."

"Not anymore. She was through with me after I gave the police my eyewitness version of Jennifer's murder. I had no idea what she was up to."

Joel trotted over. "We better get goin' If somebody saw us hit that car and called it in—"

"Sorry about your van," Marshall said. "Five days on the run, and my nerves are shot." He looked at Christine. "When you said you were working for Debra, I panicked, thinking she'd sent you after me."

"It's my fault," Christine said. "the way I said it, with no explanation. Anyone would have jumped to the wrong conclusion."

"Thanks for saying so, but I didn't give you a chance for explanations."

"Okay," Joel said. "Does this mean we can go now?"

Marshall looked at the van. "How bad is it?"

"We must have just grazed the other car. The door's not dented too bad, but the paint transfer along the scrape is pretty obvious."

"And you're willing to let me back in?"

"Yeah, I guess. We're already fugitives from a hit-and-run, whether you're with us or not."

This time Marshall climbed into the back seat, Christine up front. They headed for the 405 freeway, avoiding Ventura Boulevard.

"So how do you know Debra?" Marshall asked.

"I do charity work. I'm the project manager for a children's foundation. I met Debra at one of our fundraisers."

"Your foundation—it wouldn't happen to be the Orange Coast Children's Alliance?"

Christine strained against her seatbelt for a better look at Marshall. "How did you know?"

"My first wife, Kathleen, had been a sponsor for years. She kept a low profile, giving the donations anonymously. I mentioned it to Debra. I told her I wanted to continue supporting Kathleen's cause, in her memory. I wanted to keep it anonymous. The memory was for me. I thought about sending Jennifer to the fundraiser, but Debra volunteered."

"I'm afraid she wasn't very discreet." Christine said. "In fact, she became a rather high-profile regular. After we got to know each other, she told me about your marital problems."

"Marital problems? Was she specific, because all this is news to me."

"She said you were having an affair. She eventually persuaded me to follow you. I was on your tail Wednesday night, when you drove to the Ritz-Carlton. I was led to believe you met Jennifer."

"That's crazy," Marshall said. "I met Debra. Jennifer was busy painting her old room at my house."

"Did Jennifer normally spend much time there?"

"Not really. She had her own place. I'd see her occasionally. Out for lunch, things like that. Then last month I began a remodel. Jennifer had her own interior design business, so her involvement was only natural. That night, Debra had asked her to do some work upstairs while she was away at her parents' house."

"Then later," Christine said, "Debra was waiting for you at the hotel?"

"That's right. Debra called first and said she didn't want to drive all the way home from LA. She asked me to meet her at the Ritz and make a night of it."

"Too bad we can't prove it," Christine said.

"Why's that?"

"Your apparent rendezvous with Jennifer was all part of a pattern to establishes your relationship and my credibility."

"But there's one thing I don't understand. If you followed me to the Ritz, you know I met Debra."

"Do I?" Christine said, hanging on to maintain her tenuous position on the front seat while Joel turned onto the 405."I didn't actually see who you met. The police have a copy of Jennifer's credit card receipt for room 812, Wednesday night, substantiated by a desk clerk's description. He identified Jennifer from a photo I had taken of her a few days ago. This is more than just circumstantial evidence, it's an eyewitness account."

No one spoke. The tires droned on and the wind whistled by the windows. Christine turned to the front and looked out the windshield. Up ahead, brake lights flashed and eventually formed into a shimmering red line where the freeway stretched out beyond the bottom of the hill. Joel opened the center console and pulled out a couple of bottled waters.

"Thirsty?" he asked, looking into the rearview mirror.

Marshall reached up for one of the bottles. Joel passed the other one to Christine. "We'll have to share."

The wind and tire noise died when they caught up with the slowing traffic. Marshall said, "I guess that explains it."

Christine resumed her former position on the seat to face him. "Explains what?"

"Her disguise. She looked just like Jennifer when I met her at the dock." Marshall paused for a long swallow of water. "I still can't get it out of my head—the way she looked, the way she looked at me. Flaunting it. She seemed to be enjoying herself. I've racked my brain trying to figure out if she's some kind of long-lost relative."

"You saw a family resemblance?"

"It seemed like it at the time. Now, I don't know. Kathleen had an older sister living in LA. I think she's still there. I don't see her much. But I'm pretty sure all her kids are accounted for. Never heard so much as a rumor about an unwanted pregnancy, or anything like that. And Kathleen and me, it was only the two of us since high school. That's one thing I'm sure of."

"You've also been through a lot." Christine said, "You actually only saw Debra in her so-called disguise the one time at the dock."

"Yeah. When I saw her at the Ritz, she was her normal self."

"But she had just been parading around the lobby looking like Jennifer. Believe me, she didn't have to look that much like her. I don't think the desk clerk spent much time studying her face. When you finally met her at the dock, it was getting dark, and I'm sure it caught you by surprise."

"I see where you're going with this," Marshall said. "Maybe you're right. With a wig and a damn good makeup job she could pull off something like that. She used to be a model and probably knows how to achieve different looks. She didn't have to worry about age and size—they were pretty much the same."

Christine nodded along with him. "And I was close by, but not too close, watching the whole thing. I saw your daughter get out of her car and come on to you like a long-lost lover."

"Could you see us board my boat?"

"What happened out there?"

"I don't know. I never made it down the companionway. Somebody clubbed me from behind on my way down the stairs. I still have a sore lump behind my ear to remind me. I can't figure out why they didn't kill me when they had the chance."

"That night? With your daughter?"

"It doesn't make sense. They aren't holding back now."

"There's a reason. There's always a reason. My first guess would be money. How much are you worth?"

"A lot."

"Enough to kill for?"

"Obviously."

"And who benefits most if something happens to you?"

"Not Debra," Marshall said. "All my assets and property are tied up in a living trust. She'd receive an appropriate sum of money. Nothing big."

"Did she sign a pre-nup?"

"Of course. I might have jumped the gun marrying her, but I hadn't completely lost my mind."

"What about your daughter?"

"After Kathleen died, I made Jennifer a co-trustee. She would have inherited everything."

"How did Debra feel about that?"

"We never really discussed it. Like I said, she'd get something, but only as a beneficiary, way down on the food chain. That might have changed later, but I'd only just met the woman."

While Marshall gulped more water, Christine looked over at Joel. "What's with the traffic? It isn't rush hour yet."

"It's always rush hour around here," Joel said, "and it's always the worst around LAX. Maybe we'll get lucky on the other side of the airport."

Marshall sat up on the edge of his seat, equal distance between the two of them. "Well, there was something else included in the final draft of the trustee document. It can only go into effect upon the occurrence of specified events."

"Spoken like a true attorney." Christine said.

"I'm only parroting how it reads."

"What does it mean?"

"Debra is also listed as a contingent trustee. If she survives the deaths of both trustees, and if she's still married to me at the time, she becomes the trustee. I didn't think anything like that had a chance of actually happening. It was just a gesture."

"I thought you didn't talk to Debra about it."

"Well, I guess I did mention the trust. She didn't say much. She didn't even ask if she was included, and it had the strange effect of making me feel guilty or selfish. I told her I'd make sure she was taken care of if the worst happened."

"You have no one else to leave the business to? A brother or sister? A favorite nephew?"

"No one. There's only my mother, but she's too old to make business decisions. Anyway, she's well provided for as a beneficiary."

"So if you and Jennifer happen to die while Debra's married to you, she gets everything."

"Basically . . . yes."

"There's your motive," Christine said.

"But it still doesn't make sense," Marshall said. "I'm still alive."

"But your daughter—your co-trustee—isn't. Think about it. If you were both murdered on the boat, who'd be the prime suspect?"

"I suppose they'd take a good look at Debra."

"She wouldn't stand a chance. On the other hand, if you killed Jennifer—"

"Debra's halfway there," Marshall said.

"And nobody suspects her," Christine said. "I provided her with one hell of an alibi—practically watching you murder Jennifer while Debra's wringing her hands at home, wondering where you are."

"And all Debra has to do now is make sure that I'm dead before I change the trust."

"Believe me," Christine said, "she has the resources."

The van had come to one of its intermittent halts in the stop-and-go traffic. Joel breathed out a deep sigh. "I still think you should take this to the police."

"I wish we could," Christine said, "but we're not ready. We don't have a shred of proof to substantiate any of this. They'd probably lock us all up."

"That's no good," Marshall said. "You guys have already taken too many risks. If it comes to it, I'll go in alone." A pause. "If I do, what are my chances?"

"If you turn yourself in," Christine said, "you'll go to jail. Bail will be a problem. They probably won't allow it. You'll stay locked up all the way through the trial."

"Would there have to be a trial? What about the things we talked about, like Debra disguising herself? If the man who broke into your office—"

"Like I said, you'll need proof, and if we don't find it, you won't stand a chance. The situation with the break-in is irrelevant. It doesn't put a dent in the armor-plated evidence they have against you. The DA will laugh at your version of what happened. You know Debra passed herself off as Jennifer, but I don't. I can only take your word for it. At best I can say I think she did. I'm on record saying you met Jennifer at the Ritz and at your boat. If I change my story, I'll lose credibility. Who knows, they could claim I'm involved or got paid off."

Christine watched Marshall slump back in his seat, then said, "Well, you do have a few things going for you, if we can find a way to exploit them."

"Like what?"

"Cappannelli is linked with the boat that destroyed your slip. That's what spurred my interest to begin with. I don't know how we're going to prove it yet, but it's something we can work on without risking our lives. I'd also like to know more about the guy who came after me. I only know he worked for Cappannelli because I saw him at his house."

"When was that?"

"Saturday afternoon, when I foolishly confronted him about the boat."

"That was you knocking on Cappannelli's garage door?"

Christine gave Marshall a brief account of what had happened on her side of the garage door. When she was through talking, she looked out at the thinning traffic and said, "All we have to do now is figure out when and how did Jennifer come aboard the boat, who actually killed her, and how they got away. The timeline's tricky. Jennifer had to die when you were aboard, or the plan wouldn't work."

"By the way," Joel said, "where are we going?"

"I haven't even thought about it," Christine said.

"We need a plan," Joel said. He looked up at the mirror. "I guess its your call. You giving yourself up, or what?"

Marshall remained quiet. He watched Christine shoot Joel a private glance, barely shaking her head as she spoke.

"We need to buy a little time."

"Any ideas?"

The van was back up to speed, with Long Beach coming into view. Christine sat up. "Take the Garden Grove freeway to Anaheim. There's all kinds of motels around Disneyland. We'll find one around Katella. I'll get a room for a couple of days, a place that's not too cheap, not too expensive. A typical, nondescript motel with plenty of people coming and going." She looked back, speaking to Marshall now. "You'll never be noticed." Remembering something, she dug into her purse. "I almost forgot—here's another three hundred dollars, courtesy of Miss Phelps."

TWENTY

T HEY STOPPED at the first available fast food drive-through off the freeway.

"You wouldn't believe the stuff I've been eating for the last few days," Marshall said, "dumpster diving with my new friends. I don't think I would have made it without them."

"Where did you sleep?" Christine asked.

"In the Sepulveda Basin. My friends, an old guy named Doc and his girlfriend, had scratched out a campsite where they could set up their Coleman stove and keep their goods dry. They also have a little hideaway down an alley off Ventura Boulevard. I promised I wouldn't tell anyone about it, so that's about all I can say."

Joel brought the van up to the front of the line and ordered the food, collected it at the next window, and found a place to park around the other side of the building.

Halfway through her burger, Christine asked Marshall, "Tell me about the golf. You play with your father-in-law often?"

"Never, until the other day. It was only the second time I'd seen him. I'd met him once before, with his wife, when Debra and I drove out to his house. It was sort of a meet-the-parents get-together shortly before we were married. I got the impression Debra didn't get along too well with them."

"So why the golf?"

"Debra set it up. She didn't tell me until that night at the Ritz. She had just come from his house, and she said he'd been asking about me. One thing led to another and before she knew it she had accepted, on my behalf, his invitation to play golf the next day. I wasn't crazy about the idea, but why make waves? He was counting on me to make up their foursome. I had to drive home the next morning for my clubs, then back to his golf course off Wilshire."

"That's an interesting variation of the version Debra gave me," Christine said.

"Don't tell me you were there," Marshall said.

"Debra arranged it. I knew your tee time and got there later on. I was more interested in where you'd be going next. I stayed out of the way on the veranda that looks down on the eighteenth green. That's when I got my first look at Paul Cappannelli, when you two walked off the green together."

"You didn't notice the other two guys?"

"Not really. Only that they looked younger. You were far away, and I focused on you two. I figured Debra's father was the other old guy."

"Thanks for that," Marshall said. "Those other two guys were Luke and James."

"Was one of them the man who broke into my office?"

"If it was the same guy running after you on Cappannelli's driveway, it was Luke. Neither one of them will be a problem now."

"Why not?" What about James?"

"He's now in a cast from his crotch to his neck. He'll be lucky if he can make it back and forth to the pharmacy for more painkillers."

"Did you have anything to do with it."

"I'd like to say I put him in the hospital, but it was really more of an accident."

Christine bit into her burger. Joel showed more interest, as though he'd like to hear more about the accident. Before he could butt in to the conversation, she said to Marshall, "Were you expecting to see Debra at your boat?"

Marshall nodded. "She wanted to spend one more night away from the house. She suggested we meet at the boat, maybe take it out. When I told her about the accident, that it would be moored offshore for a while, she insisted. Thought it would be romantic."

Christine exchanged glances with Joel. "Let's find a motel."

* * *

Christine returned to the van and climbed in. "This isn't about the money."

Joel checked his mirrors and backed out of the parking space in front of room 104 at a Best Western Motel near Katella and Harbor.

"What makes you say that?"

"Marshall was right, wondering why they hadn't killed him when they had the chance."

"But you said—"

"I know what I said. But Marshall was making more sense. I started thinking about it when he mentioned them having to 'make sure that I'm dead before I change the trust.' That's what bothers me. How can Debra have any expectation of staying a contingent trustee if Marshall knows she was in on killing Jennifer? She gave herself away as soon as she met him at the boat. If he stays alive, what's stopping him from contacting his lawyers? If he's in jail, even better—he'll have all the access he needs, complete with client-lawyer privileges."

"So you believe him?"

"I believe Debra impersonated Jennifer. I can't prove it, but I *know* it was Debra who met him at the dock and boarded the boat with him the night Jennifer was killed."

"Then how did Jennifer get out there?"

"Good question. For now I'd be happy to find the reason why and worry about the how later. It all boils down to motive. We'll never get any further than guesswork until we figure out what it is."

"We?"

"A figure of speech," Christine said. She leaned back in her seat. "Just take me home, Jeeves."

"Isn't Jeeves a butler?"

"Yeah, a butler who multitasks as a chauffeur."

Joel found an on ramp for the 55. They passed under a freeway sign directing them to Beach Cities.

"When do you get your car back?"

"Today, I hope. Maybe I'll be able to pick it up when I give them my statement." She glanced at her watch. "Still plenty of time to go home first. I need to see how the Khazanoviches are doing. I never got the chance to tell them about last night."

"You mean how their dog—"

"Yeah."

Just thinking about it created a flutter of apprehension in the pit of Christine's stomach. She felt bad about not talking to her landlords. She'd had a hard enough time calming Joel down last night. Then getting up early, coming up with the plan to intercept Phelps . . . to be honest, she'd forgotten about the Khazanoviches completely.

When they turned down her alley, she told Joel, "I think it's best if I go this alone."

"Going for the sympathy angle, huh?"

Christine managed a smile. "Thanks for being there for me. For last night, and for today."

She kissed him.

"No reason for me to go," Joel said. "I can wait upstairs for you."

"Thanks, but there's nothing for you to do now. Who knows how long I'll be tied up at the station. Then I'll have to go through the car hassle—"

"You'll need someone to drive you down there."

"I've got it covered, and I've kept you away from your shop long enough. Besides, there's a lead I need to follow up on."

She kissed him again before he could summon a protest. "Don't worry. It's just some computer research."

She jumped out of the van and watched him drive off, then turned for her gate. When she opened it and looked across the back yard, there was Tuco, lying at Mrs. Khazanovich's feet.

She sat in one of her lawn chairs, an iced tea at her side, reading the morning paper. When the gate creaked open, she looked up with a concerned, sympathetic expression as Tuco sauntered over to greet Christine, gently nudging his snout against her leg and receiving a few pats on the head.

"Christine, are you all right? I was just reading the news . . ."

She left the words hanging and rose from her chair as quickly as her soft, matronly proportioned body was able and came up for a close look at Christine's face.

"Really, I'm fine, Mrs. Khazanovich. I'm a little tired, that's all. I probably look worse than I feel."

"You can't fool me. That eye has to hurt. It's awful to think what could have happened to you. What if Tuco hadn't been with you?"

Christine relaxed into a relieved smile. "I'm sorry I haven't had a chance to talk to you. I didn't want you to find out like this. Has anyone been bothering you, the media, police?"

Mrs. Khazanovich shook her head while she fussed over Christine. She clutched her hand and led her to the lawn chairs.

"It's been very quiet. Not even a call."

"The police believe Tuco is my dog," Christine said. "Actually, they just assumed it, and I went along with them. I kind of panicked when the animal control wagon pulled up, and I wanted to keep it simple"

Mrs. Khazanovich still squeezed Christine's hand. "Don't worry about a thing. I'm just glad that you're all right."

"Has Tuco been behaving himself?"

"Tuco's a good boy. Always so gentle around us. That man must have really provoked him."

"Sitting here," Christine said, "now that it's over, it all seems distant and unreal, almost like it didn't happen."

Christine brought her hand up to her face, as if to remind herself how real it had been.

"Just get some rest," Mrs. Khazanovich said, her smile unwavering as Christine smiled her appreciation.

Tuco followed Christine to her steps, then trotted back to his place at the older woman's feet. He liked it outside, and better still if he had company.

Once inside, Christine dialed her office answering machine. She fast forwarded a couple of routine messages. That was it. Nothing more from Matt. As much as she wanted to avoid contact, she felt an underlying disappointment that he hadn't called back.

She sat down at the small vanity desk and stared at the phone. What time was it in Boston? Didn't Matt say Mass General?

Maybe she could call for information on how her father was doing, if he was still there. Maybe he'd been released or set up as an outpatient. Don't they administer chemo and other treatments to outpatients?

The phone rang and she jumped, her heart hammering against her ribcage. She let it ring and tried to collect herself, then picked it up, afraid it would stop ringing before she had a chance to check the caller ID.

The voice of Lieutenant Del Hallstrom answered her tentative greeting.

"I thought I'd better check in," Hallstrom said. "See how you're doing."

"I'm all right."

"I'd like to clear up some of the paperwork on last night. When would be a good time to take your statement?"

She was slow to change gears, still thinking about Matt and her father, not paying attention to Hallstrom.

His voice crackled into the dead air. "You sure you're all right?"

"Yeah. I can come down. Will you be around for the next hour or so?"

"I should be. If not, check with the desk sergeant."

"Say listen, while I've got you on the phone, can you tell me when I can get my car back?"

"We've already cleared it. I'll check on the paperwork."

Christine broke the connection and called Walter Jenkins.

At the sound of her voice, he said, "Where have you been? I heard all about it. I've been trying to get you on your cell phone. Any hang-ups on your office answering machine are probably me. Are you all right?"

"Yeah, I'm okay. I've just had my cell turned off. Battery's about dead and I keep forgetting to recharge it."

"What happened? Did last night have anything to do with—"

"I'll tell you later. First, I have a favor to ask."

"Name it."

"I need to get to the police station. They're waiting for me to make a statement about the break-in. They've also impounded my car. They wanted to look it over, you know, part of the crime scene. I thought if you could give me a ride . . ."

"Say no more. When do you want to go?"

"The sooner the better."

Walter told her that he could leave as soon as he cleaned his brushes and changed clothes. Christine gave him directions to her place and met him at her back gate fifteen minutes later.

"You look terrible," Walter blurted out, caught off guard by the sight of her bruised face.

"You should see the other guy," Christine said. Tuco had followed her to the gate, interested in her guest. He scooted in front of her to investigate all the interesting smells coming off the newcomer. The scent of mahogany, varnish, and paint thinner was strong enough for Christine to notice. "I thought it might be a good idea to introduce you two before you barged in here for the first time."

"So this is *Cujo*," Walter said, offering his upturned hand for Tuco to examine.

"His name's Tuco. He's really a mellow dog." After a shrug, she added, "Maybe a little protective."

"Walter cast a doubtful stare a the dog. "If you say so."

Christine shooed Tuco back in the yard, then followed Walter over to his car, a well preserved 1956 Chevy Nomad.

"What is it with you and your ancient modes of transportation?" she asked, settling back into the naugahyde upholstery.

Walter was about to turn the key. He paused for a moment, as if pondering Christine's question, then dismissing it with quick shake of the head as he started the engine.

"I guess I never thought about it before," he said. "I just like what I like. Besides, this wagon wasn't ancient when I bought it."

Walter braked at the end of the alley and waited for a couple of slow-moving cars on the cross street to pass through the intersection.

Christine rolled down her window. "What I'd really like to know is how your bar manages to survive."

"My bar? What do you mean?"

"That is your bar, isn't it? The Dry Dock?"

"Sure, everybody knows that."

"How do you get away without naming it? I know everybody calls it the Dry Dock, but that's more of a rumor than anything else. I mean, when you drive by, all you see is a funky, remodeled Victorian style house separated from the highway by a small parking lot that can't handle more than seven or eight cars. There's no sign out front or anything else that would indicate what goes on, or even if it's open to the public."

Walter just sat there. The cars he'd been waiting for passed by, and he stared vacantly at the open road left in their wake. "It's kind of a long story. I guess I don't think about it much any more." He paused again, looking even more reflective as he momentarily closed his eyes. "That's not entirely true. From time to time I can't help wondering about my wife and kids. Sometimes I try to imagine what they must look like now, after all these years."

"I didn't mean to bring up bad memories, Wally. I'm sorry."

Walter shifted the car out of gear. He let it sit there in the empty alleyway, the motor idling patiently. Rather than face Christine, he stared out the windshield, as if about to report on something he could see out there, far away.

"The bar used to be called O'Brian's Bayside Grill, named after an army buddy I'd met in Korea." Walter finally looked at Christine, his eyes misty. "When we've got more time, I'll tell you about it. I promise."

He dropped the gearshift into drive and turned out of the alley. They drove on without further conversation for the next couple of blocks, until they pulled up to the stoplight on Tustin Avenue and PCH.

"I ran into Wes Marshall today," Christine said.

"Are you pulling my leg? How'd you find him?" Walter had his attention on Christine and almost missed the light when it changed.

They turned south down the highway. Christine told Walter what she'd been up to from the time she saw Miss Phelps to the present. Then she had to go back further and tell him the inside story on what had happened when she surprised Luke at her office. They were still talking about it when they turned into the lot at the Newport Beach Police Station.

"Pull over there and park for a minute,"

Walter slid the old station wagon into a parking space and turned off the engine. "Why do I have the feeling that you're going to put me back to work?"

"See how intuitive you are? That's a big plus for a detective."

Walter gave out a little groan.

"Stop your moaning," Christine said, "this won't be so bad. I just need you to look something up for me. Can you get on the Internet with that computer of yours?"

"You noticed that relic on my desk, huh? It's slow, but I can get on the web. I got an on-line service a few years ago when I was looking for my Chris Craft.

"There's a name I want you to look up for me," Christine said. "All I have is an address. Just use your browser to locate a directory. What you're looking for is a reverse lookup. You type in the address and they'll tell you the name of the resident. I'd be doing this myself—that's why I went to my office last night—but the police have my computer and I don't know when I'll be getting it back."

"I think I can handle that," Walter said. "I know my way around the web."

Christine wrote down the address. "See what you can do. I'll call you latter."

* * *

The officer behind the front desk looked over the shoulder of a citizen standing in front of him as Christine approached.

"Ms. Blake, Lieutenant Hallstrom asked me to keep an eye out for you. He's in his office right now. Do you know the way?"

"Yes I do."

The officer waved her on and continued what he was doing. Christine strode down the corridor to Hallstrom's office, hoping she appeared more confident than she felt.

Hallstrom's door was closed. She knocked lightly and the familiar voice invited her in.

Hallstrom didn't stand to greet her this time. He tilted his head at the seat facing his desk. "Your eye's already looking better. You must be a fast healer."

"Like they said—it wasn't as bad as it looked."

"Well," Hallstrom said, "The good news is your car's been released, but I'm afraid it'll be awhile before the tech boys are through with your computer."

"I hope they'll be careful. My case files and billing accounts are stored on the hard drive, and you have all my back-ups. If anything happens to the data, I'll be screwed."

"Our guys know what they're doing. They'll be careful."

Christine sensed the mood darken a shade before Hallstrom continued.

"We've identified the man who broke into your office."

She said nothing, waiting for the other shoe to drop.

"His name's Lukas Parker. Ever hear of him?"

"Christine froze. She couldn't even shake her head. I'm a lousy liar, she thought, as if she could feel Hallstrom reading her mind.

"I'll take that as a no," he said, rising from his chair. "And you know, I find that kind of odd. We did a little digging. Turns out Parker works for a loan shark named Paul Cappannelli. You know who Paul Cappannelli is, don't you?"

Christine managed an affirmative nod.

Hallstrom was pacing now, in and out of her field of vision, forcing her to turn her head if she wanted to follow his movements.

And do you still want to tell me there's no connection between the break-in and Jennifer Marshall's murder?"

"I told you last night, if there's a connection, I don't know what it is. I still don't."

"You're playing with words, Christine. I asked you if there is a connection, not what it was. I think you know the difference." He came around in front of her and half-sat on the edge of his desk. "We did some digging on you, as well—Harvard Law, a stellar record with the Boston DA. Then nothing. Your career's over, and you haven't turned thirty yet. What the hell happened?"

Hallstrom looked down on her over folded arms. Failing to elicit a response, he returned to his chair behind the desk. "I'd like to believe your still one of the good-guys, but to tell you the truth, I don't know if you're mixed up in this or just trying to do our job for us."

He had no trouble finding the recorder this time. He placed it in front of Christine, a little closer than before. "I guess this would be a good time to get your statement."

Christine told her story, word for word, as she'd done the night before. Hallstrom shut off the recorder.

"Our stenographer is out sick. I can give you a day to come back and sign the transcription."

"Can I pick up my car?

"Not a problem," Hallstrom said. "I'll have an officer take you to the impound yard. They've already received the necessary paperwork."

He stood up, signaling their meeting was over with a parting remark.

"See you soon."

TWENTY-ONE

IT WAS past four o'clock by the time Christine drove out of the impound yard. It had already been a long day. She didn't feel like going to her office, but she needed to make sure it was locked and secure after all the police activity.

She pulled into her parking lot, relieved to see everything looking back to normal. There was no yellow tape visible and the pavement had been scrubbed clean. About half of the parking spaces were in use, which was common for that time of day. The only thing that seemed out of place was the white, stretch limo taking up several spaces on the south side of the lot. The tinted rear windows were too dark to see through. She gave the limo another glance when she got out of her car a few spaces down. The driver's side window was open. A young man in a gray suit coat and white shirt sat behind the wheel, smoking a cigarette. Christine was mildly curious about who would take a limo to get her hair done, but had put it out of her mind by the time she reached her office. She had enough things to worry about without including the strange habits of the natives.

One last length of yellow tape blocked her doorway. Christine pulled it down and unlocked the door. Memories of last night wouldn't go away, and she couldn't help looking around as she walked in. The small office looked different to her, like she was seeing it for the first time. She had to laugh at herself for opening the storage closet door, but not until she'd closed it after taking a good look inside. A red digital number was blinking on the answering machine sitting on her desk. Four messages waiting for her. She was halfway through the last one when a knock on the door broke her concentration.

She normally left the door unlocked while she was there. She didn't get many walk-ins off the street, but it wasn't unusual for her clients to drop by, sometimes with an appointment, other times on their own. A few of them would knock, others would let themselves in, depending on how they reacted to the surroundings. The doors along the upstairs hallway of Christine's building looked more like they belonged to apartments than businesses.

Today, the door was locked. Christine walked over and looked through the peep-hole. She could make out the gray suit and white shirt of the limo driver through the tiny fisheye lens. She opened the door.

"Miss Blake? I just wanted to make sure you were in. These stairs are kind of a challenge for my uncle."

Before Christine could respond, the kid ran down the stairs and helped the man struggling with the first few steps. He tucked himself under the man's good arm—the one that wasn't hampered by the elaborate cast covering most of his upper body—and gave him enough support to negotiate the climb to the second floor. As soon as the man reached the top of the stairs, he leaned against the nearest wall, his face bathed in sweat. Christine stood there, silent.

"Just give me a minute to catch my breath," the man said. "That was a little trickier than I thought it would be."

Christine said, "You must be James," as she looked nervously at the stairs. No way out. The kid was standing on the landing, blocking the stairway.

"I'm not here for retribution." James held out his left palm in a gesture that said, "I come in peace." He turned to the kid. "Hey Lonnie, why don't you wait in the limo. I'll need some help getting down the stairs, so keep an eye out."

The kid said, "No problem," cheerfully enough, and walked down the stairs.

"That's my nephew," James said. "His dad—my brother—owns a limousine service in Hollywood. As you can see, I need a little help getting around."

Christine hadn't moved; she didn't know if she was in danger or not. Her pulse was still jackhammering from the aftereffects of that first jolt of adrenaline that shot through her when she recognized the man from Wes Marshall's description. "What do you want?"

"Can we go inside and talk?" When he didn't get an answer, James said, "I know you wonder what I'm doing here. That's understandable. But I mean you no harm. Besides, if anything were to happen, I'd be the one eating shit."

Christine had to admit that James didn't look like he was capable of making it back down the stairs, much less be any kind of a threat. It was daylight, the salon downstairs was open, and people were coming and going. All potential witnesses that wouldn't have any trouble remembering such a conspicuously bandaged man being helped in and out of the white limo. Christine relaxed a notch and motioned for James to come in.

Once inside the office, James said, "Do you mind if I stand? "It hurts worse when I'm sitting down."

"Pull up a wall," Christine said, taking the seat behind her desk. She glanced at the desktop and closed drawers. Not so much as a decent letter opener around that she could use to defend herself. "So, James, once again, what do you want?"

"How do you know my name?"

Christine didn't say anything.

"Look," James said, "this is uncomfortable for both of us. I'm risking a lot coming here. If you're working for the wrong person, I'm as good as dead. But I'm betting you're working for Marshall, or at least looking out for his best interests. If that's the case, maybe we can help each other."

"Why would you need help?"

"I don't think things are going to turn out well for me. I'd like for us to lay our cards on the table and see where we stand . . . maybe see what we can do about it."

Christine thought it over. If James was for real, this could be the break she needed. It would be nice if they were honest with each other, and if Christine had to make the first gesture, so be it. She said, "It's not too hard to figure out who you are. Wes Marshall told me about your accident and described the cast.

"You've been in touch with him."

"Yeah. How did you find him, anyway?"

"Paul Cappannelli—the man I work for—got a hold of me and Luke. Told us to haul ass down to Newport Beach and meet his attorney at a coffee shop by Fashion Island. When we got there, the lawyer told us about this little old lady that might lead us to Marshall. We got to Marshall's office just in time to see her leave the building. We tailed her all morning, until she finally led us to him. Luke got a little too aggressive and ran them into a ditch on PCH. I followed Marshall on foot, hooked up with Luke when he took a cab to a motel in Irvine. Then I got careless. Luke had to take me to a local hospital, and we lost him."

"What were you planning on doing with him?"

"You don't want to know. Besides, he got away. It's not important now."

"What is important, James? I'm still not sure where this conversation is leading."

"I want to distance myself from Cappannelli," James said, "and I'm not sure how to do it. If I was in better shape I'd leave town, but right now I'm a sitting duck. I can't fight and I can't run. I've never been this helpless before. All I can do now is try to use my head and find a way out."

"Did you have anything to do with Jennifer's murder?"

"No, and I've been feeling bad about it since I found out what happened. Luke was a little more involved than me, but I know he didn't actually kill her. In fact, Cappannelli, Luke, and I were having dinner the night it happened. Just the other day Luke and I were talking about how unusual it was for Cappannelli to keep us around like that. Now I know that he was establishing our alibis. The three of us played golf with Marshall that day. After he took off, we showered at the club and played gin until dinnertime. We didn't leave until midnight. Plenty of people saw us, and the guard at the front gate has a record of our coming and going."

"What about Debra?" Christine asked. "Do you know where she was?"

"No, and at the time I didn't know anything was going down. There was no reason to even be thinking about Debra. I found out later that Luke ran a boat into Marshall's slip. The next day we're playing golf with the guy. Luke hadn't said anything at that point, and I was just hangin' out, going along with Cappannelli's program, not any the wiser. Even if I'd known more, I wouldn't have thought it unusual. Over the years we've done a lot of weird things to intimidate people. It wasn't until later, after the murder, that things got tense. Cappannelli sent his wife away for the week, down to La Costa, and had us looking for Marshall, priority one."

"Now that you can look back on it," Christine said, "what do you think? Was Debra capable of killing that girl?"

"Oh yeah . . . absolutely."

Christine felt a chill run down her spine. She had never entertained the thought that Debra had done the actual killing. She didn't even know why she asked the question; it just came out. And James answered her with the calm conviction of a man who knew what he was talking about. "What can you tell me about her?"

"You want the whole story?" James asked.

"If you can help me, and if what you said is true—that you didn't have any knowledge of Jennifer's murder until after the fact—I'll do everything I can to keep you out of it." Christine paused for a moment to give James time to think, then said, "I don't know much about Debra . . . just what I've learned in the last few days, which amounts to almost nothing. If you could enlighten me, it might be useful."

"Well, I've known her for quite a while," James said. "She was just a kid when I started working for Cappannelli. I take it you know what kind of business he's in."

Christine nodded. She'd get back to Cappannelli later. Right now she didn't want to sidetrack James.

"After I'd been with him awhile and had a chance to see him with his family, he called for me. Debra had run away. She couldn't have been more than fourteen. It must have been quite a scene, because he didn't expect her to come back. He wanted me to find out where she went, make sure she was all right, and sort of keep tabs on her. I got the impression that what he really wanted was to teach her a lesson, to let her see how tough it was out on the street and that she didn't have it so rough at home. By the time I found her, I barely recognized her. She was hangin' out with punk hustlers out on Hollywood Boulevard, taking drugs, turning tricks, the whole nine yards. When I told Cappannelli, he just said, 'Fuck her.' I don't know what he told her mother. Meanwhile, I'm starting to feel sorry for the kid. I'd look her up now and then, give her a few bucks, that sort of thing."

"Cappannelli just abandoned her?" Christine asked. "He knew where she was and he didn't do anything about it?"

"That's right. Cappannelli can be pretty cold. Feeling that chill directed at me is the reason I looked you up. Anyway, Debra lived a hard life for a few years. She hooked up with an older guy, about twenty-five. His name was Raymond—never did find out his last name. He was a violent sonofabitch. I'm not sure if he beat Debra, but I know the two of them made quite a team. She'd sucker tricks into places where they could beat the shit out of 'em and take their money. They'd roll drunks or anybody else that looked like easy pickin's. Raymond thought he was a real gangster. Carried a goddamned blackjack with him and used it every chance he got. He knew just how hard to tap a guy on the head so as not to kill him, but hard enough to make sure he didn't get up right away. I lost track of her around then. Later on I heard she made the hooker big leagues—got recruited by one of those Hollywood Madam types when she turned eighteen."

"What about her modeling career?"

"Modeling career? If she did any modeling, it wasn't for Cosmo."

"So when did she show up again?"

"It couldn't have been too long ago. The first I heard of her, after all those years, was when Cappannelli called me about our golf match the other day. He said we were going to play with a guy named Wes Marshall, and mentioned that he was Debra's husband."

Christine just sat there. She'd gotten an earful and it took a while for what James had said to sink in. What amazed her most was how well Debra had presented herself. Christine would have never guessed that she had evolved from such a gruesome background.

"You've certainly shed some new light on my perception of Debra. As for Cappannelli, I think I already have a pretty good idea of where he's coming from. He wants to get rid of Marshall and cash in . . . or I guess split it with Debra when she cashes in."

"What Cappannelli wants is Marshall's business," James said. "He'd like nothing better than to strut around his country club as the president of 'Cappannelli Inc.', whatever that may happen to be. A land development company worth millions would do just fine."

"Wealth and respectability," Christine said, "what more could a hard working man ask for?" And if a couple of innocent people have to die—"

"You're getting the picture. And I'm sure Cappannelli wouldn't shed any tears if something unfortunate happened to me, either."

Christine picked up a pencil and asked, "How can I get in touch with you?"

"What have you got in mind?"

"I don't know yet. I have to find a way to prove what your boss and his daughter have been up to, find a chink in their cast iron alibis. All I've got now are bits of circumstantial evidence and hearsay. Not near enough to excite the authorities, not with all the physical evidence they have against Marshall. They found the guy alone on his boat, covered with his dead daughter's blood. When they catch him they'll lock him up and throw away the key."

"Unless Cappannelli finds him first. He's very upset that the guy's alive. If they lock Marshall up, he won't like that either. He wouldn't want Marshall talking about him. He'll do whatever is necessary to avoid that kind of attention."

"After meeting Luke, I believe you."

James shot a hard stare and Christine immediately regretted her reference to Luke. The men had probably been friends. The stern look on his face turned into a grimace as he pushed off from the wall he'd been leaning against. He gave her his phone number, telling her to only speak to him personally and not to leave a voicemail. Christine followed him out the door, locked it behind her as he made his way to the stairs, and caught up with him while he was waiting for Lonnie to help him down.

"Thanks for talking to me," James said. "I don't know if it'll do any good, but I feel better. At least I'm on record with someone about this." Lonnie reached the top step, but James paused for a moment before they started down. "I'm sorry about your run-in with Luke. He got caught up in something he didn't understand. Not to make excuses, but I've never felt like we were cold-blooded killers."

"I think I understand what you're trying to say. And if I need you I'm going to give you a call. Is that all right?"

"Yeah, I'll do what I can."

James struggled with the stairs, Lonnie staying one step in front to steady him as he gingerly took each slow step. She waited until they were gone before she climbed into her Camry and headed south down Pacific Coast Highway.

TWENTY-TWO

EVERYTHING WAS slipping away; Paul Cappannelli could feel it. It was more than just his dreams that he worried about. The very ground he walked on felt shaky. He should have taken care of Marshall when he'd had the chance—and made sure that the body wasn't too hard to find. The cops would have been more than happy to write the whole thing off as a fugitive wanted for murder killed by misadventure while on the run. Case closed.

He'd blown the best chance he was going to get. If he'd handled Marshall correctly things wouldn't have gotten out of hand. Even after that, if he'd kept Luke on a short leash and figured out the proper way to deal with Christine Blake maybe he'd still have an outside chance of pulling his shit together. All he could do now was fret about it like some helpless old lady.

He paced the slow hours away minute by minute, room by room, first at his house, then at his office in Century City. Luke was dead and James was out of commission. Both of them history, along with his only chance of finding Marshall. The odds were in favor of the cops finding him first. Cappannelli actually felt his stomach cringe when he thought of Marshall spilling his guts in a police interrogation room, telling them about the garage and how Luke had beat him up—and with the bruises to make it sound compelling. Christine Blake had Luke's body to prove her side of the story, and when the cops connected all the dots, Cappannelli knew he was finished. He just kept pacing around his office, a bottled mixture of frustration and rage, about to explode.

Then he received a call from Zack Naylor. It was the biggest mistake of Zack's life, second only to borrowing money from Cappannelli in the first place.

Zack had his own agency, an outfit that specialized in replacing whole-life insurance policies with cheaper term-life contracts attached to supposedly high yield annuities. Cappannelli knew exactly how it worked. The business relied on hard-sell tactics, carried out by a sales force armed with a canned presentation. The results were impressive.

Once the mooches—as Zack fondly referred to potential clients—were at the kitchen table, listening to the enthusiastic promise of money saved and interest earned, the battle was over. To pass on such a deal would be an act of pure stupidity. And Zack got a piece of every sale. His organization was basically a pyramid scheme requiring a steady influx of fresh salespeople to generate commission overrides to be doled out to recruiters, to sales managers, and, ultimately, to Zack, the man on top.

The business had its ups and downs. On a good month Zack knocked down as much as fifty thousand dollars. He could also have a bad month. That's when he'd call Cappannelli. But this time he wasn't asking for a loan; he was informing Cappannelli that he couldn't come up with the weekly payment on the twenty-five thousand he'd borrowed last month.

He had obviously heard that Cappannelli's collectors were out of the business. He never would have made that call if Luke or James had still been a threat. Zack was well aware of how seriously they took their job, and he knew that skipping a couple of payments was a good way to reach the top of their shit list. Zack would have found a way to come up with the needed cash, or else disappear, if there was even a remote possibility that he'd have to deal with one of them.

Cappannelli behaved himself during the phone conversation. Sure, he understood. Zack was good for the money. Not a problem. He hung up the phone with a newfound calmness. His hand wasn't even shaking. It was still steady when he locked the office door behind him. He walked with a purposeful, brisk gait. The door to the elevator opened as soon as he pushed the button. Minutes later he was in his car and pulling out of the underground parking lot.

He headed out to Long Beach. Getting busted was one thing—being pushed around by a cheap chiseler was something else. His blood pressure might have been redlining, but he was under control. He stayed focused, saw past the clogged traffic crawling around him, and savored the internal hum of adrenaline surging through his veins. He hadn't felt this alive since forever. He was firing on all eight cylinders when he came up to Zack's office and saw his car parked in the lot. He pulled in on the other side of an SUV a few spaces over. He retrieved his five iron out of the golf bag in his trunk. He slid back into his car and waited.

When Zack finally arrived, Cappannelli blew into him like an ill wind, smashing his right knee with the five iron before the man had a chance to unlock his car.

"You have the vig for me tomorrow," Cappannelli said, "or your other leg is next. When you run out of limbs, I'll tear your fuckin' heart out with my bare hands."

He left Zack writhing on the asphalt. He climbed into his car. His blood was really up now and he took a few deep breaths before starting the car. He was on a high. He wasn't ready to come down. He found his way to the 405 and headed south.

* * *

Christine pulled up in front of Joel's shop. He owned the place, located on the south side of San Clemente on El Camino Real, a few blocks from his house.

It had once been a bicycle shop, and the old Huffy Dial-a-Ride the previous owner had bolted to the roof for advertising was still in place. The bicycle was something of a landmark, and Joel had exploited it to his advantage by mounting a surfboard rack over it's rear fender and fitting it with a replica surfboard. The board made for a good sign, the way it stood on edge over the bicycle's rear tire. The name of the shop, Wishbone Surfboards, was printed across its deck.

Christine stepped out of her car. Joel was visible through the storefront window. He was shaping a polyurethane surfboard blank with an electric planer. She knew he'd be working late after spending all morning with her. He preferred to use the spacious front room for his workshop and to keep his materials and finished boards locked up in the more secure rooms in back.

He glanced her way, then pulled off his respirator and hosed off the foam dust covering his body with a blast of air from the small compressor he kept charged nearby for that purpose. She met him at the door.

"What have you got there?" he said.

Christine pulled a bottle of Cabernet out of the grocery bag she'd brought with her. She held it up for his approval.

"Thought you might have forgotten about dinner."

"So we're drinking it?"

"Come on."

Joel shut the door and they left the dust-filled room behind them and went around to the side of the building, where a fenced-in area running alongside the building accommodated a weather-beaten iron patio table and a couple of oxidized aluminum chairs. The frayed, sun-faded webbing holding the pitted frames of the chairs together may have once been green.

Christine set out the contents of the grocery bag on the table. Joel smiled at her.

"A loaf of bread, a jug of wine, and thou . . ."

"All we need is a book of verse beneath the bough."

"We've certainly got the wilderness." Joel looked around at the neglected shop debris scattered around the side-yard. "I guess it's been a while since I cleaned up around here."

"It's not so bad," Christine said. "I don't see any engine blocks or rusted out washing machines."

"I save those for the front yard."

"Plastic cups okay? This was kind of spur-of-the-moment."

Joel picked up the bottle. "Got something to open this with?"

Christine produced a cheap corkscrew. Joel opened the bottle and they broke bread and used a folding knife out of the shop to slice cheese.

Christine held up her cup and Joel poured.

"The bread and cheese was just an excuse." She saluted him with a toast-like gesture.

Their plastic cups came together with a disappointing thud and they sampled the Cabernet with wry smiles and tentative sips.

Joel raised his cup in appreciation. "The wine far surpasses the presentation." After a greedy tear off the loaf, he said, "I see you got your car back. Were you able to get your research done?"

"No, but thanks for reminding me. I've got Wally working on it for me. The police still have my computer."

"You seem to be getting along with Walter pretty well."

"When this is over, you've got to meet the guy. He owns a boatyard and a bar and a bunch of other stuff along PCH. You'd love the old Chris Craft he's restoring."

"Sounds like he's tight with Marshall."

"I'm sure they're pretty good friends. I can sense some history there."

"And what, exactly, is he doing for you?"

Christine leaned up to the table with her cup. Joel poured the remainder of the wine. She sat back and said, "Look, Joel, Wally's already involved with this. He's hired me and we have certain legal protections. But you and I . . . well, today we crossed the line. Marshall's a fugitive, wanted for murder, and we helped him."

"I didn't know we'd be hiding him out."

"I was planning on talking to him. That was going to be it. I wanted to hear his version of what had happened. But when he came up to me in the donut shop I guess I got caught up in the moment. He was nervous and scared and wanted to get out of there. The next thing you know we're driving him to a motel."

"Could they disbar you?"

"Are you kidding? They could throw us both in jail. I didn't come down here to alarm you, but you need to know the score. If you stay down here, out of the loop, there's no reason for them to find out about you. All I did was borrow your van."

"What about you. Are you going to be okay?"

"I don't know. I keep digging myself deeper into trouble. Not only have I harbored a fugitive, I've been withholding information about Luke. If I'm not careful, it's all going to come down on me."

"What can I do?" Joel said.

"Don't you get it? You need to stay away from me. That's what I've been trying to tell you. If anyone asks, you lent me your van. That's it. You don't know anything."

"So you're going ahead? On your own?"

"I do my best work alone, you know that. Didn't you tell me once that I had all the makings of a solitary surfer?"

"I believe I said soul surfer."

"There's a difference?"

Joel surrendered with a slow shrug. He tossed back the last of his wine and gathered the remains of their meal, using the grocery bag to hold the trash and the empty wine bottle.

"You better come with me," he said. "We can spend one more night together, before *I'm* the one harboring a fugitive."

He locked up the shop and carried the trash around to the Dumpster in the small parking lot out back. Christine had her car started about the time his van nosed onto the street. She followed him to his house.

As soon as they were inside, she said, "I've got to use your phone. I keep forgetting to charge my cell."

She grabbed the phone in the kitchen and punched in Walter's number. He told her he had the information she was looking for.

"A lad named Robert Woodworth lives at the address you gave me. There's more info available, but they charge you for it. You can find out all kinds of stuff: how long he's lived there, where he works, how much money he makes . . . sort of scary."

"Privacy is a thing of the past," Christine said. "You don't even need a private investigator anymore"

"Should I keep going, see if I can get into his background?"

"Not yet. The name is all I need for starters. Thanks for getting it. If I need more before I get my computer back, I'll let you know."

Joel was standing behind her when she hung up. He was in the process of opening another bottle of wine.

"If you needed a computer, you could have used mine."

"Since when?"

"Since I bought one for the shop. Thought it was time I had my books in order."

"What's next, a cell phone?"

"No way. I thought about an answering machine for a minute, then came to my senses. Don't want to spoil the customers."

"Yeah, you might make it easy for them to reach you."

"That would ruin the mystique. Supply and demand is a fragile balance. Make it difficult to buy something, and they want it all the more."

"I guess I can't argue with success," Christine said, taking the glass of wine Joel offered. "Here's to your backlog. May you always have more orders than you can fill."

"Amen to that."

TWENTY-THREE

MARSHALL STARED across the room. Reflections from passing headlight beams ghosted across the closed curtain next to the front door. The digital clock on the nightstand blinked twelve o'clock repeatedly, waiting for someone to reset it.

He couldn't sleep, and he didn't savor the prospect of watching the sun come up.

His room was situated in the center of the motel's west wing on the ground floor. The parking lot came up to the open-sided hallway in front of his door. There were the usual sounds of cars and slamming doors and people talking as they walked by, and more doors opening and closing along the hallway.

There was something comforting about it. Life went on as normal, just outside the window of his small room, completely unaware of his plight. It reminded him of how sweet it was when he had been one of them: an ordinary guy going through life, taking for granted all the insignificant things that would now mean so much to him.

Then he caught himself. He couldn't afford to start thinking about a normal life, not where it concerned him. He was a long way from anything like that. Now was not the time to slip into a melancholy funk. He needed to deal with the present and take advantage of the reprieve he'd been given. It might not last too long.

He tried to think of something positive, but nothing held up against his refreshed grief and anger. Even the dwindling thoughts of his old life had turned dark and he wasn't able to stop his mind from slogging through all the unanswerable questions about his daughter.

Why did she have to die? Was it all part of some karmic debt left over from another lifetime? Or was she paying for the sins of her father? And if that was the case, what had he done to cause such harsh reckoning? He'd give anything for an answer, an irrefutable edict handed down from a higher authority, chiseled in granite and spelled out in language he could understand.

Then he thought about retribution. It was no more than a word to him at first, and he said it out loud and he liked the way it sounded. He thought about what it really meant. No reason to dwell on God or Karma or any other rationalized explanation for his unanswerable questions. No special beliefs were needed to understand his own stripped down definition of retribution. You do something wrong, you pay for it. Simple as that.

Wheels began turning, and the simple concept adopted a life of its own, no longer thought of in abstract terms but in real-life images of flesh and blood. Marshall thought about it long and hard, disturbed by where those thoughts were taking him but unable to think about anything else.

Someone has to pay.

He reached over and picked up the telephone and called a cab before he could talk himself out of it. He hung up the phone and prayed to God, or to that higher authority, that Debra would be home when he got there.

* * *

Fifteen minutes later, headlights pulled into the space in front of his room. Marshall looked through the curtains. The cab had arrived. He walked outside with his hand over his eyes in a sort of misshapen salute to shield the glare of the headlights and to hopefully obscure his face. He climbed into the back seat on the right side of the cab to make it as difficult as possible for the driver to see him in the rear view mirror. He shut the door. "Let's go to the beach—Corona del Mar."

"You got it," the cabbie said, putting the cab into reverse and backing out of the space. "Whereabouts in Corona?"

"Driftwood Road. It's just off the Coast Highway, on the south end of town."

Marshall supposed the man driving the cab was fresh from somewhere in the Middle East. He had on a country western station and was trying to sing along with the words, stumbling here and there with some of the pronunciations. Marshall absently wondered if the guy liked the music or was just trying to improve his English. They merged onto the 55 and the cabbie continued with his performance. He seemed content to entertain himself, and possibly his fare, during the long drive.

After they'd turned down PCH and passed the center of town, Marshall broke in. "Take the second street on the right after you go through the light."

The cab turned off the highway and Marshall directed the cabbie to Driftwood Road. A dark house came up on the left, not even a porch light on. "This is it, turn in here."

Marshall waited for the cab to back into the street and turn in the direction they'd come, then walked up the sidewalk toward the front door. When the cab was out of sight he changed direction and came back to the street and headed for Shorecliff Road. It was only half a block away and the night provided plenty of cover. A thick marine layer had drifted in and settled over the coastline, and the few, intermittently spaced old street lights gave off more ambiance than actual light.

No one was around, and Marshall felt almost invisible as he walked along, the soft soles of his deck shoes padding quietly as he neared his house. He was across the street and almost in front of his driveway when the black Cadillac came into view. He recognized it immediately. It belonged to Cappannelli.

Marshall cursed under his breath and kept walking. He'd have to kill time until Cappannelli left. All he could do was walk around the neighborhood and hope he didn't run into someone who might recognize him.

He walked down to the cul-de-sac at the end of his street, praying that no one would pick that moment to come driving up to one of the houses and bathe him in headlight beams. He drew in slow, deep breaths of salt air and released them just as slowly, trying to relax as he walked.

Ten minutes later he approached his house again. Cappannelli's car was still there. Halfway up the street on the next lap, the Cadillac backed out of his driveway. It turned away from him and raced off, tail lights winking as it braked for a curve in the road.

Walking up to his house filled him with dread. He wasn't sure what he was going to do—or what he was capable of doing. A moment of truth was drawing nearer, he thought, for better or worse. When he reached the front door, he found the door knob turning in his hand.

He stood there a moment trying to calm down, breathing quietly. The sound of the blood throbbing behind his eardrums faded away and an empty stillness settled around him. He knew he wasn't alone in the house. Cappannelli's silhouette in the driver's seat had been clearly visible when he drove off, making the empty space on the passenger's side all the more obvious. There was no way Debra had gone with him. Marshall shut the door and looked around as he walked through the foyer.

It was a big house. Debra could be sitting in one of the other rooms or out on the deck. She could be taking a shower upstairs and he wouldn't be able to hear the water running from where he was. Without knowing her location, he was careful to keep quiet as he went from room to room. He wanted to catch her by surprise.

He walked into the family room. He heard a metallic sounding voice, very faint. As he came nearer to the sectional sofa, the voice grew louder but remained unintelligible. He peered around the corner of the sofa. There on the floor, lying between the sofa and the glass coffee table, was Debra, flat on her back, not moving. There was something wrong with her face. A shadow or dark liquid seemed to be covering her mouth and chin and portions of her left cheek. Marshall stepped closer. It was blood. The voice rattled out of a cordless phone receiver pressed against her chest and gripped with both hands, like a hard won bottle in the clutches of a passed out wino.

Marshall bent over her, pried the phone loose and held it against his ear. The voice was calm and urgent at the same time.

". . . if you are unable to speak, don't hang up. We want to keep the line open. Help is on the way . . ."

It was the 911 operator. Marshall pushed the phone's power button off and straightened up, not taking his eyes off of Debra. He didn't check her pulse; he didn't even touch her, other than what it had just taken to get the phone loose. He backed away slowly, until the back of one of his legs bumped into his favorite chair. Debra moaned. She seemed to have trouble lifting her head. Her eyes caught Marshall's stare.

"I thought you were my old man, coming back for more. Thought it best if I looked like I'd had enough."

She pulled herself up to a sitting position on the floor, her back against the front of the sofa. Marshall sank into his chair.

There was no reason to try to get away. The police would be there in a matter of minutes, if not sooner. There were only two exits from his neighborhood that connected with the highway, and in the time it would take him to find Debra's keys and get her car out of the garage and arrive anywhere near them, they'd be sealed off. He thought about the terraced stairway below his house, but it would only deposit him on a beach boxed in on either side by rocky cliffs that jutted well into the water. There was no way he could make a swim for it. That section of coastline was isolated for miles. It would only be a matter of time before the patrol boats or helicopters spotted him.

Debra wiped the back of her hand across her chin, below her broken nose and swollen mouth. She looked down, studying the smear of blood that had transferred onto her hand, then broke into a wide, red-stained smile, her eyes coming up to stare at Marshall with a triumphant gleam.

"This is fucking perfect."

The chirp of tires braking to a quick stop sang from the driveway. Doors slammed, a voice barked commands. The glare from all the lights found a way into the family room and lit the walls.

"I can't wait to tell them how you did this to me," Debra said, struggling to her feet.

Marshall came up and hit her squarely on the jaw before she had time to shout.

TWENTY-FOUR

CHRISTINE FELT okay other than a residual tiredness from all the wine she had consumed. She'd slept off most of it at Joel's house, then woke up and couldn't get back to sleep. She returned home before light, and it seemed she hadn't been in bed more than five minutes when the phone rang.

"Christine? I know it's early, but if you haven't heard yet, I thought you'd want to know—"

"Who is this?"

"Oh, I'm sorry. It's Miss Phelps." There was a moment of silence on the line, and Christine could feel the woman gathering herself before breaking the news. "Debra Marshall is in the hospital. It appears as if Mr. Marshall has assaulted her."

Christine tossed back the covers and swung her feet onto the floor. "Is he all right? Have they arrested him?"

"Apparently, he got away. You can read all about it in the morning paper. I wasn't sleeping very well, so I picked up mine as soon as I heard it delivered."

"I don't know what to say. Can I call you later? I need to check this out and see if there's anything I can do."

"I'll be at the office."

Christine hung up, threw on her sweats, and went outside and around to the front of the Khazanovich's house. The morning edition of the Times was sitting on the porch. She picked it up and hurried back to her kitchen to read while she brewed a pot of coffee.

According to the newspaper story, Debra had been rushed to the emergency room at Hoag Hospital, badly beaten and semiconscious. She told authorities that Wes Marshall had stormed into the house and attacked her, for no apparent reason. Debra was quoted as saying Marshall "acted crazy", and that she was barely able to get a call off to 911 and scare him away before passing out.

Christine reread the story over a second cup of coffee. She folded the paper back the way she'd found it, and returned it to the Khazanovich's porch. The sun came up while she took a shower. She put on her khaki slacks, a white, long sleeved blouse, and an off-white linen blazer.

She ate a bowl of cereal and lingered at the table. She pictured Marshall's assault on Debra, and it bothered her. Christine's recent bout with Luke made that image very real. The nature of her work also influenced her. She'd been introduced to a fair share of battered women over the years, along with a few of the men responsible. They were a great help in fostering her one true prejudice: she hated those guys, in general, and individually. Now she found herself lumping Marshall into their ranks. It might not be fair to him, especially when she considered what Debra might have done, but Christine couldn't change how she felt. She was going to have to detach herself from her feelings, or at least hang on to the favorable impression she'd had of Marshall when she'd first met him. She needed to stay focused on helping him; it was the only way to keep herself out of serious trouble.

She stayed at her apartment until eight o'clock. There was a slim chance that she could find something out at Life Care, and she wanted to wait until there was some activity in the place before she went over to snoop around. It wasn't much, but it was the only active lead she had. If nothing panned out, she could eliminate it from her short list of things to do.

Robert Woodworth, the name Walter Jenkins had matched with the Clay Street address, was probably staying at Life Care. That was Christine's best guess. The old lady she'd seen with Debra must have been Mrs. Woodworth on her way to visit her husband.

It could turn out to mean nothing, but it seemed odd to Christine that Debra had rushed to the old lady's house so quickly after attending Jennifer's funeral. Was there a significant reason for that, or did she already have prior plans to see her? It didn't appear to be an emergency. Once Debra had arrived at the house, she wasn't in a hurry, and when she reappeared with her companion, neither of them showed the kind of strain one would expect if they had been responding to a dire situation. And, as Christine thought back, she remembered the satisfied smile on Debra's face, visible from across the street. It had all been very curious.

* * *

Christine wasn't expecting much when she pulled into the parking lot at Life Care. She walked through the front door with the kind of enthusiasm it took to bet on a busted flush. Bluffing her way along, and with a little luck, she might be able to find a connection between Debra and whoever was staying there. And if there was a connection, she could only hope it would be relevant.

She was glad she'd waited until eight. There wasn't exactly a crowd of people milling around, but the hallways were fairly busy with nurses and attendants making their rounds. It was still too early for many of the patients to be up and about. The few hanging around were in wheelchairs. Her impression was that anyone under sixty and walking must be an employee. She wasn't ready to start asking questions, but she found it easy enough to walk past the reception area and march up one of the corridors that branched out behind it, carrying herself with the air of a person who knew where she was going.

As she'd expected, the names of the patients inside each room were posted in a slot on the wall next to the appropriate door. It was a matter of walking the hallways until she came across the room with Woodworth's name on it. At the end of her third hallway, she found it.

There were slots for two names but only the one for Woodworth was in use. Christine walked up to the open door to peek in. It appeared empty at first. The bed was made and the lights were off. Then she saw him. He sat on a metal chair with green padding for the seat, back, and tops of the arm rests. He faced away from her, between the bed and the far wall, looking out a window to an interior courtyard. Christine walked in quietly, feeling like she should be on her tiptoes.

"Mr. Woodworth?"

No response. Christine tried again, a little louder. Still no response.

She walked farther into the room. She craned her neck to get a good look at him. It couldn't be Woodworth. The man was too young. From the back, his steel gray hair had a youthful quality about it: very thick, cropped to an inch in length, standing straight up. It shinned like a halo backlit by filtered light streaming in through the window. Then the years piled on as Christine came around far enough to see his face. Withered flesh clung to the bone, unable to soften the skeletal contours. The skin itself had a fragile quality about it, like old parchment that hadn't been touched in years. Christine could picture herself putting her lips up close to the man's cheek and softly blowing on it, as if to blow out a candle, and sending a layer of dust swirling off in the air. The loose robe and baggy pajamas hanging from his rail-thin frame lent to his brittle appearance.

There was a scar, an angry slash on his forehead, so prominent that she wondered why it wasn't the first thing she'd noticed. It was at least three inches in length and about the width of her pinkie finger, running in a vertical direction from above the eyebrow to the man's hairline. Beneath the raised scar tissue there was a cleft, or fissure. It ran deep. His forehead was misaligned on either side of the old wound, as if his skull had been taken apart, then put back together minus a piece. That was probably the reason she wasn't getting a response from him. She crouched next to him and passed her hand in front of his eyes. They were open but they didn't follow the movement.

Christine sighed and sat down on the edge of the bed—then nearly jumped out of her skin when the lights came on and a voice that came out of nowhere said, "Good morning Robert . . . who's your friend?"

Christine turned to face the door. A uniformed attendant with a tray in her hands stood at the doorway. She'd just taken it off a cart parked in the hallway.

"Didn't mean to startle you, hon," the woman said. She was a big gal, middle aged, with a Midwestern twang. "You gave me quite a start, too. Ol' Robert, here, he don't get too many visitors." The woman fussed with the tray, setting it on a wheeled stand and removing the plastic covers that kept the contents on the plates warm.

Christine moved out of the way. "I was just passing by, when I thought I heard someone call out. I came in to see if there was anything I could do."

"Oh, that couldn't have been Mr. Woodworth here," the woman said. She stopped what she was doing and looked at Christine. "This man don't make a sound, ever. He'll open his mouth and let me shovel in his crushed peas and apple sauce but that's about it. Nobody here has heard him say a word."

"I don't know, maybe he was having a dream." Christine shrugged. "I guess I could have heard something coming from another room."

The woman shot her one of those who-are-you-trying-to-kid looks and said, "You visiting somebody here?"

Christine grasped at the first name she could remember from her search up and down the corridors.

"Yeah, my aunt. She's down the hall: Ruth Wilson." The woman seemed satisfied with her answer, giving Christine a chance to change the subject. She looked at Woodworth and said, "Do you think he can hear us?"

The woman had everything ready to start feeding him and began spooning up a green mush. When she developed a good rhythm—Woodworth opening his mouth for her and most of the food finding its mark—she answered Christine as if she were talking about a piece of furniture.

"He might be hear'n us, but it don't register. See that scar? A twenty-two rifle did that. Self-inflicted. He tried to kill himself, at least that's what I've been told. Poor guy wound up with a home-made frontal lobotomy."

"How horrible," Christine said. "And no one even visits him, huh?"

"I didn't say that. I said he don't get too many visitors. Just his mother and daughter, and they come around all the time."

"His mother and daughter? Are you sure? When were they here last?"

"Just the other day," the woman snapped. "You don't think I know who's visiting my own patients?" Heated anger showed in her efforts to ignore Christine and concentrate on feeding Woodworth. Her eyes widened as she put down the spoon and looked up. "Say . . . why all the questions, anyway? Who the hell are you?"

"Sorry," Christine said. "I guess I'm just naturally nosy. I didn't mean to upset you."

She turned on her heel and made for the hallway. She didn't have to look back to know the woman was watching her from the doorway as she marched once again down the long corridor. She was almost running when she got to the front door. Not to get away from Life Care, but in a hurry to prove a theory that had just crystallized in her mind. She ignored the two pay phones at the end of the corridor—she'd wait to get to her office. She still hadn't recharged her cell phone.

Pulling out of the lot, she noticed a white Ford sedan parked at the curb, a silhouette behind the wheel. She turned down the street without giving it a second glance. She made her way to PCH and headed south for her office, too preoccupied with thoughts of the call she wanted to make than to direct much attention to her rearview mirror.

Her lot was full. A customer from the hair salon was walking out the front door as Christine pulled in. She waited the minute or two it took for the woman to fiddle with her keys, start the car, and back out of the way before she could slide her Camry into the momentarily available space. She had barely gotten her door open when the white Ford sedan pulled up behind her, blocking her in. She walked over to find Dennis Ash behind the wheel. He rolled down his window and said, "Glad I caught you, Ms. Blake."

"What are you doing here, Ash?" Christine stared at his car. "Have you been following me?"

"No, it's nothing like that. I've got something for you."

Ash hopped out and opened his back door to retrieve Christine's computer. He placed the CPU, along with a plastic bag containing her back-up drives, on the hood of his car.

"Lieutenant Hallstrom asked me to return this stuff to you."

"Why does he have a detective out running errands? Have you been a bad boy?"

"I just do what I'm told. I happened to be around and Hallstrom said you were in a hurry to get this back."

Christine didn't push it any further. Ash wasn't the type of guy to kid around with. No sense of humor. Neither of them mentioned Marshall's name or said anything about what had happened Monday night, not ten feet from where they were now standing. Ash unfolded a paper and laid it on the hood, next to her computer.

"Why don't you make sure everything's here and sign this release form for me?"

Christine glanced it over, saw that the number of flash drives in the bag corresponded with the number stated on the form, then threw her shoulder bag next to everything else on the makeshift table to look for a pen.

"Here, use mine," Ash said, handing her a ballpoint.

They completed the transaction. Ash kept the paperwork and Christine grabbed the CPU, tucking it under her arm while she used her free hand to jam the bag full of disks into one of the pockets in her blazer. She looked at her shoulder bag still sitting on the hood of the car.

"Let me help you with that," Ash said. "Besides, we need to talk."

"All right," Christine said, handing Ash the CPU and grabbing her shoulder bag. "Come on up."

As they walked through the door, Ash said, "I shouldn't be telling you this, but Hallstrom is not a happy guy."

"Why not?"

"We figure somebody must be helping Marshall. The Lieutenant has this crazy idea it's you. Not only that, he's sure you're holding back information about the break-in and resulting death here at you office. He's ready to ask for a warrant. He just has to decide whether to bring you in on criminal charges or as a material witness."

"That is crazy."

"Is it?"

"Okay," Christine said, "Have a seat."

Ash set her CPU on the desk and sat in the facing chair. Christine placed everything she was carrying next to the CPU and moved the whole pile out of the way so she had a clear view of Ash over the desktop when she took her place behind it.

"How long have I got?" Christine said.

"Before Hallstrom makes up his mind? Not long. He's taking a lot of heat from the brass to bring Marshall's reign of terror to an end."

"So you were following me."

"You're on a short leash, Ms. Blake. It might be best for you to come in on your own and maybe revise some of the statements you've given Hallstrom. He'd like to know the real reason you're mixed up in this. If you're heart is in the right place, I think he'll give you a break."

"That's reassuring, Ash. But what if I told you Marshall didn't kill his daughter? That there's a conspiracy to frame him for the murder and eventually have him killed as well?"

"And you can provide evidence of this?" Ash said.

"I'm close to nailing it down. I just need the rest of the day, then I'll come in."

"What can you give me now?"

"Nothing I can prove. That's why I need the time."

"We don't work like that. You've got something, or you don't. We're not going to let you run around and foul this up. If you know where Marshall is, tell us. Give us everything else you've got and we'll look into it. Don't try to be a part of this."

"I've been a part of this since the get-go, set up to provide Debra Marshall with an alibi and cover her tracks."

"You're saying Debra Marshall had her stepdaughter killed?"

"Yes. And Debra's father, Paul Cappannelli, has a hand in this. If you want to arrest someone, start with him. I've talked with one of the men who work for him, and he's ready to turn."

Ash pulled out a notebook and pen. "What's his name?"

"James. I don't know his last name. But his partner was Luke Parker, the man who broke into my office."

"The dead guy," Ash said.

"That's right. Their main function was to collect debts for Cappannelli. James wants out."

"And you know him how?"

"It's a long story. And everything I've got is circumstantial. What we need is a wiretap on Debra."

"There is no we," Ash said. "How many times do I have to remind you?"

"Okay, you get the wiretap. Isn't what I'm giving you enough for a warrant?"

"That could take time. We'd have to run down James what's-his-name and bring him in—"

"How about a wiretap on Wes Marshall?"

Ash looked up from his notebook. "How would that help?"

"Come on Ash, get creative. All you need is a roving wiretap. The Fed's use them all the time. Any phone Marshall uses is fair game, including cell phones. I'll bet he pays for Debra's, and if her number isn't on his billing statement, I can give it to you myself."

"That's not a bad idea," Ash said. "We should have pursued this as soon as Marshall resurfaced at his house."

"We?"

"You know what I mean." Ash stood up and pocketed his notebook. "The premise of the wiretap has to be for finding Marshall. I don't know if we'll be able to use any collateral information coming from Debra."

"Maybe not in court," Christine said, "but proof is proof. It could turn your investigation in the right direction."

"Just get it together," Ash said. "Hallstrom could be having your own warrant drawn up as we speak."

Christine watched through her office window as Ash drove away. She hurried down to her car, slid behind the wheel, and headed for Walter's shop.

TWENTY-FIVE

CHRISTINE TURNED down the adjacent driveway next to the hardware store, all the way back, past where she'd seen Marshall and Debra park the other night, to a space on the far side of Walter's old station wagon. She climbed out and surveyed her surroundings to make sure that her Camry would be virtually impossible to see from the highway.

The pleasant quietness of the small boatyard calmed her down. The only signs of life were a few seagulls perched on the dockside railings, seemingly content to sit and watch the occasional boat drift by. Beyond the harbor and the rooftops on the peninsula, a large fog bank loomed against the blue sky, the water in front of it turning gray as it rolled shoreward. She turned away and walked toward the tall doors at Walter's shop.

She found Walter where she'd first met him, at work on his Chris Craft. She watched him from the doorway, not wanting to interrupt while he pulled a paintbrush across the deck of the wooden boat in long, practiced strokes. When he stood back to scrutinize his progress, she walked in and said, "Looks like you're about finished, Wally. It's beautiful."

Walter looked over to the doorway. "Yeah, I think I can wrap it up by this afternoon. I'll give it a couple of days to cure and have her in the water by this weekend."

"You must be excited. After all this time you've spent on her, you'll finally get to show her off."

"To tell you the truth, I'm just trying to keep busy and take my mind off everything. My goddamned meddling in Marshall's affairs almost got you killed. Now they say he was trying to beat Debra to death. I don't want to think about it anymore."

"Don't be so hard on yourself. You might have spurred me on, but it was my decision to get involved. Now I've finally stumbled onto something and need to check it out while I'm still free."

"What do you mean by that."

"Let's just say I'm not making any friends over at police headquarters. To be on the safe side, I parked out back where they aren't as likely to spot my car."

"You sound a little paranoid," Walter said.

"I just want to make sure I have enough time to finish what I've started. With a little luck, I might be able to establish Debra's motive. Okay if I use your office?"

"Sure, help yourself. The door's unlocked."

Walter turned back to his boat and Christine walked over to his office next door. Once inside, she sat behind his desk and pulled her notebook and pen out of her bag. She picked up the telephone and called the Los Angeles County Registrar's Office. Christine had a contact there, only knew her by her extension number and first name, but had worked with her in the past.

"Hey, Susan, how are they treating you?"

"Can't complain. Well, I could, but it wouldn't do me any good. We're integrating a new software program and I'm really buried."

"Then I'll cut to the chase. I'm in a real bind and need your help. Do you have time to dig up a birth certificate?"

"When do you need it?"

"Yesterday. Sorry to throw this at you, but it's important and I don't have much time."

"What's the name?"

"Debra Cappannelli."

"Mother's maiden name?"

"I don't have it. That's the name I'm interested in. The father's name is Paul Cappannelli. Debra's around thirty years old. I don't need a copy of the certificate, just the mother's name."

"I'll have to put you on hold for a minute," Susan said, then clicked off. A couple of minutes later she came back on and told her the certificate listed Paul Cappannelli as the father and Marianne Butler as the mother's maiden name.

Christine thanked her, then pressed for another favor. "I also need to get into the marriage certificate data base. I'd do it myself if my computer wasn't down, but I really need—"

"Let me guess. You want the parents' marriage records?"

Christine smiled into the phone and said, "I owe you."

The wait was shorter this time. Susan said, "Do you want me to fax you a copy?"

"I don't have one here. Just read me the date they were married."

Christine jotted down the date, expressed her thanks again, and stayed on the phone after Susan disconnected to call Marshall's office. She was put on hold while a woman whose voice she didn't recognize went off to find Miss Phelps. Christine sat at the desk, doodling in her notebook, when the woman returned to say that Miss Phelps was tied up in a meeting upstairs.

"Could you do me a big favor?" Christine asked. "Go up and slip her a note that says Christine Blake called and that she needs to hear from her as soon as possible."

The person on the other end agreed to carry out Christine's wishes. Ten minutes later Miss Phelps returned the call. Christine figured she was busy with Marshall's business and promised not to take up too much of her time.

"I need to find out all I can about a man named Robert Woodworth. Does the name mean anything to you? Could Woodworth have been someone Mr. Marshall has done business with?"

The faint hum of the open line was the only sound Christine heard while Miss Phelps thought over the questions. Christine started talking again to help her along.

"The man looks like he's about Wes's age. He's being taken care of at a nursing home in Newport Heights. His mother lives over on Clay Street—"

"Did you say Clay Street?"

"Yeah, could that mean something?"

"Mr. Marshall grew up on Clay Street."

Christine had a local's knowledge of Clay Street. Her garage-top apartment was only a couple of blocks from its west end. The street stretched about half a mile to the east from where she lived, then curved into Fifteenth Street near the south end of Newport Harbor High School.

"How old is Wes, Miss Phelps?"

"He must be close to fifty."

"And I assume he went to Newport Harbor High."

"Yes, I believe he did."

Christine thanked her and hung up. She jotted down some numbers, did the math and came up with 1978 or thereabouts as the year Wes graduated from high school. She crumpled up the paper she'd been writing on and threw it in a waste basket on her way out the door and back to Walter's shop. He stopped what he was doing when she walked in.

"How did it go?" he asked.

Christine walked over and sat on one of the stools next to the workbench. She said, "Well, for one thing, Cappannelli isn't Debra's real father."

"So what? What does that prove?"

"I'm not sure. It might have something to do with a man named Robert Woodworth lying in a nursing home over by Hoag Hospital."

Walter's eyebrows shot up. "The lad from Clay street?"

"Not exactly. The man in the nursing home is Robert Jr., the son of the man you found for me on the Internet. But they all lived on Clay Street, still do for that matter, at least Mrs. Woodworth does. She's Debra's grandmother, and the two of them visit young Robert on a regular basis."

"So you think Robert Woodworth Jr. is Debra's father?"

"It's common knowledge at the nursing home. I can't think of a reason why Debra or Mrs. Woodworth would lie about it. To double check, I just called the registrar's office to see what I could find out. Paul Cappannelli and Marianne Butler are the names of the parents on Debra's birth certificate. Then I checked the marriage certificate data base to see how long they had been married."

"You're losing me, Christine. If Woodworth is Debra's father, why is Cappannelli named as the father on her birth certificate? And what does the length of their marriage have to do with anything?"

"First of all, when a child is adopted as a newborn, the adoptive parents are named on the birth certificate. But it's a secondary birth certificate. The birth parents are named on the original, which is sealed by the courts. The secondary certificate becomes the one on record, the one I found at the registrar's office."

Walter still looked confused. "What about the time and place of birth." he said. "Do they mess with that too?"

"No, that remains the same as the original. The registrar's office keeps track of all this with internal earmarks. It takes a court order to see the original."

"So where does that leave you?"

"With only the secondary certificate, but that's okay."

Walter stroked his beard for a few moments, then said, "I get it. You're sure Woodworth is Debra's father, but Debra calls Cappannelli dad and he's the one on the birth certificate. So Cappannelli must have adopted her.

"That's right. But what interests me is the mother. Cappannelli's wife could be the mother—from a prior marriage, an unwed teenage pregnancy, whatever. But Cappannelli's marriage certificate pretty much rules that out. They've been married for thirty-five years."

"And how old is Debra?"

"Around thirty."

"I'm still not sure where you're going with this."

"I'm not sure either, Wally. It's still sketchy. But I think I can put together enough evidence to interest Lieutenant Hallstrom. He can get that court order and find out who Debra's real mother is."

"Which will prove . . .?"

"By itself, nothing. But it might prove there's a very close connection between Debra and Jennifer. A connection that could reveal a motive for murder."

Christine slid off the stool before Walter could say anything.

"I've just got one more thing to do, then I'll drop all this in Hallstrom's lap."

She tossed Walter a preoccupied wave and headed for the doors. At the threshold, the first patchy wisps of the advancing fog bank caught her eye as they drifted up to the open doorway overhead and clashed with the warmer air rising from inside the shop. She stepped into a damp breeze, the buildings across the bay dissolving into obscure shadows before disappearing. Within seconds everything beyond fifty feet of her was gone, replaced by varying shades of gray. The fog was so thick it even seemed to muffle the familiar noises around the harbor. The traffic on nearby PCH had slowed to a crawl, emphasizing the stillness that settled in as the breeze died.

* * *

She was back in the clear as soon as she crossed PCH and drove a few blocks up the hill. She was on her way to Newport Harbor

High School, trying to think of a way to avoid the administration office. Those kind of places weren't very stranger-friendly, and she didn't want to waste a lot of time explaining why she wanted to rummage around in their archives.

She had been on campus before, about a year ago, working on a child abuse case. Christine remembered the teacher she worked with and tried to recall her name as she pulled into the visitor's parking lot.

"Rachel . . . Rachel something," Christine said aloud, striding up to the main building, a stately two story structure with an impressive tower rising above the front entrance. It appeared very old, the architecture reminding her of the East Coast despite the tile roof and surrounding palm trees. She climbed the stairs to the second floor and prowled the corridors until a bell rang, signaling the end of a period. Doors swung open and a flood of students poured out of the classrooms. Christine snaked her way through the tide of bodies. The teacher's last name came to her just as the woman came out of her room.

"Christine, what a surprise."

"Hello, Rachel. I didn't know if you'd remember me."

"I hope I'm not getting that old."

Rachel said it with an ironic wink, looking no older than Christine. She was wearing her dark hair up, off her neck, and she self-consciously replaced a fallen strand, then smoothed out her blouse that was trying to come untucked from her skirt. As she finished rearranging herself, she continued, "Besides, I still think of you once in a while, when I see Joanne Martin in one of the hallways. She'd had a rough time, and I remember how you helped her." A concerned look crossed Rachel's face. "I hope that's not why you're here."

"No, it isn't," Christine said. "Have you got a minute? Maybe we could step inside your classroom."

Without going into details, Christine told Rachel about wanting to look at some old yearbooks without wasting a lot of time going about it.

"Come with me," Rachel said. "I've got a few minutes before my next class. I'll take you to the library and introduce to our librarian."

The two women marched out of the main building and across campus to the library. By the time the bell for the next class rang, Christine had the '77, '78, and '79 yearbooks in front of her on an otherwise empty table flanked by tall, stuffed bookshelves. She opened the book for 1978, holding her breath while she flipped through pages of student portraits. She found what she was looking for on the last page of the senior class photos. There, at the bottom of the page, under the last black and white picture, was the name Robert Woodworth, Jr. She quickly worked her way back to the M's, and sure enough, there was Wes Marshall.

She spent a little while longer skimming through the book, stopping here and there to glance over pictures and their brief, printed descriptions. A photo of the varsity football team caught her attention, and closer examination revealed Marshall and Woodworth standing next to each other among the crush of players.

A few pages later, in one of those pseudo-candid photos of campus life that yearbooks were so fond of printing, Wes Marshall and an attractive girl in a cheerleader sweater mugged for the camera. The caption identified the girl as Kathleen Connaker. Her resemblance to Debra was unsettling. How was it that Marshall hadn't noticed?

Christine looked closer at Kathleen's picture. It was a black and white print, which obscured differences between hair color and skin tones and allowed the similar bone structure and facial features shared by Kathleen and Debra to shine through. She might have missed the similarities if the picture had been in color. It was taken a long time ago and Marshall's recent memories of Kathleen were of a much older version, but even still, Christine couldn't help but wonder.

She was about to turn the page when she noticed the expression of one of the onlookers in the background. It was Robert Woodworth. He probably wasn't aware of being photographed, but the camera had caught his unabashed stare. It was unmistakably zeroed in on Kathleen. And now, over thirty years later, that stare rose goose flesh on the back of Christine's neck.

TWENTY-SIX

DEBRA MARSHALL rode a taxi home from Hoag Hospital. It was close to noon when she climbed out. The morning fog hadn't burned off yet. It still threatened the shoreline, covering the water but leaving most of the land mass in sunshine.

Shadows blossomed and faded along the brick pathway that led to the front door, the sun beating down on her one moment and hiding behind the ragged, leading edge of the fog bank the next. She pushed open the door, then froze.

"Come in," Marshall said. "I've been waiting for you."

"What the hell are you doing here?" Debra said, steadying herself with a hand on the doorjamb.

"I never left," Marshall said. "After all, it is still my house." He grabbed her arm to assist her inside. His voice sounded forced. "Let's go out back and talk."

Debra let him prod her through the house, ending up on the deck beyond the family room. It felt like walking out on a lofty pier, with nothing but gray shades of ocean and sky stretched out before her.

Marshall motioned her toward an outdoor teak table and matching chairs by the railing. On the table were a bottle of Patron tequila and a shot glass next to a couple of whole limes, the spent wedges of another, and a carving knife. She took a seat and felt the sun through the thin layers of fog that continued to drift overhead.

"Sit tight," Marshall said, reaching over for the knife and taking it with him. "I'll bring you a glass."

Debra placed her handbag on the table and felt inside for her cell phone. She barely had time to palm it before Marshall returned.

He sat across from her and went to work on one of the limes, slicing it into quarters. The carving knife was overkill. Debra would have preferred to see a small paring knife in his hand. When he was through with the lime, he poured a shot of tequila into the fresh glass, leaving his own glass empty.

"Go ahead," he said. "I'll give you a chance to catch up."

Debra picked up the glass. "What are we drinking to?"

"Your execution."

The glass stopped halfway to her lips. She set it back on the table. "Then I'll have to pass. I'm not that thirsty."

"Your choice," Marshall said.

"And who's the executioner? You?"

"That's your choice as well. You can turn yourself in, or we can end this right now. I've got nothing to lose."

Marshall stared at her, rock steady. He had a look on his face she'd never seen, as if his eyes were already dead, waiting for the deadness to spread through the rest of his body. It scared her. Then he was out of his chair, leaning across the table, his face uncomfortably close.

"Who are you?" he said.

Debra sat back as far as she could. He grabbed the front of her blouse to keep her close.

"Who are you?" he repeated. "Why are you doing this? What makes you hate me so much?"

"Get your hands off me," Debra said, a surge of anger coming to her rescue. "Letting you touch me, not to mention fuck me, has been the hardest thing I've ever had to do. Just go fuck off and die."

"Don't tempt me," Marshall said. "Because I'll take you with me."

He released his grip, letting her drop into the chair. He picked up the glass he'd offered her and the tossed back the tequila himself. Debra watched him sit down, while out of the corner of her eye she measured the distance to the knife.

"Just tell me why you did it," Marshall said.

"Why did I do what?" Debra said. "Kill Jennifer? Or why did I kill your fucking wife?"

They both shot out of their chairs—Marshall reaching for Debra's throat, Debra grabbing the knife before he got to her. She slashed at his rib cage as soon as she had her fingers around the handle. She felt the blade scrape across bone.

"Back off," she said, keeping the blade in front of her, aiming it at Marshall.

He fell back into his chair, ignoring the swelling red line darkening his white polo shirt, his eyes no longer a dull glaze but now burning with a bright glow.

Debra inched away from the table, keeping watch on Marshall while she retrieved her cell phone that had fallen from her lap. She speed-dialed Cappannelli.

When he answered, she said, "He's here. At the house."

"What?"

"You heard me. He's sitting right in front of me."

"Alive?"

"And kicking. You better get over here."

"I'm twenty minutes away. Just make sure he's still around when I get there, or that little dance we had last night? It'll be a pleasant memory compared with what happens next."

Debra closed the phone and set it on the table, staying within lunging distance to Marshall in case he moved. His shirt was soaked with more blood but the flow seemed to be slowing.

He said, "How can you talk to him so easily, after what he did to you?"

"Did what?"

"He beat you to a pulp. You look like hell. It must be painful"

"I'm used to it. He'd been beating me all my life. I don't see why you're so concerned. You didn't seem to have any trouble joining in last night."

"I had to buy some time. Besides, I'm not your father."

"Neither his he."

Debra pulled her chair out from the table and sat down with a clear space between them. If anyone was hurting right now, it had to be Marshall. Maybe too hurt to try anything. If he did, she was ready with the knife. In the meantime, she didn't mind talking, keeping him preoccupied until Cappannelli arrived. Cappannelli had more experience with this sort of thing, and she wanted to avoid another bloodbath. She also wanted to enjoy these last remaining minutes with Marshall.

"I'm surprised you never noticed how much I look like my mother. Or maybe you did, and just couldn't admit that's what attracted you."

Marshall stared at her. Most of the fire had left his eyes, as if snuffed out by defeat. "If you're referring to Kathleen, that's not possible."

"It's more than possible. I was born during your senior year in high school." Debra watched Marshall's eyes while she spoke. This was getting good. "Remember the guy down the street, your friend, Woody?"

"I don't believe you," Marshall said. "Kathleen and Woody? No way."

"How blind can a person be?" Debra said, shaking her head in mock sympathy. "You want to spend what little time you have left in denial, so be it. At least you heard it from me."

"Even if it's true," Marshall said, "Why kill my family? They didn't deserve to die."

"Why not? Kathleen killed my father. He just hasn't quit breathing yet. He spends his days in diapers, a catheter bag hanging next to him, unable to feed himself. He's been that way for thirty years. I doubt if he knows who I am."

"What does that have to do with Kathleen?"

Debra sat up on the edge of her chair. "Kathleen told Woody he got her pregnant, that he ruined everything and that she didn't want to see him again. She told him she was getting an abortion. A week later, Woody shot himself in the head."

"I still don't believe you," Marshall said. "If there was a baby, it would have been mine."

"When was the first time you fucked Kathleen?"

Debra watched Marshall's facial expression change. He was getting it, doing the math. He said, "How can you possibly know all this?"

"I'm very close to my grandmother, Woody's mother. She still lives in the old house on Clay. Woody told her everything. And when I learned who my birth parents were and found her, she told me. I've been paying Woody's bills since my grandpa died."

"And Jennifer?" Marshall said. "Why her. She was just an innocent kid."

"Innocent my ass. She should have never been born." Debra was on her feet again. "That was supposed to have been me. It was my birthright. I should have been growing up on the beach, going to college, getting all the breaks. Not hustling tricks on Hollywood Boulevard after running away from my pig of a so-called father and his flaky wife.

"I spent years watching your innocent little girl. When I'd drive out to see Grandma, sometimes I'd pull over on Irvine Avenue and check out the kids at Newport Harbor High, fantasizing what it would be like, one of those rich kids in the suburbs. And I watched Kathleen even closer—all her little routines, the golf and tennis and shopping. The jogging before dawn. Sometimes I'd stay overnight at Grandma's so I could get up early and sort of accidentally-on-purpose run into her, like one of her buddies trying to keep in shape. After a while, she'd recognize me with a little wave or a nod. I think she might have said hello once. Then one morning, everything fell into place. I was coming up behind her on the sidewalk that curves around those benches overlooking the main beach. All it took was a little shove. No one saw a thing."

Marshall's face reddened, his breath huffing from his nostrils. Debra couldn't help scolding him. "Better watch the blood pressure. You're going to start bleeding again, and I don't want you to die yet. I'm just getting to the good part. You want to hear how I did it, don't you? How I left you out there on the boat with your dead daughter?"

Debra looked down on Marshall and felt a wave of satisfaction course through her veins. This is what she'd been after all along—seeing the look on his face when she broke him, watching him crumble. She had missed it with Kathleen and Jennifer. She had seen only Kathleen's back and Jennifer had been unconscious at the moment of truth. But this was sweet. She couldn't stop talking, savoring every word as it left her mouth.

"I'll bet you're dying to know how I set Jennifer up—how I went by her studio, dropped off a key to the cabin of your boat and told her that you needed someone to pick up the briefcase you'd left onboard and bring it to the office, as you were in the middle of an important meeting and needed it by two o'clock. I apologized for not doing it myself. I would have been glad to if I knew how to handle the skiff. Jennifer understood. Of course she'd be happy to take care of this during lunch.

"That gave me plenty of time to drive out to the Peninsula and park on the other side of the bay, get into a wetsuit and swim out to the boat. I was waiting in the cabin when she arrived, and knocked the shit out of her when she came down the stairs. You remember how that feels, don't you? Do you know that I always carry a blackjack in the bottom of my purse. I guess it's a security thing. Anyway, I hit her pretty hard, probably did some permanent brain damage. That was all right. It was better for me if she didn't regain consciousness. She only needed to stay alive until that evening, so she could die when you were there. Time of death was important. I stripped off her clothes and tied her up on the bed, using the sheets so there wouldn't be any ligature marks. Then I stashed the wetsuit, put on Jennifer's clothes and got the wig out of the plastic bag I'd brought with me."

Marshall's face was turning redder. He seemed hard pressed to control his voice when he spoke. "So Jennifer went out to the boat on her own, and you returned to the dock later in her place, looking just like her, right down to the clothes."

"I'm glad you can appreciate the plan. I haven't been able to share it with anyone."

"Not even Cappannelli?"

"Especially not him. That would have ruined everything. He would have never gone along with it. I had to appeal to his business aspirations in order for him to help me."

"What about Christine Blake?" Marshall said.

"What about her? She's already played her part."

"I wouldn't count on it. She's on to you. She's been suspicious since the night she followed me to the Ritz-Carlton and saw Jennifer's car in my driveway, when Jennifer was supposed to have been meeting me there. I can see how you could have overlooked a small detail like that. You had a lot of balls in the air. The important thing was to keep Jennifer occupied at the house, alone, while you strolled through the Ritz-Carlton in your disguise, booking a room with Jennifer's credit card. It wouldn't have been good if Jennifer was seen somewhere else at the time. You faced the same problem with me the next day. You had to keep me away from the boat, so you had Cappannelli watch over me at the golf course. And then you used Christine to establish the proper motives, alibis, and eyewitness accounts."

"So you figured it out," Debra said. "It doesn't matter now."

"Yeah it does. Christine and I had a long talk, and we've compared notes. She knows about the impersonation. We know you used Jennifer's credit card at the Ritz. Christine knows about you meeting me at the boat. You've got more than just me to worry about."

"I don't care about that," Debra said, upset with herself for letting Marshall get to her. This was her moment, and he was ruining it for her. She pointed the knife at him and said, "The damage has been done. Jennifer's dead. And I'll have to admit, once we were on the boat and I had everything set up, I really enjoyed myself. I'd never stabbed anyone before. But as soon as I started in on Jennifer I felt like I was going to come. I used a chef's knife from the galley, and it slammed into her so easily, slick with all that blood, over and over . . . it was pure bliss."

Debra relaxed her grip on the knife. She'd been holding it too tight, talking too loud.

"When I was through," she said, dropping her voice, "it was just a matter of swimming back to the Peninsula. I'd had on the wetsuit when I stabbed her—hood, gloves, booties, the works. I even tied plastic bags around my feet so there wouldn't be any tread marks from the boots tracking through the blood. I left the clothes I'd been wearing on board. They were Jennifer's. When I reached shore I used a pay phone down by the Pavilion to report a horrible sounding fight coming from the Salty Swan. Then I drove home."

Marshall stared at her in silence. When she blinked, he sprang out of the chair, grabbing the hand holding the knife with both of his own. They tumbled onto the deck and struggled in a desperate silence. The only sounds they made were husky grunts and ragged gasps for breath, as if they were impassioned lovers trying not to wake up the rest of the household.

TWENTY-SEVEN

PAUL CAPPANNELLI sat behind the wheel of his black Cadillac, punctuating his fuming anger with rants and curses every time he had to change lanes to pass a slower vehicle. When he pulled off the freeway, thirty minutes had elapsed since his phone conversation with Debra. But if he could keep cool as he drove down the surface streets, and not do anything stupid enough to attract a traffic cop, he'd be on Shorecliff Road in a few more minutes.

He didn't have much of a plan. He'd grown too accustomed to the luxury of contemplating his woes from behind the desk in his Century City office. When a problem came up, all he would have to do is pick up the phone—problem solved. Now he had to think on his feet, with no one waiting by a phone to carry out his wishes. He was on his own, and how he handled himself was going to determine his future. He was going to do his best to make sure he had one.

When he reached PCH he calmed down. He didn't get to where he was in life by accident. He was a fighter and a taker. He'd had to scratch and claw his way off the street and into that fancy office. The closer he got to Debra's house, the more he could feel the person he used to be, the fighter, bristling to take over. He reached into the glove box and pulled out a thirty-eight caliber revolver. It was a little snub nosed throwaway, meant to be used once and then discarded. There was no way it could be traced back to him. He tucked it into his waistband, just to the left of his belt buckle, and kept on driving. He was almost there.

* * *

Marshall had his back against the railing and his butt planted on the deck. There was blood all over him. He didn't know how much of it was his or how much of it was Debra's. Along with the still-leaking swipe across his chest, both of his forearms were cut, but the lack of any arterial blood flow allowed him to worry about other things.

Debra lay a few feet away, rolled up into a fetal position, still clutching the knife handle protruding from just below her rib cage. She hadn't moved or made a sound since Marshall had crawled over to the railing. He wasn't aware of how long he'd been sitting there, staring at the body, replaying the last moments of the struggle. At the time, Marshall's only thought was keeping the blade pointed away from him. It had been between them when they started rolling over each other. Then he watched it disappear, the weight of their bodies forcing it deep into Debra's midsection.

As bad as that image was, it faded when Marshall realized what was going to happen next. Nothing could save him now. It didn't matter that he knew every detail surrounding the murder of his family. The only source for those details, the person who so eloquently confessed to everything, was in fact, dead. The police weren't going to listen to his crazy accusations. If there's an afterlife, Marshall thought, Debra's having a good laugh. Her death put him back at square one: alone with a murdered body, covered with the victim's blood.

As for Christine Blake, he could already hear the DA's office spinning out conspiracy theories linking the two of them together. The wildest speculation would sound more believable than anything he had to say.

Marshall glanced at the cell phone on the table, knowing he had to call 911. He was through running. He rose to his feet, accepting his fate. The worst of it was over. Then he saw Paul Cappannelli, taking up most of the space behind the sliding glass door.

"There must be a God after all," Cappannelli said, sliding the door open. "And who would've thought he'd ever smile down on an asshole like me?"

How long has he been there? Did he see what happened? Did he watch Debra die?

It didn't matter. What he probably saw was a way out of his involvement. When the handle of the revolver sticking out of Cappannelli's waistband flashed into view, Marshall knew what the man must be thinking—shoot Marshall, then go over to Debra's body and wrap her hand around the revolver's grip and squeeze off another round. What a nice, tidy ending that would make.

Marshall backed up against the railing. Any thoughts of running for cover were out of the question. He'd free-fall at least fifty feet if he jumped off the deck. Cappannelli blocked the only exit he could walk or run through. Marshall couldn't take his eyes off him. Cappannelli met his gaze with a cold stare. Marshall knew his life was over.

So this is what it's like to die, he thought, feeling an uncanny sense of relief. He closed his eyes and waited, not with apprehension, but with a strange and merciful acceptance.

Instead of a gunshot, a shout came from inside the house. Marshall opened his eyes in time to see Cappannelli drop to his knees and clasp his hands behind his head. A man in a blazer and gray trousers roughly assisted Cappannelli into a face-down position on the floor. He cuffed Cappannelli while two uniformed patrolmen covered him with drawn weapons. After Cappannelli was secure, a man in a dark suit drifted into view and came out to the deck.

"Are you okay?" the man said. "Any of that blood yours?"

Marshall stood there, speechless, wondering why they weren't shouting him down, weapons out, brandishing handcuffs.

The man in the blazer walked past him to check on Debra's body. The other man introduced himself to Marshall.

"I'm Lieutenant Hallstrom, Newport PD. You've given us quite a chase."

Get on with it, Marshall thought. Read me my rights and take me outta here—

"Ash," Hallstrom said, looking closer at Marshall "We need an ambulance, ASAP. This man's hurt." He righted an overturned deck chair, moved it away from the blood spatters, and gently guided Marshall over to sit down. Hallstrom pulled on a pair of latex gloves from out of a coat pocket and widened the tear across Marshall's shirt.

After a quick examination of Marshall's chest, Hallstrom said, "I know it looks messy, but they call stuff like this superficial." Hallstrom then glanced over Marshall's forearms. "Same with the arms. You'll be okay after they stitch you up."

Marshall felt lightheaded, whether from blood loss or confusion, he couldn't tell. Maybe he was just tired, or already asleep, dreaming.

Hallstrom held up a finger in front of Marshall's face, a gesture that said, Hold that thought, and walked over to pick up Debra's cell phone.

"No need to record any more of this," Hallstrom said. He pulled off the phone's back cover and took out the battery. "Where were we? Oh yeah, seeing about patching you up."

Still confused, Marshall said, "Aren't you going to arrest me?"

"I don't think so. Not since we recorded Debra's confession." Hallstrom looked around slowly as he spoke. "As for all this—a clear case of self defense. Along with everything being recorded, you're defensive wounds back it up."

"I don't understand," Marshall said.

Hallstrom held up the cell phone. "You know, these phones are actually miniature computers. Unprotected, unable to block viruses or spy ware. We had the carrier download a program that turned this phone into an open mike, activated by us. The user's none the wiser. And the beauty of it is the mike's always on, even when the phone's turned off. The only way to shut it down is to take out the battery."

"Is that legal?"

"Depends on who you talk to. In this case it won't matter. We're only using the information we've gathered to exonerate you, kind of like passing a lie detector test, only stronger. No one's going to court, so . . ."

Marshall looked past Hallstrom, through the open glass door to the family room. The uniformed patrolmen had taken Cappannelli away.

Hallstrom followed Marshall's gaze. "Don't worry about Mr. Cappannelli. He *will* be going to court. Christine Blake has supplied us with all we need to nail him for motive, conspiracy, you name it. She was at the station, filling me in with what she'd learned, when Ash called in for backup."

Hallstrom put the phone together, minus the battery, and replaced it on the table. He peeled off his gloves and brought up another chair. "I'd like to know how you managed to show up here. We swept the place several times looking for you after the ambulance picked up Mrs. Marshall last night."

"This is a big place," Marshall said, "The property runs all the way down to the beach. Jennifer was just a kid when we moved here, always exploring. She loved to play hide-and-seek, and I learned where to look. Your men didn't have that luxury."

"Kind of like hiding in plain sight," Hallstrom said.

"I figured you didn't expect me to stay here. And I knew Debra would be back. She was badly beaten when I first showed up, but when I saw the look on her face as he came around and recognized me, I knew this wouldn't end until one of us was dead."

"That must have been the way she wanted it," Hallstrom said. "She refused protection. I should have been more suspicious about it when she insisted that we stand down. She didn't want any of my men at the house. I had them make one last sweep through the place before she was released from the hospital, and then she came back here by herself."

"You're right. She was glad I was here."

Marshall didn't notice the paramedics until they were hurrying onto the deck. They prepped him where he sat, then escorted him out to the waiting ambulance.

TWENTY-EIGHT

MARSHALL WALKED out the door and breathed in a lungful of freedom. It couldn't have tasted sweeter . . . or felt more empty. Christine waited next to her car. She walked over to meet him at the bottom of the ramp leading up to the emergency room doors. She drifted within arm's reach and gave him a warm hug. Neither of them spoke until they were inside her car and out of the parking lot.

Finally, Marshall said, "I need to see her—" He stopped to clear his throat and tried again. "I need to see her grave. Would you mind?"

"I know the way," Christine said.

They drove out to Pacific View Memorial Park. Christine stayed by the car and watched Marshall make his way down the hill to his family plot. She felt uneasy watching him walk away, as if reminded of something not out of the past, but of something yet to happen. She didn't attempt to hold back the tears. They weren't really for her, and that somehow made a difference. She gave him all the time he needed, and when he came back, he was ready to talk.

"Hallstrom spent a lot of time with me, Marshall said. "He covered legal stuff and filled me in on some of the details of what happened. He said you'd know more than he did."

"How much did he tell you?"

"He showed me a copy of Debra's original birth certificate. Kathleen was down as the mother."

"You never knew about it?"

"Not a clue." Marshall looked out his window. They were halfway down Marguerite Avenue, a wide band of the Pacific Ocean rising into view. "How did Debra find out?"

"About the adoption? She must have hired an investigator."

"She seemed to know the whole story, Marshall said. "She'd been stalking my family for years. Do you know that it was Jennifer who introduced us?"

"You and Debra?"

"That's right. They were friends. After I married her, Jennifer never forgave me."

"I can see why you were attracted to her."

"It's spooky, looking back on it. There was something familiar about her, right from the beginning. I wanted to believe it started out as one of those magic moments—you know, how you meet someone and think it's all about fate. A lost soul from another lifetime. She really knew how to play me."

"Her planning and execution was almost flawless," Christine said, "including her choice to use me to confirm your guilt. After you told me about Debra's interest in the children's alliance, it got me to thinking. My bio is posted on our website, along with the other officers and committee members. I'll bet Debra checked us out, and my background must have appealed to her. I'd make a credible witness. I can't believe how quickly she had me eating out of her hand."

"I'm glad you finally saw through her."

"I never did, really, until I stumbled onto Robert Woodworth and the secondary birth certificate. Good thing Jennifer was born in LA."

"That was more happenstance than anything else. Kathleen's family moved to Minnesota during the summer before our senior year at high school. Nothing suspicious about it. Her father worked for 3M and received a promotion. He said they needed him at corporate headquarters, at least that's how the story went.

There must have been something to it, because her family never moved back to California. But Kathleen's sister lived in LA. Best I can figure, she had the baby there, then joined her parents in Minnesota to finish out high school. We didn't get back together until after we graduated."

"Makes sense," Christine said. "Nobody was the wiser—the old friends in Newport Beach or the new ones in Minnesota."

"Good way to shield her pregnancy," Marshall said. "She sure didn't want me to know."

"How well did you know Woodworth?"

"Woody? Hell, we were pals . . . I thought. He lived down the street where I grew up. He knew I had a thing for Kathleen. I'd sure like to know how he got her pregnant."

"I can understand why she'd want to keep it from you."

"I remember when Woody had his accident," Marshall said. "It happened during the summer, but everyone was still talking about it the next school year. I guess we didn't know the half of it. I'd just like to know why Kathleen told him she was having an abortion. Why lie to him about it?"

"It makes sense to me," Christine said. "She could have been mad at him. Maybe she wanted to hurt him. Telling him she was getting rid of the baby would be a good way to do it and get him out of her life, all with that one little lie."

"I don't know," Marshall said. "It's all speculation now. I'll never know what really happened."

They drove down Marguerite to PCH. When they came up to the stoplight, Marshall told her to drive straight ahead.

"There's one more place I'd like to go."

They crossed the highway when the light changed. Marguerite ended two blocks later at Ocean Boulevard, a residential street with long gentle curves skirting the edge of a seaside bluff.

They turned south and drove past ranks of well-kept homes standing tall, shoulder to shoulder, on the inland side of the street. Their windows looked out over prime Orange County coastline, and beyond. Across the street a scattering of rooftops was all that could be seen of the homes clinging to the far side of the bluff. Tree-shaded common areas flourished within a few narrow strips of curbside real estate, where the public was allowed a taste of the privileged vistas.

Marshall hadn't been anywhere near Ocean Boulevard all year, but he knew exactly where he was going. He felt as if he'd just been there yesterday. Up ahead he saw his destination and showed Christine where to pull over.

This time there were plenty of places to park along the curb: no police and emergency vehicles blocking the way; no crime scene tape strung in front of the three park benches out on the promontory overlooking the main beach; no strong hands of a uniformed patrolman to steady him after he looked out over the edge of the bluff and recognized the lifeless body down below, dressed in the familiar navy blue jogging suit.

This time he didn't have to rush past the onlookers and duck under the yellow tape. There was no one nearby as he walked slowly along the empty sidewalk, past the benches, out to the edge of the bluff, where he continued pacing back and forth a few times before looking down. All he saw over the edge were leftover footprints along a lonely stretch of sand.

He stood there a long while, until Christine came up and joined him. They both sat down on one of the empty benches.

"This is where it happened?" she asked.

He answered with a silent nod, looking toward the jetties protecting the harbor entrance and at the blue water sparkling in the channel.

"I've sailed by here a million times, but this is the first time I've actually been here since it happened. That last day I went sailing the conditions were pretty rough, probably more than I should have taken on by myself, but I was compelled to go out. I wanted to tell Jennifer about it afterwards, when I ran into her at the house.

"She always thought the sailing was an escape, and she reminded me once again how she felt about it. Our conversation went sideways and we moved on to other stuff. That's when Debra called, and I never got the chance to tell Jennifer what it was really about."

Marshall leaned against the backrest of the bench. With a soft voice, he said, "When someone close to you dies, you don't stop loving them. If anything, you love them even more. That's all you have left to hold on to. And since she's been gone, whenever I think of Kathleen it's always the same moment frozen in time—the two of us, alone, saying goodbye, just before she left for Minnesota. The last thing she said was, 'I wish we could get on a boat and sail away.'

"The way she said it, and the way she looked at me, her eyes glistening with tears, shinning with an inner light that words can't begin to describe . . . man, it hit me like some kind of telepathic laser beam. In that one moment, we got each other. It just about broke my heart. That's when I realized how much I loved her.

"And I'll admit, since she died, maybe I was looking for an escape. Your problems on shore seem less significant when you're under sail, your mind occupied with the direction of the wind and the effect of the seas and how to best set the sails to your advantage. Shore-bound problems have a way of disappearing completely when the weather kicks up and you're worried about staying afloat, not to mention staying alive.

"But last Wednesday, on the second anniversary of Kathleen's death, something happened when I took the boat out. It was as if my mind had been washed clean and I could see clearly. I wasn't running away or trying to forget. I was keeping a half-forgotten promise I'd sworn to myself on that day we said goodbye. I knew it was only a dream, even back then. The wishful thinking of a heartsick kid. But for these last two years it was all I could think about. It gave me a reason to look forward to another day. To keep living. It's why I bought the boat and worked so hard at learning how to handle her. Then last Wednesday it all came together. I finally got a taste of how it could have been. A dream that almost came true."

And Jennifer never heard about it, Christine thought, realizing she was a stand-in for Marshall's daughter.

They stayed on the bench for a few more minutes, then, without a word, they walked back to Christine's car. They drove back to PCH and then on to Shorecliff Drive.

Christine pulled into Marshall's driveway. He remained seated, and she turned off the engine.

"Are you ready for this?"

"I have to go home sooner or later." Marshall was looking away at something beyond his house that Christine couldn't see, then turned toward her, his eyes clear and steady. "There's no way I can repay you for what you've done. You put your life on the line for me, a stranger you knew nothing about—"

Christine reached out and touched his arm. He smiled quietly, clasping her hand just long enough to say goodbye.

* * *

On her way through Corona del Mar Christine pulled over in front of a bar still open for lunch. It was dark enough inside to suit her mood. She ordered a glass of wine and a sandwich and didn't eat much of the sandwich.

Her eyes needed a minute to readjust to the harsh light when she stepped back into the real world outside the bar, but her thoughts remained dark. She thought about a young woman she'd never met, lying under a flat stone on a gentle slope a few blocks away. She thought about Marshall, and the emptiness he'd have to deal with. She felt lost. She wished there was more she could do than say she was sorry and walk away.

She lingered at the curb before getting into her car.

That's all it took, a couple of seconds. Maybe she was having one of those moments, like Marshall on his boat, seeing everything clearly.

She could almost hear Matt's voice. He'd been right. She would regret it if she chose not to see her father again. She'd end up like Marshall, visiting the grave after it was too late, telling stories to strangers that were meant for someone she loved.

That's not going to happen.

She stepped off the curb and into to her car, tossing her purse onto the passenger seat. She pulled out and merged with the traffic flowing along Pacific Coast Highway and from time to time she glanced at the purse holding her dead cell phone.

No reason to panic. Her office was only five minutes away.

Hold on, Dad. I'm coming home.